THE 4TH REICH

- Book Two-

Patrick Laughy

Patrick Laughy

DEDICATION

*This book is dedicated to all Second World War history buffs
out there who, from time to time wonder...what if?*

ACKNOWLEDGEMENTS

Thanks to Suzy for her hours of research and editing, David for another great cover and Linette for her continued support.

CHAPTER ONE

- Gabriella –

Erika, Count Karl von Stauffer's wife, had kept him awake well into the early morning hours of September twenty-fifth nineteen-forty.

To suggest that the Countess had become obsessed with the determination to see their youngest daughter Gabriella safely married off and leading life as a proper German wife, inclusive of producing several grandchildren, was of course, old hat by this point in the evening and Karl saw no point in rehashing that issue.

Instead he simply let his wife re-vent her concerns and when she had run out of steam he patiently offered his support for each of these in turn.

Yes, the current situation had gone on far too long.

Yes Gabriella was spoiled and out of control.

Yes, she needed a good husband, someone who could rein her in and keep her properly contented.

Yes, she needed to have a change of venue and become a good and productive citizen within the new Reich...and yes he would see to it that the discussions that the family had engaged in during the previous evening in that regard would produce action which would reach fruition quickly.

* * * * *

- The Internment Camps –

The first standard internment camps constructed after the Nazis came to power in Germany were those at Dachau near Munich and at Oranienburg, a small town located in Brandenburg, Germany.

The Nazi party did not invent the concept of building this type of restrictive internment facility that has, since that time, been generally encapsulated within the term *'concentration camp'*.

That particular name for this type of confinement resource likely came from what had been referred to as *'re-concentration camps'*. These facilities had been set up in Cuba by General Valeriano Weyler in eighteen ninety-seven.

Institutions of this nature, of various sizes and forms have existed throughout history, being constructed and utilized to house and contain citizens whose political actions or beliefs were considered by those in power to be of a disposition that was a danger to the security of the state.

For example, the British used the concept historically as a matter of course, prime examples being the Tower of London, transport of criminals to Australia and containment camps used during the Boer wars; and the British were far from the only exception. The United States and Canada stripped their Japanese citizens of their property and interred them at the outbreak of war with that nation, and Australia interred what they classed as *'enemy aliens'* as well.

Without question, the idea of locking up political prisoners was far from being a *'new phenomenon'* at the time Hitler came to power.

It had been going on for centuries.

As has always been the state of affairs when political power is absolute, as was the case in a true dictatorship like that of Nazi Germany, such containment facilities tended to be more numerous and much larger than would be either palatable or acceptable within a democratic state.

However it is highly unlikely that any country can claim a complete lack of involvement in some degree of such historical activity.

In a democracy those in power often lock up politically motivated anarchists or terrorists. In an autocratic dictatorship anyone who doesn't agree with the governing party's policies in either expressed thought and/or action risks being locked up.

Right or wrong, common sense tells you that there are going to be far more offenders in the latter than in the former.

So it was to be in Nazi Germany, arguably one of the strongest Dictatorships ever formed in the history of our world.

* * * * *

- Nazi Judicial System –

After the Nazis rise to power the judicial system, not unlike the medical and teaching systems, underwent a period of rapid transition.

Initially this consisted of a two-pronged approach to justice. The democratically enshrined judicial system the Nazis had inherited when they came to power was allowed to continue to function but it underwent some very rapid changes.

Adolf Hitler became Chancellor of Germany on the thirtieth of January nineteen thirty-three and immediately began to structure the legal system to simplify his long held intention to facilitate the incarceration of his political opponents.

Exactly one month later, on the twenty-eighth of February of that year, a Presidential Order, *Reichsgesetzblatt Nr. 17* (Legal Bulletin of the Reich No.17) was signed. This order was justified by the need to curtail the rampant political unrest that had become commonplace in Germany.

It was announced as a short term necessity.

Among other things, the Order stipulated that articles 114,115,117,118, 123, 124 and 153 of the Constitution were invalid until further notice. These changes related to freedom of the individual, the right to free speech, freedom of the press, right of assembly, and right to form groups, personal privacy rights regarding the mail, telegraph and telephone communications as well as house searches.

Additionally confiscation and constraint of property ownership which had previously been restricted by specified limitations under law were now permissible. The order also specified that those who endangered human life by their opposition would be sentenced to penal servitude or a term of imprisonment of not less than six months.

In addition to these changes in the laws, the inherited legal system was almost immediately forced to coexist with the new and definitely arbitrary arrest powers the Nazis quickly provided to the police.

These came about by way of the Nazis reinterpretation of the *Schutzhaft* (protective custody) section of the law in nineteen thirty-three whereby they determined that 'protective custody' was now to mean legal arrest without judicial review of not only real, but also *'potential'* opponents of the regime. They also determined that persons so arrested were not to be confined within the in-place prison system but were to be confined in camps under the exclusive authority and control of the *Schutzstaffel* (SS).

Less than three months after coming to power the Nazis had eradicated all political unrest by either eliminating or severely curtailing the enshrined basic and inalienable civil rights of the average German citizen.

Hitler and the Nazi party hierarchy were incensed by the *'not guilty'* verdicts rendered by the *Reichsgericht* (Supreme Court) with regard to charges laid as a result of the infamous Reichstag fire. These decisions, in their view, only served to fortify their opinion that the *'political'* reliability of the courts was sadly lacking.

As a result Hitler ordered the immediate establishment of special new courts throughout Germany whose sole function would be the trying of politically sensitive cases.

In a further step, he created the *Volksgerichtshof* (People's Court) in Berlin in nineteen thirty-four, and mandated it to try all treason and other important *'political'* cases.

In addition to these immediate steps to deal with the Nazi recognized shortcomings of the legal system, the entire process was destined to be restructured and indoctrinated in order to better reflect the goals and aspirations of the New Germany.

All professional legal associations in the administration of German justice were forthwith merged into what was designated to be the National Socialist League of German Jurists.

In April of thirty-three the Nazis purged the legal profession of all Jewish and socialist judges, lawyers and other court officers. They also instructed the Academy of German Law to immediately Nazify German law, removing what they referred to as *'all Jewish influence'*.

All judges appointed to the revamped legal system were then

instructed to let *'gesundes Volksempfinden'* (healthy folk sentiment) guide them in reaching all future decisions.

* * * * *

- Protective Custody –

By July of nineteen thirty-three the number of so called *'protective custody'* detainees had reached just short of fifteen thousand in Prussia and nearly twenty-seven thousand spread throughout the Reich.

These men were housed in approximately fifty temporary internment centers under the control of various agencies including those of the police, the SA and the SS.

At that early stage of development the disorganized and inconsistent methods of arrest and incarceration began to raise some alarm in the newly Nazified Reich. In response to pressure from the judiciary the Nazis began to look into ways to standardize and better administer the process.

* * * * *

- Dachau –

The first internment camp of its kind constructed by the Nazi government, Dachau was used by the Nazis as a model for all such further institutions which were over time to be erected in many locations within the confines of the steadily expanding territory of the New German Reich.

Established in March of nineteen thirty-three Dachau was built ten miles northwest of Munich on the grounds of a long-abandoned munitions factory located just northeast of the town of Dachau.

Its purpose was to house the political opponents of the newly elected Nazi regime.

At the time of its construction Dachau was officially described by Heinrich Himmler, then head of the Munich police, as "the first concentration camp for political prisoners".

At this early date, the existence of Dachau was not something that the Nazi Party was ashamed of or wanted to hide from the general population of Germany; quite the opposite actually. Its construction was widely heralded with a view to making the public aware that the injuries, deaths and property damage brought about by political unrest and anti-Nazi sentiment which had become routine in previous years would not be tolerated by their newly-elected government.

As was the case with all of the early camps constructed by the Nazis, Dachau was created initially to fulfill the function of temporarily containing dissidents for the purpose of interrogating, harassing, terrorizing and torturing those who had previously openly disagreed with or challenged the Party's policies.

These so called 'wild concentration camps' were initiated and controlled by the various Nazi government paramilitary organizations, primarily the Gestapo, SS, and SA.

The camps were not set up with a view to either long-term incarceration or the extermination of those imprisoned, although deaths did occasionally occur.

The camps were designed to be used as tools calculated with the intention of bringing about the,'re-education' of inmates, who had been found wanting by Nazi standards and had then been subsequently adjudicated by some form of a judicial process.

After prisoners had been found guilty of the charges against them they were then sent to a camp where they could complete a course of 'rehabilitation' after which they would be released back into German society and an expected return to a productive lifestyle within the new Reich.

During its first year of operation, Dachau held just under five thousand prisoners. Generally speaking, those interred at that time were German social-democrats, communists, trade unionists and any other active political opponents to Nazi ideology, of whatever stripe.

Conditions inside the camps were less than desirable to say the least and those, 're-educated' and 'rehabilitated' were then released back into the mainstream population of German society.

Once free they were not only decidedly unlikely to wish to repeat the process but were also more than eager to warn others to avoid such pitfall.

Within a short period of time Dachau was performing its intended task credibly. It had become infamous and a new saying, *"Dear God, make me dumb, that I may not to Dachau come"*, had been coined and was being echoed throughout the new Reich.

CHAPTER TWO

- Inspection Assignment –

After the von Stauffer's family dinner of September twenty-fourth nineteen-forty, SS-Obersturmfuhrer Wilhelm von Stauffer had gone directly to the train station to join two other Himmler aides aboard the night train to Munich.

With a view to broadening his general knowledge of SS responsibilities, Wilhelm, along with one of the other new Himmler aides, a medical doctor holding the SS rank of Hauptsturmfuhrer (Captain), had been ordered by the Reichsfuhrer to join a group of SS officers he'd assigned to conduct an impromptu inspection tour of the concentration camp located at Dachau.

The Reichsfuhrer's senior aide, SS-Hauptsturmfuhrer, Joachim Peiper had, after passing on the order from Himmler to Wilhelm earlier in the day, offered to introduce Wilhelm to the recently graduated and newly recruited thirty year old Medical Captain who would be accompanying him on the trip to Munich. Here it was intended that they would join up with the new head of the *Inspektion der Konzentrationslager* (Concentration Camps Inspectorate), SS-Brigadefuhrer (Brigadier General) Richard Glucks and his entourage.

Glucks, Theodor Eicke's deputy, had replaced the SS-Gruppenfuhrer as Inspector of camps in the autumn of nineteen thirty-nine.

Wilhelm was pleasantly surprised to find that he'd already had the pleasure of meeting the doctor.

The Hauptsturmfuhrer, who entered Peiper's office in response to a summoning phone call, struck Wilhelm as somewhat ill at ease in his crisp new uniform.

However, any apparent sense of unease the newcomer felt with regard to his new mode of dress as he entered the office was immediately deflected by the broad smile that formed on his handsome features when he spotted Wilhelm, who at the sound of the opening door had stood and turned to face the newcomer as he entered the room.

Wilhelm returned the Captain's warm smile with one of his own.

"Konrad…"

Peiper laid down the document he had been reading and looked up from his desk as Wilhelm flushed and then snapped his heels together and raised his right arm in salute.

"Heil Hitler! My apologies Herr Hauptsturmfuhrer, congratulations are in order I see."

Wilhelm turned to glance at Peiper.

"Hauptsturmfuhrer Kauffmann and I met a short time ago. He was interning under an old family friend SS-Sturmbannfuhrer (Major) doctor Baron Heinrich von Kliest at the Kaiser Wilhelm Institute of Anthropology, Human Heredity and Eugenics."

Kauffmann returned the salute somewhat awkwardly and then extended his hand, which Wilhelm shook warmly.

"Yes, Wilhelm and I managed to find the time to share many a late evening stein while I was taking instruction under Doctor von Kliest."

Peiper nodded and bid the two men to be seated.

* * * * *

- Arbeitslager –

As the growing bureaucracy within the various organizations who were responsible for dealing with the number of openly political opponents within the Reich began to work effectively, the early *'wild'* camps began to expand in number.

Subsequently these internment camps began to morph to restructure with a view to meet this new requirement for housing the increase in interment.

After the Reichstag fire of February twenty-seventh, nineteen thirty-three a state of emergency was declared.

This resulted in a mass arrest of communist opposition
members who requiring restricted housing.

After the '*Ermaechtigtungsgesetz*' (Enabling Act) was
proclaimed on March twenty-third of thirty-three the non-Nazi
politically active leaders, members of the socialist and civil party
affiliates and trade-union leaders were also arrested.

These so called '*protective-custody*' detainees reached fifteen
thousand by July of nineteen thirty-three.

One '*Totenkopfverbande*' (SS-Deaths-Head) unit was
assigned to act as guards at each camp after April of nineteen
thirty-six and the entire administrative staff, including the
Commandant, was also absorbed into the '*Totenkopf*'organization.

At the time all the members of SS units wore the Deaths-
Head symbol on their caps but only these newly created
'*Totenkopfverbande*' units were additionally authorized to wear the
symbol on their uniform lapels.

It was not until the later formation of the first militarily
trained Waffen-SS forces, which had been formed solely from the
members of the '*Totenkopfverbande*' in nineteen-forty, that any
frontline fighting troops were allowed to sport the symbol on their
lapels.

The need for new and larger concentration camps grew as the
Nazis began to identify additional groups that were considered by
the party as '*undesirable*'.

Various '*undesirables*' began to appear on the ruling Nazis
Party's radar.

Repeat criminal offenders, Jehovah's Witnesses, Gypsies,
homosexuals, the homeless and other '*asocial*' personages came
into contention and unlike their predecessors; these new inmates
did not necessarily receive any form, however cursory, of judicial
redress before finding themselves sentenced to a camp.

Under the new laws such inferior creatures could also rarely,
if ever, expect to be released back into the mainstream of German
society as free citizens.

Early on the Nazis had placed this type of individual in the
category of sub-human: those who should at all costs be prevented
from breeding either through sterilization or by way of a gender-

divided incarceration.

By nineteen thirty-nine, a new and different type of camp was needed in order to house this much larger element of what were now being loosely designated as *'Unzuverlassige Elemente'* (Undesirables).

Each of these new camps, a mirror image of what had proven successful in Dachau, was staffed by one *SS- 'Totenkopfverbande'* unit which was divided into two unique groups.

The first group consisted of:

A) The Commandant who held authority over the heads of division and his personal staff, a security Gestapo officer and his assistant who were responsible for the maintenance and update of all inmate records.

B) The 'Schutzhaftlagerfuhrer' or Commandant of the protective detention camp that housed the actual prisoners and his staff which included the labour allocation officer.

C) The roll call officer and the 'Blockfuhrer' (Block Leader) who had the direct responsibly for the order and discipline of the prisoner barracks as well as an administrative staff responsible to look after the fiscal and supply administration of the camp.

D) An SS-Physician and two 'SS-Sanitation officers' or medical orderlies whose duty it was to maintain the camp infirmary.

The second group was the *'SS-Wachbataillion'* force which was the actual guard component required for the internment facility.

After nineteen thirty-eight the authority to incarcerate persons within the confines of the camps was officially designated as exclusively a privilege of the *'German Security Police'* (Criminal Police and Gestapo).

The legal processes for these arrests were covered in the terms of either *'Schutzhaft'* (Protective Detention), used by the Gestapo or *'Vorbeugungshaft'* used by the Criminal Police after nineteen thirty-seven against habitual offenders or those defined as of *'asocial'* behaviour.

A judicial review was not required by those enforcing these two arrest procedures.

Under the new laws, the only review possible was one to be made by the Germany Security Police and unsurprisingly they were not at all interested in becoming involved at that point in the arrest process.

As the numbers of targeted individuals within the Reich grew, more camps were built.

In nineteen thirty-seven the SS, using inmate labour, initiated construction of a large complex of buildings on the grounds of the original Dachau camp. Prisoners housed within the camp itself were utilized to complete this work, starting with the destruction of the old munitions factory.

The new construction was completed in mid August of thirty-eight.

Between nineteen thirty-eight and nineteen thirty-nine, several new camps were built.

Sachsenhausen was constructed in thirty-six and Buchenwald in thirty-seven.

Flossenburg and Ravensbruck, a camp for the internment of female inmates, were completed in thirty-eight/nine.

The earlier experiments using prisoners for forced labour on SS projects such as camp renovation and construction, which had begun in nineteen thirty-four, had been deemed a great success.

By thirty-eight this concept was in general use at all camps and some later camps were specifically constructed near quarries or mines, with a view to using the forced labour of future prisoners to work these sites and beginning the commercialization of the concentration camp labour force as a source of income for the SS.

These new encampments were classified by the Nazis as *Arbeitslager* (Labour Camps).

At the time of their incarceration, inmates who fell within the earlier mentioned categories were now placed into these detention centres with the specific intention that they were to be used as slave labourers and obligated to work, without recompense, for the good of the State until they died.

From this point on, the unworthy of Germany would work, all-be-it unwillingly, for the betterment of the Reich.

Although no specific guidelines were ever officially

promulgated in writing, these internees would be destined to live in meagre conditions and fed a diet that was realistically insufficient to sustain human life, thereby insuring the inmates would be quite literally, over time, worked to death.

CHAPTER THREE

- Night Train to Munich –

Wilhelm von Stauffer and Dr. Konrad Kauffmann arrived together at the busy Berlin Bahnhof station early and found time to enjoy a beer together before they made their way through the crowded waiting room to meet with Obersturmfuhrer Helmut Muller who had been designated their liaison for the scheduled inspection tour of the internment camp at Dachau by '*SS-Brigadefuhrer*' (Brigadier General) Richard Glucks, head of the Concentration Camps Inspectorate.

Muller arrived at the predetermined meeting place a few minutes late and apologized for his tardiness,

He quickly provided them with their travel documents and tickets before leading them to the train which was by then building steam and in the final stages of loading.

They made their way through the Party-banner-hung and poster-strewn station to join a sea of moving uniforms and purposefully striding civilians to the platform indicated and then alongside the standing train to the first class coaches to board.

The three men, all tall and broadly built, stood out in their well-tailored, distinct and readily recognizable black uniforms.

Upon their formation as an elite organization, Hitler's original bodyguard unit had adopted the black uniforms and '*Totenkopf*' (Death-head) or skull and crossbones insignia which had originated within the Prussian army cavalry under Frederick the Great.

For the average German, the distinctive black uniform and the ominous Death-head badge insignia worn on the peaked cap of an SS officer was, in Germany by this point in time, associated with an elite force backed by tremendous authority and one which demonstrated little or no sense of humour.

Not surprisingly, Wilhelm and his two associates experienced little difficulty moving forward unimpeded along the crowded platform; those in front of or approaching them averting their eyes as they moved to one side, actively taking care not to obstruct the SS officer's forward progress.

These examples of submissive behaviour toward those in SS uniform had been commonplace for some time in the *'New Reich'* and yet each of the three men reacted differently to it.

Muller took it as his due.

Wilhelm felt a surge of pride.

The doctor, very new to the uniform and the experience of public exposure to it, felt a little uncomfortable.

They boarded their car.

Shortly thereafter Wilhelm was pleasantly surprised to find himself waved into a luxurious self-contained compartment offering not only comfortable seating but also sleeping quarters for four.

Muller noted the appreciative looks on the faces of his SS - uniformed companions and laughed.

"It pays to be the Reichsfuhrer's aide when arranging transportation."

He closed the door behind them and in so doing, muted the sound given off by those moving about in the corridor and then casually tossed his case up onto the luggage rack provided before dropping down into one of the seats.

"Best accommodation available and the car immediately forward is the dining car."

* * * * *

- The Jewish Question –

Unless they happened to fall into the specific politically-unacceptable categories mentioned earlier, persons of Jewish extraction had not been specifically targeted for incarceration in any of the early internment camps types.

This was not because the Nazis had not predetermined them as *'unworthy of German citizenship'*. They definitely did consider them as such, as evidenced by the passing of the Nuremberg Laws of nineteen thirty-five.

However, based on Nazi thinking at the time, the Jews were considered a unique, very special and extremely dangerous group of undesirables.

Only those of a pure Aryan type were to become a permanent part of a new Nazified Germany.

As far as the Nazis were concerned the Jews were a cancer on the body of the German state, a race of contemptible sub-humans unworthy of the slightest consideration for possible future occupancy within the borders of a wonderfully new and expanded German Reich.

Jews were to be considered for incarceration.

They were to be completely removed from German soil.

Subsequently in those first few years the Nazis worked very diligently at encouraging all those of Jewish decent to leave Germany. Increasingly they did this by making the very existence for Jews residing in Germany a living hell.

No consideration whatsoever was given to the thought of interning a Jew with the aim of attempting to, 're-educate' him or her, with the intention of returning them to the mainstream of German society. The Nazi Party was adamant about achieving this cleansing of the Fatherland of all Jews to the extent that, at this point in time, they were not even to be considered as of sufficient value for utilization as potential slave labourers.

In those early years Nazi policy was strictly aimed at forcing every Jew out of Germany and the sooner the better.

* * * * *

- Allied Agreement –

In March of nineteen-forty the French and British concluded an agreement that stipulated that neither country would ever sign a separate peace treaty with the Nazis.

When, three months later, Paris had been overrun by the German *'Blitzkrieg'*, the disheartened French Premier, Paul

Reynaud, was forced by the furious onslaught of the German military machine to ask Winston Churchill to release the French from the recently agreed joint-pact.

When it came, Churchill had grave concerns over the request.

For Churchill, the possibility that the French fleet, the world's fourth largest naval force, might fall into German hands was alarming to say the least.

He responded to Reynaud by suggesting that it would be possible for the French to be relieved of their responsibilities under the agreement if the French Navy was ordered to immediately set sail for British ports prior to any such attempt to explore a possible separate armistice with the Germans.

In his responding communiqué to the French leader Churchill additionally proposed that the two countries should also sign a document cementing an '*indissoluble union*' between Great Britain and France.

Reynaud was taken completely aback by these suggestions.

The French forces were being soundly beaten back and the British expeditionary forces in France were retreating with them.

France was being trampled under the Nazi boot.

The French Premier was currently facing a losing battle in an attempt to hold on to some vestige of sovereignty over the south-eastern half of his overrun nation and certainly not inclined to unnecessarily irritate the Germans with whom he firmly believed, if conditions did not change, he would shortly have to negotiate an armistice.

On the thirteenth of June nineteen-forty the final meeting of a series of the Anglo French War Council, which had been going on sporadically for several months, took place at the Prefecture in Tours, France.

In this case the British delegation of the War Council was composed of Churchill, Lord Halifax, Sir Alexander Cadogan, General Ismay and General Spears. The French in attendance were the Prime Minister, Paul Reynaud and Paul Baudoin.

Spears, who had attended earlier such meetings found the British approach to this last meeting of the group different in that whereas Churchill had earlier demonstrated empathy and good will, he now took a more businesslike and definitely self-interested approach to the talks.

From Churchill's perspective, the British Empire was determined to fight on, and it naturally followed that their ally France must fight on at their side.

The French had signed an agreement that no separate armistice could be made with Germany without the agreement of both signatories to that agreement and he wanted to hold them to it.

The French were literally under the gun by this point. They simply couldn't stop the Nazi blitzkrieg which was steamrolling over their dwindling defences with the power and determination of an inexorable tidal wave.

Reynaud's back was against the wall.

With trembling hands and a soft voice, he readily acknowledged that France had agreed to never conclude a separate peace but now surely the British could see that the situation had changed to the point that France no longer had the option of choice.

His country was physically incapable of continuing the war and had no option but to seek an armistice with Germany.

It was a bombshell that the British had not been expecting. There was a pregnant pause as looks of shock and horror filled the faces of the English delegates.

Finally Churchill broke the silence.

"We must fight, we will fight, and that is why we must ask our friends to fight on."

Reynaud nodded, acknowledging that the British would of course continue the war. He went so far as to suggest that France would also continue the struggle from its North African colonies if necessary, but only if there were a reasonable chance for success.

He further stated that, from his perspective, success could only come about if the United States were to choose to join the Allied cause.

Churchill was under no illusion that the Americans were prepared to join the fight in the near future. The isolationists held sway in the USA and the President would have been tarred and feathered and ridden out of town on a rail if he had so much as suggested such a thing.

Churchill was confident that it was true that Roosevelt himself was sympathetic and doing his best to set the stage for his country's eventual entry into the battle but that would be some time off.

At the end of the meeting the French leader again called for the British to release them from their obligation and allow them to sue for a separate peace now that there was no other choice.

Earlier in the conference Churchill had been offered the opportunity to address the French cabinet before the British left for home.

He had initially intended to deal with the question of the agreement at that time; however the current discussion had ended in such confusion and lack of cohesion that, for whatever reason, the French made no offer to honour such an opportunity.

The earlier offer was no longer on the table.

On the flight home the British group, singularly depressed, were all of the opinion that any remaining possibility that France would remain in the war against Germany was rapidly evaporating.

However, during their stay in France, the French Marine Minister, Admiral Darlan had privately and personally given his word to Churchill that the French fleet would never be allowed to fall into the hands of the Nazis.

Both men had a sound naval background. Neither had considered for a moment that Germany might not desire the takeover of the French fleet.

But in fact, Hitler had no such intention.

When it came to the French fleet, the Nazi leader simply wanted it neutralized, either by scuttling or by interment for the duration of the war in French ports *under German or Italian supervision*.

Hitler's naval interest was in submarine warfare and he had neither the desire nor the trained manpower required to staff an additional fleet of seven battleships, twenty cruisers, two aircraft carriers and a horde of destroyers and auxiliary ships.

He simply wanted them destroyed or mothballed and under his watchful eyes.

CHAPTER FOUR

- A Sleepless night –

Count von Stauffer had spent several restless hours, tossing and turning fitfully in his bed after he'd left his wife's boudoir to return to his own bedroom suite.

This matter with Gabriella was becoming insufferable.

Erika could think of nothing else and he was only too well aware that his wife, famous throughout the family for her determination and resolve in directing family matters, would no more let it lie than a dog would willingly give up a new-found bone.

He let out a frustrated sigh and rolled over to switch on his bedside lamp, momentarily raising his hand to protect his eyes as the bulb burst into life.

When his eyes had become acclimatised to the illumination he glanced at the clock resting on the bedside table beside the lamp.

Three-forty...

He reached out to pick up the glass of water beside the clock and took a sip. As he was setting the glass down he swung his legs out from under the covers and let his feet drop to the thickly carpeted floor.

He was in the midst of stifling a yawn when he heard a vehicle pulling up in front of the mansion. This was followed by the sound of a car door opening.

Curious, he pushed the covers aside, reached for the robe on the chair next to the table holding the lamp, slipped into it and shuffled over to the large window which overlooked the street at the front of the house four stories below and raised a hand to part the heavy blackout drapes.

An SS-licensed staff car sat at the curb, exhaust burbling out in a gentle stream, as its motor idled. The passenger door stood open and it took him only a moment to recognize his youngest daughter who had just unsteadily exited the vehicle and stood teetering for a moment before turning to lean her upper body back into the gaping door of the vehicle.

Obviously drunk...my God almost four in the morning...she has to be up in just over an hour to go to her classes at the hospital. Yes, Erika was right - it has gotten completely out of hand.

He watched from his elevated viewpoint for a few seconds as Gabriella, using the frame of the open door for purchase, eased her head back out of the car and then pushed the door closed.

The car's engine roared into life and the long black vehicle surged back into the roadway.

Gabriella stood for a few seconds, watching the vehicle pull away before she turned and made her way across the sidewalk toward the front of the house.

With a heavy sigh, the Count let the blind fall closed and turned away from the window.

He eased his feet into his slippers and adjusted the robe slightly before tying it firmly and then started across toward his bedroom door.

Well it stops now. Enough is enough.

* * * * *

- Adolph Eichmann –

Adolf Eichmann was born in Solingen, an industrial city in the Rhineland in nineteen-six. At the time of his birth, his father was employed with a local power company.

In nineteen-thirteen his father was given a promotion that meant the family was obliged to move to Linz in Austria.

Adolf's father and therein the entire family, were German nationalists.

As was the case with many Germans, The elder Eichmann had lost his wealth during the post Great War period of economic crisis and had been forced to rebuild his fortunes from scratch.

He was a very bitter man.

In consequence he enrolled young Adolf in the 'Wandervogel', a popular youth group of the time.

This and later groups Adolf Eichmann joined as he grew to manhood exposed him to many of the concepts and ideas that he was to strongly embrace in his later life.

The 'Wandervogel' group was purportedly apolitical; however it was laced with the nationalistic and romantic beliefs of the 'Volkisch' movement. The German word Volkisch means folklore and ethnicity.

When he was a little older Adolf moved up to join the Linz branch of the 'Heimschutz' (Homeland Protection), a blatantly right-leaning paramilitary association made up primarily of German army veterans.

'Heimschutz' groups first formed in Austria after the end of the Great War and promoted the idea that 'homeland protection' was not just the protection of geographical borders but also required the defence of the society's culture as well.

At the time Eichmann, a strong anti-Semitic, also considered, but due to other considerations, subsequently rejected, joining the 'Masons'; for the simple reason that the organization excluded Jews.

Eichmann's father was a senior member of the Evangelical Church.

From the time of his birth, young Adolf was in awe of his father, with the result that he was strongly influenced by and easily moulded by several older male authority figures throughout his life.

Eichmann did not do well in school and when the time came, his father, who had recently opened his own business in the field of oil-extraction, put him to work in the new family business.

Adolf worked on the surface and below ground in oil-shale tunnels for a short time and then moved on to take up an apprenticeship in an electrical engineering firm.

In nineteen twenty-seven Eichmann senior found a position for Adolf with another firm, the Vacuum Oil Company.

While a poor student when in school, Adolf excelled at picking up practical skills when being given on-the-job-training under the direction of older males whom he respected.

He did well with the new company and was soon travelling about Upper Austria selling oil products, searching out new sites for, and overseeing the construction of, gas stations and fuel supply depots.

Impressed by both his diligence and administrative ability his new employers transferred him to the Saltsburg region, where he continued to astound them with his abilities when it came to interpersonal human relations, his capacity to identify excellent traffic hubs, sell a product and administer effectively.

By nineteen thirty-three, after five years in the field, Eichmann was no longer finding himself challenged by his work.

He was becoming bored with his new job.

As chance would have it, he was laid off shortly after reaching this plateau and found himself eagerly packing his bags with the intention of travelling north to Austria to seek his fortune.

As a natural progression from his earlier membership in various right-leaning groups and his entry into manhood, Adolf Eichmann joined the Nazi Party on April first, nineteen thirty-two.

While attending a Nazi rally he was approached by a member of the SS, Ernst Kaltenbrunner, a tall (standing at just over six foot seven) and facially scarred lawyer who was three years his senior.

At the time Kaltenbrunner was the 'Gauredner' (District Speaker) and 'Rechtsvberater' (Legal Consultant) of the SS Division VIII.

Kaltenbrunner, whose father was a business acquaintance of Eichmann's own father was already a member of the Nazi party and had joined the SS in Austria in nineteen thirty-two.

The two men had met previously and happily exchanged greetings when they ran into each other at the rally.

They immediately hit it off.

Before the day was through, Kaltenbrunner told Eichmann *"you belong to us"* and from that day onward Adolf actively combined political activism in the Austrian SS with commerce until nineteen thirty-three, when the Nazi party was outlawed there.

In January of nineteen thirty-four, along with numerous other

National Socialists, Kaltenbrunner was charged and jailed by the Dollfuss government and subsequently sentenced to incarceration within the 'Kaisersteinbruch' concentration camp.

Before he was arrested he arranged for Eichmann to clear out of Austria and make his way into Germany.

Once safely in Germany, Adolf joined an SS training centre and initially served with an exiled Austrian SS unit before being posted to Dachau.

While assigned to Dachau, he applied to join the *'Sicherheitsdienst des Reichsfuhrer's-SS'* (Security Service) or SD, the intelligence agency of the SS and the Nazi Party.

Between thirty-three and thirty-nine the SD was administered as an independent SS office. After thirty-nine it was transferred to the *'Reichssicherheitshauptanmt'* or RSHA (Reich Main Security Office) as one of its seven departments.

This organization was formed in nineteen thirty-one as the *'Ic-Dienst'*. At that time it was operated out of a single small office and reported directly to Heinrich Himmler.

Himmler had appointed the former naval officer, Reinhardt Heydrich, to create and manage the small agency.

The office was renamed SD in the summer of thirty-two.

The SD was the initial intelligence unit to be established in Germany and was closely tied to the Gestapo, an organization which the SS brazenly worked to infiltrate with great success after nineteen thirty-four.

The SD was perfectly suited for Adolf Eichmann's talents and abilities. He worked there as a clerk and spent the majority of his time monitoring Freemasons before he was spotted by the head of the Jewish section, Leopold Itz Edler von Mildenstein, who was soon to become his next mentor.

Born in Prague, then part of Austria-Hungary, in nineteen-two, von Mildenstein was a member of the bottom rank of the Austrian nobility. He was raised as a Roman Catholic.

Von Mildenstein was educated as an engineer and joined the Nazi Party in nineteen twenty-nine. He joined the SS in nineteen thirty-two, the first Austrian to do so.

Early on in his career, von Mildenstein took an interest in

Zionism, going so far as to attend Zionist conferences to gain a greater understanding of the movement.

He actively promoted the concept of Zionism and the creation of a Jewish state as the answer to the German *'Jewish question'*, which was the creation of a Jew-free Germany.

Von Mildenstein encouraged Eichmann to take up the study of Jewish society and history so as to better understand the makeup of this *'subhuman'* enemy race.

Eichmann, as was his nature, instantly began to emulate his elder mentor and threw himself into the task.

The SD at the time was only a minor cog in the SS machine, and the Jewish section an even smaller puddle within the SD pond.

He had done this because, despite those realities with regard to the size of the fledgling unit, the SD was being run by Reinhardt Heydrich, a Himmler stalwart and favourite.

Eichmann foresaw a bright future ahead for the *'Jewish section'*.

From the mid-thirties onward, Heydrich had directly targeted Jewish issues and had built his personal empire on that basis to the point where it had a reputation within the Nazi Party as a centre for clear, scientific understanding and thinking on the methods of dealing with this ominous and dangerous *'Jewish subhuman race'*.

Thanks to Heydrich's mentorship, Eichmann began to stand out and started to receive a series of promotions.

During this period, the propaganda machine wielded by Joseph Goebbels was continually harping away at the Jewish plague, steadily upping the rhetoric, suggesting through notably directionless measures that more and more extreme and stringent steps needed to be implemented to deal with the problem.

Heydrich did not take this tack, instead his office quietly but determinedly, advocated and worked toward facilitating mass Jewish emigration.

In so doing, he pushed Eichmann to contact Zionist representatives and sent him to Palestine in nineteen thirty-seven to see what could be done to assist and advance the flow of Jews out of Germany and into the holy land.

In order to accomplish this task, Eichmann frantically

acquired a basic understanding of Yiddish and Hebrew before he headed out the door.

Eichmann was of course anti-Semitic. Like the rest of his group, he had no real sympathy for Zionism and was simply using the façade as a ploy to get the Jews out of Germany.

When he returned from Palestine he warned Heydrich that the SD would be foolish to promote a strong Jewish state and should instead encourage Jewish emigration only to third world countries where they would have no chance to educate and conspire to form a nation of their own.

Germany occupied Austria in nineteen thirty-eight. The Nazis thereby inherited an additional large Jewish contingent into the Reich.

For the Nazis, Austria was a natural and wonderful addition to the new Reich. However the inheritance of yet more Jews was certainly seen as untenable.

What in Gods name where they going to do with them all?

Upon his return from Palestine, Eichmann was soundly applauded by Heydrich, appointed assistant to the SD leader in the SS main region, Danube and immediately reassigned to the SD in Vienna with instructions to clean up the problem of these additional Jews.

Instructed to speed up Jewish emigration out of Austria, which was now part of the German Reich, Eichmann threw himself wholeheartedly into his assigned task the instant he arrived.

Using his impressive administrative experience to smooth the way out for the Jews, he went to work on the problem areas, removing roadblocks, wherever he found them, faced by Jews who wished to emigrate.

He concentrated on identifying all the agencies aspiring to get the Jews out of what had been Austria. He then ordered these various agencies to jointly occupy a single office.

He set up a new Central Jewish Organization in order deal directly with the leaders of the Jewish community and negotiated with them to see to it that the whole idea of Jewish emigration was organized and efficient from the grass roots up. He ordered that the wealthy Jews of Austria immediately pony up and fund the cost of sending the mass of poor Jews out of the country as quickly as was practicable.

Eichmann was not only dedicated and good at his job, he was absolutely committed and from the get-go no one even considered questioning his determination to get the job done.

Within weeks he had established an *'assembly line'* whose sole purpose was getting rid of every Jew.

His accomplishment was impressive.

When a Jew walked into the Central Emigration Office with his papers, he was moved efficiently in an orderly fashion along a line of desks. The individual involved was passed from desk to desk until he arrived at the very last of them at which time he was handed a passport and an exit visa and then shown the door.

During the process the participant was effectively and determinedly stripped of his citizenship, cash, rights and property.

Over the period of a few months the office shoved over one hundred and fifty thousand Jews out the back door of the office and thereby out of Austria while pocketing a fortune in cash and seizing a considerable amount of personal possessions and real estate property for the SS and the Reich.

Heydrich was pleased beyond belief and absolutely enthralled by Eichmann's accomplishment.

In October of nineteen thirty-nine he ordered Eichmann to set up a parallel office in Prague and appointed him to Department IV D 4 of the Gestapo in Berlin which was authorized to handle all Jewish emigration from the New Reich.

As a result of Eichmann's success in Vienna the SD's rational *'Jewish Policy'* had demonstrated itself to be the only acceptable solution to the Jewish question and was very strongly supported by Reichsfuhrer Himmler.

The SS had many irons in the fire by this point in time and the demands on manpower that would be needed to fulfill the ongoing obligations of Eichmann's programme of emigration was growing daily.

Sustaining it was becoming difficult

CHAPTER FIVE

- Night Train –

Wilhelm, as did his two companions, now sat in shirtsleeves and was nursing a beer. He allowed himself a short yawn and a wistful glance at one of the bunks before he turned his full attention back to the ongoing discussion which was being carried out between the two Hauptsturmfuhrer's.

For the moment Muller was holding the floor, expostulating on the abrupt effect of an earlier visit that had been accomplished through the use of the Reichsfuhrer-SS's special train and was conducted on September twentieth nineteen thirty-nine at Blomberg.

"On the occasion of that early visit to Blomberg by Himmler, I was one of the accompanying staff officers. As it happened we, as official visitors, were offered the opportunity to view the execution of twenty Poles.

Himmler accepted the offer on behalf of our group and we were promptly taken to the site of the killings."

All colour drained from the Reichsfuhrer's face during the executions and there were only twenty of them mind you.

The effect of viewing the terminations was instantaneous with him. He blanched and stood with his hands clasped tightly together and his lips quivering for a few seconds before abruptly turning away.

He was unable to speak for several minutes.

The rest of us silently followed him as he walked some distance away from the twitching bodies. No one spoke, unsure of what to say to him. It was obvious to all of us that he had been seriously affected by the sight of the executions.

He was speechless for several days thereafter and when he brought up the visit later, his only comment was that we had to find a better way. He said there would of necessity be many more of these terminations and our men could not be repeatedly put through this type of operation. They were good men, strong men, but less direct ways must be found to execute prisoners, methods that did not involve this type of hands-on involvement by Germany's finest soldiers."

Doctor Kauffmann nodded his head in instant agreement as he drained off the last of the contents of his stein.

"Yes, I can well imagine it must have been pretty barbaric and messy as well as mentally hard on those who carried it out."

Muller smiled.

"Yes, and as is usually the case, the Reichsfuhrer was correct in his assessment and as a result of his wishes to have the matter rectified we have recently developed several   more refined methods of dealing with those who require '*special treatment*' as punishment for their activities against the new Reich.

If you're interested, perhaps I will have an opportunity to arrange for us to oversee a demonstration of these during our visit."

While not prepared to openly express it, both Wilhelm and Konrad found the idea unpalatable and despite the fact that Muller was obviously quite proud of whatever new methods the camp was now using for the handling of the necessary executions, neither man was of a mind to respond to the offer.

Wilhelm set his empty stein down on the small table beside him.

"I don't know about you two, but I would like to grab a couple of hours sleep before we arrive."

Muller shrugged.

"Ok, but before we do I want to read something to you. It's something that you should be aware of before we visit the camp."

Both tired, Wilhelm and Konrad nodded acceptance with little enthusiasm.

Muller didn't look up at them but continued to speak.

"The first Commandant of Dachau, Theodore Eicke, created a '*Disciplinary and Penal Code for the Prison Camp*' which he issued on October first of nineteen thirty-three."

Muller shifted slightly in his seat and leaned down to flip

---

open his black leather document case which he then brought up into his lap. He fished through the contents for a few seconds and then pulled out a file which he opened and spread across his knees.

"Here, I have a copy; let me just read you a part of it."

"Any person who at work, in the living quarters, kitchen, workshops, toilets or rest places engages in subversive politics, holds provocative speeches, congregates with others for this purpose, forms cliques, loiters, collects of receives or buries information, repeats or smuggles out of the camp by means of a note or some other method to a camp visitor information, either true of false, concerning the camp, to be used in our enemies horror propaganda, or who sends written or verbal messages through released or transferred prisoners, conceals them in items of clothing or other objects, throws them over the wall, writes coded messages, or any person who in order to incite rebellion climbs onto the roof of the huts, or up trees, or transmits signals with a lamp or by any other means, seeks outside contact, or advises, supports or aids others in escape or crime, will be hanged as a subversive instigator under the terms of the revolutionary law."

Muller slid the sheet of paper back into the file and returned it to the document case before looking back up at his companions.

* * * * *

- Jewish Population Explosion –

A large portion of Poland had been absorbed into the Reich, courtesy of the Nazi military conquest of that country and with that considerable territorial grab the Nazis now found themselves again inheriting more Jews into the Reich - in excess of a million of them.

Himmler informed Heydrich that he could no longer provide the manpower necessary to continue with Eichmann's system of deportation and as a result Heydrich met with Eichmann and laid the facts out before him.

He then ordered Adolf to come up with yet another new solution to the continually burgeoning Jewish problem.

Eichmann's emotional makeup and upbringing meant that he longed to deal with challenges that respected older men presented to him.

He simply *had* to solve such problems in order to please them.

He began to explore new options and quickly settled on a plan to ship the Jews as far east as possible, within what had been Poland to a single, designated Jewish territory, where they could be placed in a secure concentration point and from there eventually shipped entirely out of the Reich.

He went to what had been Poland and searched for an appropriate location and having found what he wanted he then issued the order that would send thousands of Polish, Czech and Viennese Jews eastward to be housed in an operation which he called his new '*territorial solution*' to the Jewish Problem.

Unfortunately for Eichmann, this answer too, required a great deal of personnel and although it was warmly accepted by both Heydrich and his boss SS-Reichsfuhrer Himmler as the correct and reasonable thing to do, this plan too was soon to suffer from the simple fact that the SS simply had too many irons in the fire.

There was not sufficient manpower available to physically put such an endeavour into action.

Despite this situation, a determined Eichmann continued on with his problem solving.

One of his responsibilities was to ensure that the hundreds of thousands of ethnic Germans from Eastern Europe who, under Hitler's orders, where to be moved into the newly taken Polish lands as '*Aryan Settlers*' of pure blood, had land and housing to move to.

Eichmann, with his usual administrative efficiency and resolve, was busily working at removing a sufficient number of Jews and Poles from the needed territory in order to meet this need.

He packed the displaced Jews into ghettos, where they could be fenced off from the rest of the population and after the fall of France he began to push the idea that been formed earlier in the German Foreign Office and which recommended that any of the four million European Jews, who had failed to emigrate earlier on, should be rounded up and forcefully shipped to Madagascar.

* * * * *

- Brazil –

During the eighteen hundreds a massive emigration of Europeans to different parts of the new world began. Between eighteen forty-six and nineteen thirty-two approximately sixty million people migrated.

Germans nationals made up a good part of that emigration.

After the failed revolutions within the German states in eighteen forty-eight, many of those on the losing side chose to leave the Fatherland rather than stay under the current conditions

A fair number of these Germans, who were primarily farmers, made their way to the South American countries and Brazil had been one of the more popular choices.

By the nineteen-thirties, Brazil had become home to one of the largest German speaking populations outside Germany itself.

It consisted of one hundred thousand German-born citizens and a larger community of approximately one million persons of German descent whose ancestors had been settling in Brazil since eighteen twenty-four.

The country also had the largest number of members of the Nazi Party residing outside of Germany's borders, and generally speaking, tended to avoid integration with the native population, choosing instead to band together in large groups whenever possible.

After nineteen-thirty, successive Brazilian governments worked toward expanding industrial and agricultural growth within the country's vast interior. Getulio Vargas led a military junta to take control of the country in that year and as its new
President, backed by the military, he assumed dictatorial powers.

His tenure in office was not unlike many South American military dictatorships. It faced an internal Constitutionalist revolt in nineteen thirty-two and two separate coup d'état attempts by, first the Communists in nineteen thirty-five and then the Fascists in nineteen thirty-eight.

After a period of relative isolation during the early years of the thirties, due primarily to the effect of the Great Depression, Brazil actively sought export opportunities with the fascist regimes of both Italy and Germany.

These efforts served to help cement ties between Brazil and Germany.

The attempted fascist coup in nineteen thirty-eight coupled with the British blockade of Italy and Germany at the outbreak of the war interrupted this export trade.

Brazil, as did most South American counties, chose to remain neutral in the war.

At that time there were approximately one and a half million ethnic Germans living in South America, two-thirds of whom resided in Brazil.

German migrants had not assimilated in Brazil as they had in many other countries; for example the airlines in Brazil were totally controlled by Germans.

This tendency to maintain their own ethnic communities and businesses made the Germans living in Brazil much more sympathetic toward the Nazi cause than those of their brothers and sisters who had emigrated to settle elsewhere in the world.

The German ethnic community had influence in Brazil, especially strong in the southern regions and in general terms, the country's sympathies lay with the Nazis.

CHAPTER SIX

- A Father's Advice –

The Count, a stiff, fortifying drink in hand, was sitting in the dark on a chair standing below the blackout-curtained window in his daughter's bedroom which was located on the fourth floor at the back of the house when Gabriella entered and switched on the light.

She didn't see him at first and it wasn't until he cleared his throat that she realized someone else was in the room.

She started slightly, giving forth a small cry, but upon realizing who it was she calmly dropped her handbag into the chair beside the door and tossed her coat on top.

"Father! What a nice surprise. I don't suppose you came to read me a bedtime story though, did you?"

The Count took a slug from his glass and swallowed. Gabriella used the time to move across the room to her bed and sit down on the edge. Her father studied her for a second before he responded.

"No, I haven't done that for a very long time have I Gabriella? Perhaps I should have been doing it all along."

When did she lose her way? Why didn't we catch it early on - nip it in the bud? Is it too late for her to change? Is it possible for me to get back that perfect little girl I loved so much?

Gabriella's shoulders drooped and she shook her head.

"Really Daddy, it was very nice of you to wait up for me, but I'm a woman now and I don't need bedtime stories any more. It's late and I have to get some sleep."

The Count, carrying his near empty glass, stood and began to pace as he spoke.

"Are you Gabriella? Are you a woman grown now? God knows, you look like one but you don't act like one."

* * * * *

- French Premier –

Paul Reynaud became Premier of France on March twenty-first nineteen-forty.

He made de Gaulle his undersecretary of state for war and as the Germans began to crush the French army in May of that year he urged the continuation of French resistance and held to the alliance with Great Britain.

At that time, he had, of political necessity, Marshal Philippe Petain as his deputy premier. He did this to strengthen his cabinet but Petain, a French hero of the Great War, did not support Reynaud in his desire to continue the battle against the Germans and Petain, with the support of several other ministers of the embattled government, had been openly pushing for an armistice with the Nazis.

Reynaud, a man of character and his word, refused to support this policy and rather than be part of such a suggestion he chose to resign his position on June sixteenth, nineteen-forty.

Shortly after his resignation he was arrested and held in captivity for the duration of the war.

Petain, the old war-horse, who preferred occupation to war, immediately stepped into the leadership of the new *'Vichy French'* government.

His request for an armistice was almost instantaneous.

* * * * *

- Armistice at Compiegne –

The French raised the white flag that ended the Battle of France on June twenty-first nineteen-forty and at 18:50 hours on June twenty-second the Nazi scripted *'Second Armistice at Compiegne'* was signed between Germany and France.

Upon receipt of word from the French that they wished to negotiate the terms of an armistice Hitler had selected the forest near Compiegne as the meeting place for the negotiations.

Compiegne was the location where the armistice of nineteen-eighteen, which ended the Great War, had been signed shortly after the humiliating defeat suffered by the Germans.

The selection of Compiegne was Hitler's way of enjoying his moment of revenge for Germany over the French.

He went so far as to order that the new armistice between the Nazis and the French was to be signed in the very same rail carriage that had been used for that purpose after the Great War in nineteen-eighteen.

The rail carriage was promptly removed from a French museum and transported back to the very spot where it had been located on the occasion of the nineteen-eighteen armistice negotiations.

Hitler took his revenge a step further.

For the official signing he seated himself in the identical chair in which Marshal Foch had sat to face the representative of the defeated German Empire in nineteen-eighteen, and after listening to the reading of the preamble of the agreement, which the Germans had drawn up, Hitler drove the point home, distaining the French representatives by standing up, as Foch had done in nineteen-eighteen and leaving the rail car.

He left the negotiations in the hands of his '*Oberkommando der Wehrmacht*' (Chief of the High Command of the Armed Forces), General Wilhelm Keitel.

The French, who had been previously presented with a copy of the document in their own language, did at one point attempt to negotiate but were cut off sharply and told in no uncertain terms, that there was to be no negotiation.

The French could accept the terms as written or they would have to suffer the consequences.

* * * * *

- Terms of the Armistice –

Germany would occupy approximately three-fifths of what

had been France.

The border of this occupation force was to be north and west of a line through Geneva, Tours and the Spanish border. This would give the German Kriegsmarine access to all French Channel and Atlantic ports.

Any persons who had been granted political asylum by the French were to be turned over to the Germans.

All occupation costs would be borne by the French at a cost of four hundred million French francs per day. The maintenance of a minimal French army was to be allowed with a view to keeping internal order.

With the intention of pacifying the French and in an attempt to discourage the creation of guerrilla groups among the French military units remaining in the French colonies, Hitler had ordered that the document not ask for the surrender of the French Navy. Instead it was specified that the French Navy was to be disarmed and was to remain interred and neutral until the end of the war.

The armistice document allowed for an unoccupied region, the *'Zone Libre'*. This area was to be governed by a French administration based in Vichy which would also be responsible for the administration of the occupied zone but only under an absolute German overview.

In the belief that the war would only last for a few more weeks before the British would have to join the French and throw in the towel, the French made no attempt to argue against the clause that determined that all French prisoners of war would remain in German custody until the end of all hostilities with the British. Their hesitation to question that clause meant that almost a million French prisoners of war would spend the next five years in German containment camps.

This agreement was to last until a final peace treaty could be successfully negotiated. The ceasefire went into effect on June twenty-fifth, nineteen-forty at 00:35 hours.

* * * * *

- The Dust Settles-

The successful German invasion of France left the Nazis in absolute control of the country's north and effectively overseeing a sympathetic puppet regime in the Vichy-governed south.

Before the defeat of the French, the Allies intended that in the event of war the French fleet in the Mediterranean would be used to counter the Axis Italian Navy, thereby freeing up the British Navy to concentrate the efforts of its fleet in the Atlantic and North Sea.

The armistice signed between the French and Nazi Germany did not however, leave the Germans in direct control of the French military forces billeted in the French colonies.

Not surprisingly, some of the members of the French Military serving in those colonies did not welcome the Nazi invasion and victory over their country. In some cases their allegiance leaned toward the Free French Forces under the leadership of French General, Charles de Gaulle.

Based on the division of German control in France there was good reason for some confusion as to which side the colonies were on. Needless to say this situation was of great concern to both the Nazis and the British. Both countries had a definite need to bring these uncommitted forces under their sole control.

After the signing of the armistice between France and Germany, French Equatorial Africa and French Cameroun joined the Free French. French North Africa, French Indochina, Syria and French West Africa aligned themselves with Vichy France.

* * * * *

– Crematoria –

J.A. Topf und Sohne (J.A. Topf and Sons) was an engineering company which specialized in the manufacture of customized incinerator and malting equipment. It was founded in Erfurt, Germany in eighteen, seventy-eight.

In the nineteen-twenties, cremation as a burial right became increasingly more popular in Germany.

By nineteen thirty-four the cremation method of dealing with a passing was commonplace and the government, concerned that a naked flame should not come in contact with the coffin during the process, passed rigorous regulations in order to standardize the form of cremation and directed that it was to be a smoke and odour free practice.

As a result the firm's chief engineer, Kurt Prufer applied himself to the creation of a crematoria oven that would meet the stringent new government regulations.

Hans Loritz joined the SS in nineteen-thirty and had by nineteen thirty-three been assigned to Dachau. In July of thirty-four he was transferred to take command of 'KZ Esterwegen' where he spent two years before returning to Dachau with the rank of Oberfuhrer to take up his new duties as the camp Commandant.

Acting in his capacity as Commandant, Loritz, in the summer of nineteen thirty-seven, wrote to Himmler with a request for the installation of a Crematorium at Dachau.

Up to this point in time, the camp dead had been placed in coffins for storage within a building equipped with a Christian Cross and candles.

After a short service if applicable, the coffins were then taken to Munich for cremation.

Loritz indicated in his letter that the number of bodies being dealt with had reached numbers that suggested it would be far more expedient to cremate them on-site rather than be continually running back and forth to Munich.

Himmler's office agreed and negotiations were opened with the firm Muller of Munich-Allach to provide the facility.

In nineteen-forty the crematorium sporting the newly developed Topf company two-chamber oven, opened for business at Dachau. It was an extremely efficient design in that several bodies could be consumed at one time depending on the sizes of the corpses.

The oven was housed in a small one-room, half-timbered, cabin-like structure which was located in a dense stand of trees and at some distance from the other camp buildings.

The small edifice offered no insight as to its purpose when

viewed from the outside and when its double barn doors were closed.

At this point in time, the Nazis no longer publically acknowledged the existence or operation of the internment camps. Under the control of the SS, the entire program was now to be kept secret from everyday Germans.

Legally, all deaths in Germany had to be reported to the Public Registrar.

The Reichsfuhrer's office was aware of the growing death-rate in the enlarged camp system and it was decided that giving the Public Registrar an accounting of the rising mortality rates within the camps was no longer a prudent mechanism.

With typical German practicality Himmler's staff solved the problem by establishing an SS office that was then given the legal authority to ignore the lawful system of reporting death and further, this new entity was forthwith authorized to issue its own death certificates.

The camp at Buchenwald suffered a massive outbreak of Typhus in nineteen thirty-nine. Himmler's staff contacted Topf and Sons to see if they could provide a solution to the large numbers of dead left in the wake of the disease.

Topf immediately provided the camp with one of their mobile incineration ovens. The company had previously developed this type of product for use in the agriculture field to facilitate the need to incinerate large numbers of animal carcasses.

The mobile unit was later replaced with a permanent construct which was both larger and more efficient, a unit that could handle twice the previous incinerator's load.

After nineteen thirty-nine, Topf, who had now demonstrated the proficiency of their products, became the go-to people for the SS when it came to supplying the ovens for all camp crematoria needs.

CHAPTER SEVEN

- Clipped Wings –

The Count paced the length of Gabriella's bedroom slowly. His voice was calm and to her attuned ears, subdued.

"Recently your chosen lifestyle had become common knowledge to the extent that it is affecting the entire family. Times are changing in Germany. Each of us must re-evaluate our day to day lives, while keeping those changes in mind. What may have been considered acceptable conduct on the part of single women of your age and station just a few months ago is now clearly totally unacceptable."

Gabriella rolled her eyes and leaned back, spread-eagling herself across the top of her bed.

"For heavens sake Father, I'm simply enjoying life"

The Count stopped moving and turned to face her. His features hardened and his voice rose both in pitch and firmness.

"No Gabriella, you are not. You are making a mockery of your education and upbringing and the historic character of this family. You are recklessly throwing away your future prospects and quite frankly, you are infringing upon the prospects of those of us who love you and it has to stop now. From this point on you will do as you are told or you will relinquish your birthright."

Obviously somewhat taken aback Gabriella rolled forward into an upright sitting position on the bed eyes flashing.

"Exactly what are you threatening me with Father? Are you suggesting that if I do not do as I am told you will throw me out onto the street? Am I to be disinherited?"

"I'm not threatening you. The time for that has long past. I am chastising you for your recent demonstrated behaviour that is of a socially unacceptable and destructive nature and will, if it continues, garner you a dismal future and cost you all you hold dear as well as bring our entire family into disrepute. I'm simply stating facts. It's long past time for you to mature and take responsibility for your life and for the position you hold in German society. If you are incapable of understanding, as appears the case, if you are unable to do that on your own, then I and your mother have a responsibility to you and the rest of the family to ensure you come to your senses before it is too late."

Gabriella shook her head slowly and raised her hands to rub her red rimmed eyes. The alcohol induced headache that had been threatening for the past hour was gaining strength and she wanted nothing more than sleep.

"Could we put this discussion off until tomorrow please father."

The Count's grim features softened slightly but then returned with firmness.

"You need to understand Gabriella that this is neither a discussion nor a negotiation. The time for either of those things has passed. Tomorrow after your classes you will come to me at my office and I will outline to you what changes you must make and what your future will be. At that time you will have the option of gracefully accepting my advice and forging a new life for yourself or you can chose to go your own way, bereft of all the protection and support your family have lovingly supplied you since birth."

Glabellas' eyes began to mist but her mouth firmed.

"You forget father that I have my own income."

The Count took no offence at her remark. He let his eyes meet hers and hold them.

"No Gabriella, you do not. You receive an allowance from your trust, it's true, but, as head of this family, I administer that trust and when I am gone your brother will assume the title and it will fall to him to administer it. You are a very rich woman in your own right Gabriella, but that wealth is family wealth and it is structured to be administered by the family in perpetuity. If you so choose you will always have whatever you need but that guarantee does not come without responsibility and if you decide to continue along this path of irresponsibility to the detriment of yourself and your family, then you should not expect to share in our future security and prosperity."

Gabriella opened her mouth to speak and he cut her short.

"Yes, your aunt has promised for years that she will see that you are cared for after her passing and she is getting old. But she is not dead yet and far more importantly she is my sister and she will be leaving her wealth to our family, not to you personally. It will not go directly to you, but it will become part of the future income you may expect to receive, if and I repeat if, you come to you senses and are prepared to reasonably moderate your lifestyle to achieve a respectable and socially acceptable level."

Her mouth opened to speak and again he cut her off.

"We are both tired and nothing will be accomplished by dragging this out. Your mother is at her wit's end over your recent activities and I ask that you not raise this issue with her as it will only lead to bad feelings. We will talk again tomorrow afternoon and you can give me your decision at that time. I know that this was not the best time to have this conversation. However I'm afraid your recent lifestyle has left me without an option.

I want you to know that your mother and I love you and want only the best for you and I want you to take some time to reflect on that before you come in to see me. I sincerely hope that once you've had an opportunity to sleep on and consider what I've said, you will realize that it offers you a second chance at a good life and is the proper course for you.

Tomorrow is a bright new day and it offers you a bright new future if only you will give it a chance."

He crossed to where she was sitting, kissed her lightly on the forehead then turned.

A tear glistened in his eye as he left her room.

* * * * *

- Operation Catapult –

The British got their hands on a copy of the French version of the German/French armistice shortly after it was signed.

They scrutinized it carefully, their biggest concern being that of the disposition of the French fleet.

Admiral Darlan had promised Churchill that he would never allow the fleet to fall into German hands but based on their last meeting with the French, the British were afraid that at some point the Germans, perhaps under threat of the torching of Paris, could force the issue and demand the turnover of the fleet.

In the English translation from the French document they found the words *'neutralized under German or Italian supervision'* in article eight of the armistice. The original document was in French and had used the word *'controle'* after the word *'Italian'* and this had subsequently been translated into the English word *'supervision'*. The French version was studied carefully, after the reading of the English version and Churchill was aghast at the use of the French word *'controle'* in the original text.

In French, the word *'controle'* meant to keep custody or inspect, but not to have operational control. However, *'control'* in English meant something altogether different.

For the British, the very idea that the Germans and/or the Italians were to have control of the French fleet was absolutely unthinkable.

Something had to be done and it had to be done quickly.

At the start of the war the French fleet had formations in English ports, mainland French ports, in Egypt and in various ports in the eastern Mediterranean.

There were two battleships, four cruisers, eight destroyers, several submarines and support craft berthed in Plymouth and Portsmouth.

Already anchored in a British port, these were not of particular concern to the British.

Twenty some odd French destroyers were at ports along the North African coast. These were not a major threat.

The French Atlantic Squadron, consisting of the battleships *Bretagne* and *Provence*, the battle cruisers *Dunquerque* and *Strasbourg,* a screening force of thirteen destroyers, four submarines and a seaplane carrier were anchored in Mers-el-Kebir and Oran in Algeria. These were of concern.

Under *'Operation Catapult* 'Churchill ordered that, wherever feasible, French ships must be brought under British control or destroyed.

On the night of July third, nineteen-forty *'Catapult'* was launched.

The French ships in the English ports were boarded. The British were forcefully resisted on only one craft, the largest submarine in the world, the *Surcouf.* One French sailor was killed and two British officers and one seaman died in the exchange.

The same night, the British *'Force H'* under the command of Admiral James Somerville arrived at the port of Mers-el-Kebir in Algeria. The French fleet anchored there was under the command of Admiral Marcel-Bruno Gensoul.

Somerville had been ordered by Churchill to deliver an ultimatum to the French.

It read:

"It is impossible for us, your comrades up to now, to allow your fine ships to fall into the polder of the German enemy. We are determined to fight on until the end, and if we win, as we think we shall, we shall never forget that France was our Ally, that our interests are the same as hers, and that our common enemy is Germany. Should we conquer we solemnly declare that we shall restore the greatness and territory of France. For this purpose we must make sure that the best ships of the French Navy are not used against us by the common foe. In these circumstances, His Majesty's Government have instructed me to demand that the French Fleet now at Mers el Kebir and Oran shall act in accordance with one of the following alternatives;

(a) Sail with us and continue the fight until victory against the Germans.

(b) Sail with reduced crews under our control to a British port. The reduced crews would be repatriated at the earliest moment.

If either of these courses is adopted by you we will restore your ships to France at the conclusion of the war or pay full compensation if they are damaged meanwhile.

(c) Alternatively if you feel bound to stipulate that your ships should not be used against the Germans unless they break the

Armistice, then sail them with us with reduced crew to some French port in the West Indies - Martinique for instance - where they can be demilitarised to our satisfaction, or perhaps be entrusted to the United States and remain safe until the end of the war, the crews being repatriated.

If you refuse these fair offers, I must with profound regret, require you to sink your ships within 6 hours.

Finally, failing the above, I have the orders from His Majesty's Government to use whatever force may be necessary to prevent your ships from falling into German hands."

Somerville did not speak French. He therefore decided to delegate the handover of the ultimatum to the commanding officer of the *Ark Royal*, Captain Cedric Holland who did speak French.

While seeming a reasonable decision, it proved be the first step in a series of etiquette-related choices and communication blunders between the two Admirals.

Gensoul, insulted by the fact that he would not be sitting down with the commander of the British fleet, refused to attend personally and sent his Lieutenant, Bernard Dufay to meet with Captain Holland.

The two junior officers attempted to negotiate the ultimatum, but were hampered by having to continually seek guidance from the two Admirals. The discussions ground on for hours.

Gensoul, negotiating from his flagship through his Lieutenant was in constant contact with the French Naval Minister, Admiral Darlan but he failed to apprise Darlan of the full content of the ultimatum, specifically the option of removing his fleet to American ports.

Darlan had anticipated the possibility that a foreign power might attempt to seize French ships and had previously specifically ordered his fleet commanders that if such a situation was to come to pass, they should instead attempt to flee to ports under United States control.

The fact that the opposing fleets present were of more of less equal strength also added to the tension in regard to any negotiation of an '*ultimatum*'.

Neither side wanted a fight.

The British Commander's heart was not in it. These were an Ally's ships and perhaps more importantly they were not manned by enemy sailors.

The French were absolutely shocked and dumbfounded by the threat offered by the ultimatum. This coming from comrades in arms: an Allied force.

Negotiations dragged on and in an attempt to fortify his position Somerville ordered the Ark Royal to launch and drop magnetic mines across the outside of the port to remove the option of the French fleet from putting to sea.

In response the French sent fighters against the British aircraft and one of the English airships was shot down and crashed at sea killing its two man crew, resulting in the only casualties on the British side during the conflict.

Despite the fact that the two forces were relatively balanced, the British had the advantage in that the French fleet was at anchor in the narrow harbour and in no way prepared for battle. The main armament of the two French battle cruisers, grouped on their bows could not be brought to bear on the British without having the ships manoeuvre and the British capital ships with fifteen inch guns fired a heavier volley than their French counterparts.

Churchill had been kept informed of the lack of progress and shortly after the incident with the aircraft he personally ordered the British ships to open fire on the French at 17:54 hours.

Two salvos missed their mark but the third hit the battleship *Bretagne* which sank at 18:09 with the loss of nine hundred and seventy-seven of her crew. The French began to respond but after the British had fired off thirty salvos the French ceased action.

In order to get out of range of the French shore batteries the British fleet moved out to sea after *Provence, Dunkerque* and *Mogador* were damaged and run aground.

Accompanied by four destroyers, the Strasbourg made for the open sea and *Ark Royal* sent bombers out after them but the escaping French opened up with anti-aircraft fire and shot down two of the planes. The air attack had little effect on the fleeing French who raced successfully for the French port of Toulon.

Somerville felt no pride in the action and pursued the

escaping ships with less than heartfelt enthusiasm, breaking off the chase at 20:20 hours after asserting that his ships were not properly deployed for a night engagement.

On July fourth a British sub sank a French gunboat sailing from Oran. On July sixth *Ark Royal* launched aircraft against the *Dunkerque* and *Provence* in the belief that they had not been seriously damaged in the earlier engagement. As a result *Dunkerque* was badly damaged. *Dunkerque, Provence* and *Mogador* were given emergency repairs and eventually sailed to the port of Toulon.

On July eighth the British carrier *Hermes* launched aircraft against the French battleship *Richelieu* anchored at Dakar. A single torpedo struck and damaged the big ship.

The British blockaded the French ships anchored at Alexandria on July third and the French Admiral Rene-Emile Godfroy was offered the identical terms as had the fleet at *Mers-el-Kebir*. These negotiations went far more smoothly and on the seventh the French agreed to disarm the fleet and stay in port until the end of the war.

The French retaliated to these various attacks by sending the air force on several bombing raids against Gibraltar but these were also half-hearted and caused little or no damage.

The altercation at *Mers-el-Kebir* left thirteen hundred French sailors dead and over three hundred injured.

Relations between Great Britain and France had been severely damaged by what the French saw as England's treachery with regard to the Allied French fleet.

Needless to say, the Nazi's Propaganda machine had a field day as a result of the British attack against the Allied French fleet.

CHAPTER EIGHT

- Arrival at Munich –

A light drizzling rain was falling as the train pulled into the hectically congested Munich station.

Wilhelm and his companions made their way out onto the, even at this relatively early hour, noisy, bustling platform and were promptly greeted by a smartly uniformed officer of the SS-Totenkopfverbande.

The Untersturrmfuhrer (Lieutenant) had two empty luggage carts lined up beside him. These were attended by two uniformed non-commissioned officers and after delivering a snap salute to the visitors he promptly identified himself, welcomed them and moved to relieve them of their baggage.

While both Konrad and Wilhelm were surprised at this reception, Muller took it as his due.

Noting the reaction on the part of his companions, he grinned and turning to face them directly, spoke for their ears only.

"SS-Gruppenfuhrer Glucks, Chief of the SS-Wachverbande is aware that we will be joining him and his staff this morning on what will be for him the second day of his inspections at Dachau.

He owes much to the support of the SS-Reichsfuhrer and as we will be acting as Herr Himmler's personal representatives, his eyes and ears if you like, in today's stopover here, the Gruppenfuhrer will be taking personal responsibility for our transport and care for the duration of our stay.

He jealously guards his authority within the camps and although this trip has been billed to him as a *'cursory familiarization SS-officers visit only'* he will in all likelihood wish to ensure that our impression of the camp is a very positive one."

He turned back to face the *'SS Wachverbande'* officer and dropped in behind the man as he led the way off the platform and toward the doors which opened into the cavernous station.

Followed by their luggage they made rapid progress despite the crowd milling about on the platform, the result of other trains having recently arrived at the busy station.

Once again the ominous black SS uniforms appeared to instil a sense of expected entitlement and the throng eagerly parted ahead of them as the group approached the doors.

Once inside the station, which, like all major stations in Germany, was characteristically festooned with Nazi propaganda posters and banners, the small party regrouped momentarily and then the guests were guided through the massive building and out onto the sidewalk in front where they found two waiting closed staff cars parked at the curb.

The two corporals loaded the luggage into the rear of the first vehicle and then, task completed, each moved to open the rear door of his respective car.

The SS-Wachverbande aide waved Wilhelm and Konrad into the second vehicle and once they were comfortably ensconced the driver closed the door behind them and climbed in behind the wheel.

In the meantime the aide had quickly led Muller to the first car at the curb and the two of them ascended into the luxuriously appointed interior. Their driver closed the door and climbed into the front seat of the lead car.

A few moments later the vehicles pulled up in front of Munich's Hotel Torhaus.

Both uniformed chauffeurs leapt out and smartly moved to open the read doors in preparation for their occupants exit.

The aide led the three of them into the grand hotel.

While escorting them to their rooms he indicated they had plenty of time to settle in and mentioned that SS-Gruppenfuhrer Glucks was hosting breakfast in just over an hour and they were cordially invited to attend.

They were also advised that the inspection entourage would not be leaving for Dachau until after the completion of the meal.

* * * * *

- Dakar –

The strategic port of Dakar located in French West Africa was home port for the Mediterranean French fleet. It was loyal to Vichy France and therefore it remained quite possible that it would eventually come under German influence.

Subsequently between the twenty-third and twenty-fifth of September nineteen-forty, British and Free French forces moved against the port of Dakar in *'Operation Menace'*.

De Gaulle was very much onside with the move. A portentous man, he was absolutely confident that he could convince the French forces billeted in Dakar to join the Allied cause, without the use of military force.

He had full British support because if he could pull it off the effect of bringing one of the uncommitted French colonies over to the Allied cause would have great political impact.

Also of interest to the British was the fact that the gold reserves of the *Banque de France* and also those of the Polish government in exile were stored in Dakar. In addition, if the ploy was successful it would give the Allies a far superior port in the Mediterranean than their current one which was located at Freetown in Sierra Leone and was the only Allied port in the area.

Accordingly a task force was put together. Based around the aircraft carrier *Ark Royal* it consisted of a supporting screen of two battleships, *Resolution* and *Barham*, five cruisers, ten destroyers and transports carrying a total force of eight thousand troops.

Prior to the armistice, the British carrier *Hermes* had been operating with the French fleet at Dakar. She had been ordered by the British Admiralty to leave the port shortly after the Vichy government was put into place by the triumphant Nazis and had remained in nearby waters where she had been joined by the Australian heavy cruiser *Australia*.

They would later join the ships of the task force of *'Operation Menace'* when it arrived at Dakar.

The task force orders specified that the fleet was to negotiate a peaceful occupation with the French Governor and if this failed they were to take the city by force.

If force was necessary, only French troops were to be landed, while the British would supply support.

In the harbour at Dakar, allayed against the British task force was the unfinished battleship *Richelieu*. She was one of the most advanced warships of the French fleet and was nearing completion. With the *Richelieu* were three French submarines and a myriad of support ships.

A force of three French cruisers, the *Gloire, Geeorges Leygues* and *Montcalm* accompanied by three destroyers had departed from Toulon for the port of Dakar prior to the arrival of the task force and the *Gloire* suffered mechanical trouble and was left straggling. *Australia* intercepted the *Gloire* and ordered her to change course to Casablanca immediately or face the consequences. The rest of the ships were able to complete the voyage and make Dakar in support of the *Richelieu*.

Upon arrival at Dakar, aircraft from the British carriers dropped propaganda leaflets over the city, before Free French aircraft lifted off the *Ark Royal* and landed at the airport.

These aircraft crews were promptly taken prisoner.

Things were not going as well as de Gaulle had confidently predicted.

The Free French General boarded a small craft and headed into the port. The craft he was riding in was immediately fired on and it promptly returned to the task force.

The French fleet got up steam and began an attempt to break out of the port. The *Australia* opened fire with warning shots. The French fleet demurred and returned to port but moments later the French shore batteries from the forts opened fire on *Australia*.

A stalemate ensued and nothing further happened until later in the day when the French destroyer *L'Audacieux* made a break for the open sea and the *Australia's* guns opened up again, this time setting the smaller ship on fire and forcing the French crew to run the damaged ship up onto the beach to prevent it from sinking.

Shortly thereafter Free French forces were sent ashore at *Rufisque* beach to the south of the city. They landed under heavy fog conditions and strong fire from dug-in bunkers defending the beach.

De Gaulle, confidence shattered, called off the attack. He stated he was not prepared to '*shed the blood of Frenchmen for Frenchmen*'.

The battle between the forces continued sporadically over the next two days.

Richelieu received two hits from the *Barham's* fifteen inch guns, two French subs were sunk, *and Resolution* was hit by a torpedo launched by *Beveziers*. The shore batteries made hits on *Barham* and two of the British cruisers received damage.

The British fleet was stalemated by the shore batteries and a determined Vichy French defence and the Free French troops hadn't the strength to go on the offensive.

Neither side was making any progress. Dakar was quite obviously not going to roll over because de Gaulle was asking them to.

Eventually the combination British/Free French task force broke off from the attack and licking its wounds, limped away from the port of Dakar.

In retaliation for the British attacks on their fleets the Vichy French retaliated with several land based air attacks on Gibraltar but caused little lasting damage.

CHAPTER NINE

- Super Sub –

Light rain was falling when a tired but determined Count Karl von Stauffer reached his office at seven-thirty.

By seven forty-five he was behind his desk nursing a fresh cup of coffee which was doing wonders to push aside his lack of sleep and generally improve his mood.

His son Eric, who was slated as his father's first appointment of the day at eight o'clock, had ridden in with him and was seated across from his father, a steaming cup of his own sitting on the desk and a freshly lit cigarillo dangling from his lips.

The expression registered on his boy's face was one of wonder mingled with disbelief and the sight was enough to bring a smile to the Count's face.

One of several massive rolls of engineering blueprints was lying open and held in place by paperweights in the center of the large desk between them. Eric's complete attention was held by this top schematic.

"My God, Father. This thing is humongous! I know the Fuhrer has hinted at such things, but this…this, to think something like this is even possible. It boggles the mind. "

The Count's job entailed advising Hitler on all new developments with regard to weaponry and scientific advancement and he was only too aware of The Fuhrer's tendency to periodically expound upon his plans for the future.

He nodded his head and waved his hand toward the other rolls of drawings and designs leaning against his desk.

"Well, let me assure you, this particular one is very real. You have a great deal of reading to do to get up to speed on this specific submarine design. That will be necessary in view of the fact that you are to oversee the construction and will command the first of the four of these behemoths, which happens, by the way, to be already under construction.

Eric removed the paperweights and flipped the top sheet over and then the next several sheets in turn.

"What can be the purpose of subs this size? The design shows only four torpedo tubes, two in the bow and two in the stern. The cargo capacity is enormous; it's almost as if it's designed to act as some type of cargo ship."

The Count's smile broadened and then he laughed.

"Very good Eric - you provide an apt description. Yes, very apt indeed. You will note that it is marked as '*Top Secret*' and I will tell you now that the construction of four of these special craft, at this specific point in the war, will be a part of '*Operation Fatherland*'. Their construction will be financed from funds separate from the general war effort and although construction of the four will be part of overall war planning, its purpose is to be kept under the radar as far as anyone outside our special group is concerned.

Do I make myself clear?"

Still flipping pages, Eric nodded but his mind was obviously elsewhere.

The Count raised his voice slightly.

"Eric did you hear what I said? The construction of these four submarines will be undertaken by '*Operation Fatherland*' and their purpose is not to be discussed in a general sense."

Eric nodded absently.

"Yes Father, I understand…what kind of cargo will these subs be carrying and to where…my God, look at the power plants and the specifications indicate that they can remain under water for days and days…no need to surface each night to charge batteries.

What the hell is a '*Schnorchel*'?"

* * * * *

- Theodor Eicke –

An understanding of the history and mindset of some of those who took early responsibility for the creation of the internment systems which would be utilized by the Nazis as time went on, is helpful in achieving a better insight into both the structure and administration the concentration camps were to receive.

Theodor Eicke was one of the prime figures involved in the design, development and operation of all the concentration camps created within the growing Nazi Reich.

Born in eighteen ninety-two, the youngest of eleven children, Eicke did poorly in school. He dropped out at age seventeen, before graduation, and joined a Bavarian Infantry Regiment as a volunteer.

During the Great War he became a regimental paymaster and in nineteen-fourteen was awarded the Iron Cross for bravery.

He resigned from the military in nineteen-nineteen and went back to school briefly before dropping out again with the intention of pursuing a career in policing.

He managed to get into the police through the back door by beginning as an informer and then over time being brought on as a regular.

As his views on the Weimar Republic mirrored those postulated by Adolf Hitler and the Nazi party, Eicke eagerly joined the party on December the first in nineteen twenty-eight. He joined the SA on the same date.

Eicke had a strong dislike for the government of the ruling Weimar Republic and often took part in violent political demonstrations against them. Subsequently his police career was short-lived and, jobless in nineteen twenty-three; he managed to secure employment with IG Farben, one of the largest chemical companies in the world.

In August of nineteen-thirty he left the SA to join the SS.

Despite his lack of higher education, he had a knack for organization and served as a prolific recruiter for the SS.

Like many of Himmler's early cronies, his resulting rise through the ranks of the fledgling SS was absolutely astounding.

He went from an SS-Private on July twenty-ninth nineteen thirty to that of SS-Major by January thirtieth nineteen thirty-one.

Himmler was so pleased with Eicke's diligence and loyalty

that he personally promoted him again to the rank of *SS-Standartenfuhrer* (Colonel) on November eleventh of nineteen thirty-one.

To help understand the reasons behind this rapid advancement within the SS one has to understand the man who headed it.

As well as being a small fish in the big sea which constituted Hitler's hangers-on, who were always angling for more favour, Reichsfuhrer Heinrich Himmler was also a determined empire builder.

There were others within that ever shifting power struggle among those of the inner court seeking Hitler's praise and support, who shared that dream of wider and lager responsibility, notably Field Marshal Herman Goering. However, Himmler's aspirations knew no bounds.

Hitler wanted to change the world, starting with Germany and he therefore needed a myriad of things done quickly and quietly.

Many of these things were of a nature that clearly suggested the avoidance of a written record. Hitler hated to put anything in writing if it could be avoided.

Whenever these situations arose, and they came up often, Himmler was determined to be the man for the job whenever possible.

A casual comment in passing addressed from Hitler to Himmler in regard to a problem that the Fuhrer would like solved and Himmler was on it like a hungry flea leaping for a passing dog.

Take this process a step farther and you soon find Himmler whispering into the ear of his loyal subordinate Theodore Eicke and like magic Hitler's problem would slip quietly into oblivion.

Over time and after a string of successes using this process Hitler came to Himmler with his problems more and more often and Himmler, after having experienced the same success with his subordinate, quietly passed them on to Eicke.

Eicke was a man who never asked questions, never wavered and repeatedly demonstrated toward his fellow man the empathy and sympathy worthy of a slab of granite.

Following this sensational rise up the promotional ladder his rash political activities came to the attention of his employer and in early nineteen thirty-two he was laid off by IG Farben.

A short time later he was arrested by the police for his part in the preparation of a bomb attack aimed at political enemies within Bavaria and he subsequently received a two year prison sentence for his activities in July of nineteen thirty-two.

On orders from Heinrich Himmler and with the protection and assistance of Franz Gurtner, the Bavarian Minister of Justice, Eicke was able to flee to Italy and avoid prison.

In March of nineteen thirty-three a little less than three months after Hitler's rise to power, Eicke returned to Germany.

His nature soon led him into political quarrels with the then Gauleiter of Vienna, Joseph Burckel. The Gauleiter promptly had him arrested and as a result Eicke was judged and sentenced to several months of confinement in a mental asylum.

During the same month Hitler mentioned to Himmler that it was time to set up the first internment camp designed to house political prisoners. He strongly indicated that this was to be a special camp and not simply another prison.

Himmler decided to set the camp up at Dachau and he appointed *SS-Sturmbannfuhrer* (Lieutenant Colonel) Hilmar Wackerle as its first Commandant.

In June of nineteen thirty-three Himmler obtained Eicke's release and promptly promoted him to the rank of SS-Oberfuhrer (Senior Leader).

Following the sudden death of several detainees at Dachau who had been receiving '*punishment*' and some resulting unwanted negative complaints and questions, a displeased Himmler quickly moved to remove Wackerle and he knew exactly where to lay his hands on the man to replace the outgoing Camp Commandant. Just the man for the job: a man with all the necessary qualifications.

On June twenty-sixth nineteen thirty-three Himmler appointed Theodore Eicke Commandant of Dachau.

Upon his arrival at the camp Eicke took one look at the structure and administration and then contacted Himmler.

He informed the Reichsfuhrer that any future complaints with regard to activities going on within the confines of the camp could be avoided by the installation of a proper administration of trained and qualified staff. He requested and was granted the authority to form a permanent guard-force unit.

As a result of this decision the 'SS-Wachverbande' (Guard Unit) came into being.

An excellent organizer, Eicke warmed to the task of reorganizing the running of the camp.

He established new guarding provisions, demanded absolute discipline from his staff and unequivocal obedience to all orders. He had them wear a uniform he designed himself. The staff uniforms had a death's head insignia displayed on the collars.

He moved quickly to revise and strengthen the discipline and punishment regulations for detainees and had standard prison garb issued for all prisoners.

Reports on progress being achieved regularly passed across Himmler's desk and he was delighted with Eicke's diligence and dedication to duty.

Eicke was strongly anti-Semitic and anti-Bolshevism, both qualities that the Reichsfuhrer strongly appreciated and his insistence on unconditional obedience towards him, the SS and the Fuhrer served to strengthen Himmler's original gut feeling that he had chosen the right man for the job.

He promptly promoted Eicke to the rank of 'SS-Brigadefuhrer' (Brigadier General) on the thirtieth of January nineteen thirty-four and gave him a free hand in devising a camp system that would be used as a model for all future camps constructed within the New Reich.

Himmler so trusted Eicke's ability to handle 'sensitive' problems that when Hitler determined that a purge of the SA leadership was necessary and gave the Reichsfuhrer and his SS the job of carrying it out on the so called 'Night of the Long Knives', he turned to Eicke and a hand-chosen band of Dachau guards, supported by Sepp Dietrich's 'SS-Leibstandarte Adolf Hitler' (Hitler's personal bodyguard unit) to do the job.

After the Chief of the SA Ernst Rohm was arrested, Hitler ordered that he be offered the choice to commit suicide or be shot.

Rohm refused to do himself in and was promptly shot to death by Eicke and his adjutant Michael Lippert, on July first nineteen thirty-four.

Himmler was so pleased with how smoothly the purge had gone and the part Eicke had played in it that he promoted his star yet again on July eleventh nineteen thirty-four, this time, up to the rank of *'SS-Gruppenführer'* (Major General).

He then appointed him to the command of the *'SS-Wachverbande'* (Camp Guards) and named him chief of the *'Inspektion der Konzentrationslager'* (Concentration Camps Inspectorate).

In consideration of the fact that the aftermath of the *'Night of the Long Knives'* had determined that the SA would no longer be allowed to run any of the internment camps which they had set up and that all camps were to now be taken over by the SS, this turned out to be a very sizable promotion for the efficient, cold and undeniably loyal Himmler subordinate.

In nineteen thirty-five Dachau officially become the training centre for all future camp personal and on March twenty-ninth of that year all camp guards and administration units were designated as the *'SS-Totenkopfverbande'* (SS-TV).

Eicke's forceful personality and administrative improvements coupled with the introduction of forced labour turned Dachau into a SS showplace and greatly impressed Himmler, who had coveted control of the facility for what seemed to him as ages but had been unsuccessful up to that time in his attempt to bring it directly under the sole and direct dictate of the SS.

Warming to his role as camp inspector, Eicke began a rigorous reorganization of the existing facilities in nineteen thirty-five.

The mishmash of small camps that had been formed by the various different organizations, the SA, Gestapo etc. now came under SS control and being the empire builder he was, Eicke had full intention of making the best use of his new-found power.

Dachau, the jewel in the SS crown remained but the majority of the smaller camps were dismantled.

Under the watchful eyes of the SS-Gruppenfuhrer and newly

appointed Chief of the *'Inspektion der Konzentrationslager'* several new camps were constructed within Germany.

Sachesenhausen opened in the summer of nineteen thirty-six, Buchenwald a year later and Ravensbruck in May of nineteen thirty-nine.

He also opened other new camps in Austria where the Mauthausen-Gusen camp came into being in nineteen thirty-eight.

All the new camps followed the model Eicke had created in Dachau and all staff followed the regulations he had created for Dachau when he revamped it. Uniforms for the guards and administrative staff operating these facilities were the same as the one created for Dachau and so was the apparel supplied for all detainees.

These designated labour camps began to create a substantial amount of income for the personal coffers of the SS and Himmler soon had complete confidence in and was more than pleased with the activities under taken by Eicke.

He fully supported his golden boy every step of the way.

At the outbreak of war in nineteen thirty-nine, the *'Totenkopf's'* sister SS-formations, the SS-Infanterie-Regiment (Leibstandarte SS Adolf Hitler), in addition to the three *'Standarten'* (Regimental Standard) units of the SS-*'Verfugungstruppe'* (SS-VT) (Dispositional Troops); all primary units of the General SS, had preformed with a great deal of success.

Formed in nineteen thirty-four as Combat Troops for the Nazi Party, the *SS-VT* had been decreed by Hitler to be neither part of the police nor of the Wehrmacht (Army), but a military trained body of men who were at the personal disposal of the Fuhrer in times of both peace and war.

As a result of these units success under fire at the front and always looking to expand his personal empire, Himmler recommended to Hitler the creation of three *'Waffen-SS'* (Armed-SS) Divisions in nineteen thirty-nine and Hitler agreed to the concept.

Himmler quickly formed SS-Division *'Totenkopf'*.

The Division was made up of three *'Standarten' (Regiments),*

Patrick Laughy

'*First Division*' (Oberbayern), '*Second Division*' (Brandenburg) and '*Third Division*' (Thuringen) of the *SS-'Totenkopfverbande'* (SS-TV) (Death's Head Units) which had been formed from manpower from the camp guards and the soldiers from the *SS-'Heimwehr Danzig'*. Each Regiment had a '*Standartenfuhrer*' (Colonel) as its commanding officer.

This was a wonderful opportunity for Himmler to expand his SS and he had just the man to take command of the Division, a man he had come to rely on, SS-Gruppenfuhrer, Theodor Eicke.

Having assigned Eicke to combat duty, Himmler chose Eicke's deputy at the new '*Inspektion der Konzentrationslager*' (Concentration Camps Inspectorate) (CCI), SS-Brigadefuhrer Richard Glucks, to replace his departing boss.

CHAPTER TEN

- Baron Friedriech von Bauer –

The second appointment for the day scheduled for Count Karl von Stauffer was with the well known German industrialist, Baron von Bauer.

Eric had no sooner left his father's office and headed for his own in the company of an SS-Sergeant pushing a cart loaded with rolls of design specification for the new *'Super Sub'*, when the Count's secretary buzzed through on the intercom to notify him of the Baron's arrival.

The Count got up and crossed to the connecting door that led from his secretary's office into his own and offered a broad smile to the Baron as he shook his hand and waved him inside.

"Ah Friedriech, right on time!"

Closing the door behind him, he motioned the Baron into one of the chairs across from his desk and buzzed his secretary for fresh coffee before sitting down.

"I know you are a very busy man these days so I will make this short and let you get back to your work."

A great deal of experience in deal-negotiating behind him, the Baron settled into the comfortable leather chair, accepted a proffered cigarette from the silver box and a light then drew in a deep drag and exhaled before he smiled.

"Yes and now it will be necessary for me to go abroad for a short period of time. The arrangements have been made?"

The Count nodded.

"Yes…you will begin the first leg of your trip to Rio de Janeiro in the morning. I have reserved four seats as you requested."

The Baron allowed a narrow smile to form on his face. "

"Ah…it is to be Brazil then."

Von Stauffer nodded.

"Yes, a representative of the large German expatriate community of that country has already spoken privately to Brazil's President, Getulio Vargas. He has been good enough to smooth the way with for us.

Here is that gentleman's card. He is a well known and wealthy member of the expatriate community in Brazil and will be meeting you and your team at the airport in Reo de Janeiro and seeing to your comfort during your stay.

I am pleased to tell you that I have been advised that the President is supportive of our endeavours and warmly welcomes our long-term investment in his country.

I have been assured that he will provide us with any and all assistance that we may find necessary in completing our plans.

The President will not deal with you directly, as he understandably wishes to hold our undertakings at arms length, however, he has offered us a direct contact within his government in the form of one General Jose Carlos Eduardo Galleti and he has assured us that the General will have his full backing and all the decision making authority necessary to fulfill their end of the deal.

I have also been personally assured that the General will see to it that all our needs are met and that any dealings that may arise between us and the government of Brazil will remain of a very private nature.

As you have already arranged for the necessary transfer in gold to be made to a South American bank, it would seem that you will have little to do upon your arrival other then to arrange for the purchase of the land in question, and to see to it that the mechanisms for ensuring that the President, and of course, the General, receive the previously agreed upon ongoing monthly payments, are in place.

As agreed, we will open and staff an office in the name of the company in Rio and the shares in the mining operation anticipated will be jointly held between our consortium of industrialists and the government of Brazil, who will act in the capacity of a silent partner only, at a respective ninety percent for us and ten percent for the Brazilian government in perpetuity."

The Baron nodded and flicked his ash into the silver astray

beside his coffee cup.

"And the area on the coast indicated by our geological studies as suitable for our purposes has been cleared by the government of Brazil for our purchase?"

The Count smiled.

"Yes and as luck would have it our initial negotiations have produced a better result than we had hoped for.

For the planned financial investment, plus our agreement to provide some military advisors to the Brazilian Armed Forces, we are to receive the mineral rights as well as the deed to almost twice the land mass we had originally selected.

Basically, we have managed to purchase an entire mountain and most of the expansive valley beyond.

If all our future endeavours go as well as this one has, I see little reason why we should not reach the initial phase of our final goal within the next five years."

Von Bauer tilted his head slightly.

"And the President understands that we do not...um... have any direct ties with the government here in Germany, that we are an independent group of like thinkers and businessmen who are prepared to look beyond the current world conflict."

The Count chose his words just as carefully as his guest had done.

"Yes, the President understands that ours is a more permanent institution than one of government, that while we are loyal to our fatherland, we will be taking a longer view and he is very comfortable with that."

The Count smiled.

"Or at least he has indicated that he will be comfortable with our relationship, providing the financing that has been promised to him, his country and those among his supporters involved, continues on a regular basis.

He has been assured that will be the case and I'm certain you will be able to press that point home much more firmly when you meet his representative and tell him so in person.

After all my dear Baron, your name, personal wealth and reputation are not unknown, even in a backward country located in far away South America."

The Baron allowed himself a small smile in acknowledgement of the statement.

"It will be my first visit there. I am looking forward to it."

Karl von Stauffer let out a soft sigh as he ground out his cigarette in the astray before him,

"I know I do not have to explain to you that the President has been led to believe that we are solely interested in creating a mining enterprise in his country. But I must ask you to please take great care to ensure that he is still holding to that opinion when it comes time for you to leave him and return to us."

* * * * *

- Oswald Pohl –

Another big player in the early development of the Nazi concentration camp system was Oswald Ludwig Pohl.

Pohl was born in Duisburg-Ruhrort in the western Ruhr on the thirtieth of June eighteen ninety-two. He was the fifth born into a family of eight children.

He graduated in nineteen twelve and joined the Imperial Navy, and served in both the Caribbean and Southeast Asia.

During the Great War he spent time in the Baltic Sea region and off the coast of Flanders. He attended navy school and became a paymaster in mid nineteen-eighteen and spent the remainder of the war based in Kiel.

After the war, Pohl attended courses at a trade school and began to study law and State theory at the '*Christian-Albrechts-Universitat in Kiel'*. He didn't remain long at his studies and soon took up the position of paymaster with the Freikorps '*Brigade Lowenfeld* 'in Berlin.

As a member of the Freikorps he took part in the '*Luttwitz-Kapp Putsch'* in Berlin.

In nineteen twenty he was accepted into the Weimar Republic's new navy and in nineteen twenty-four served in Swinemunde.

A year later Pohl joined the SA and in nineteen twenty-six he joined the Nazi party.

It was there that he met Heinrich Himmler in thirty-three and soon after became his protégé with the result that he was named chief of the administration department on the staff of the new Reichsfuhrer-SS with the rank of SS-Standartenfuhrer on the first of February nineteen thirty-four.

He soon found himself deeply involved in the administration of the new Reich's internment camps, and a Himmler favourite.

Pohl, a practicing Catholic, left the church in nineteen thirty-five.

On June first of that year he was named to the position of '*Verwaltungschef*'(Chief of Administration) and appointed '*Reichskassenverwalter*' (Reich Treasurer) for the SS.

It was Pohl who initiated the concept of '*Inspection der Konzentrationslager*' to organize and oversee the camps and founded the '*Gesellschaft zur Forderung und Pflege deuscher Kulturdenkmaler*' (Society for the preservation and fostering of German cultural monuments) which he used primarily for the purpose of restoring of the ancient castle of Wewelsburg that Himmler had ordered him to transform into a new cultural and scientific headquarters for the SS.

In June of thirty-nine Pohl was appointed chief of the '*Hauptamt Verwaltung und Wirtschaft*' (Main Bureau, Administration and Economy), an SS position as well as '*Hauptamt Haushalt und Bauten*' (Main Bureau, Budget and Construction) which was part of the Reich's Ministry for the Interior.

He quickly proved himself to be a very able administrator and an indispensable financial manager for the SS.

* * * * *

- Richard Glucks –

Born in Dusseldorf in eighteen eighty-nine, Richard Glucks was another major player in the development of the camps.

Glucks had served in the Great War as an artillery officer. After the war he was appointed a liaison officer with the armistice commission and from there went on to join a Freikorps in the Ruhr district.

Glucks was an early Nazi party member.

He joined the SS at the first opportunity and held the rank of *SS-Brigadefuhrer* (Brigadier General) prior to the Second World War, serving as a staff officer in the Senior Sector West and then took command of a regiment of the general SS in Schneidenmuhl.

Definitely a staff officer rather than a combat officer, Glucks was an able enough organizer and administrator - providing he was employed in a support capacity.

Glucks was a typical bureaucrat who had often proved himself lacking in independent leadership qualities.

In nineteen thirty-six he became Theodor Eicke's deputy and worked as a staff officer on the Concentration Camp Inspectorate (CCI).

Glucks liked to spend his time in his office, close to the amenities that provided.

He was a typical administrator, carrying out his instructions unquestioningly and to the letter, but he exhibited no desire whatsoever for the practical experience to be gained by being *'out in the field'*.

He kept a low profile under Eicke, rarely making an actual inspection trip to a camp unless specifically ordered to do so by his Boss.

On the few occasions that he was directed to accompany Eicke to one of the camps, he maintained his low profile, staying in his Bosses' shadow, his only thought being *'how soon the whole thing would be over'* so he could return to his paperwork and the safe confines of his office.

He did not appear to be particularity interested in, nor did he ever try to gain any real practical experience from these sporadic camp tours.

Eicke was a hands-on leader.

He rarely found the need to use a go-between to communicate with his camp commanders, more often than not preferring to speak to them personally while inspecting their camps. Subsequently he was satisfied with how Glucks performed his duties. Glucks did what he was told and he did it efficiently and without question.

SS-Gruppenfuhrer Theodor Eicke had no interest in having others making decisions for him. He made his own decisions and was quite happy in having, what was in a practical sense, a very subservient, efficient and high-ranking bureaucrat as his deputy.

Eicke was an extrovert and an excellent problem solver.

He welcomed making decisions and creating policy and he was good at it. He was also arrogant, autocratic and demanded absolute and unquestioning obedience from his subordinates.

Glucks did not like having to '*solve*' problems or to make decisions.

He did not like to have to think '*outside the box*', but was a good administrator and was at his best when he was feeding someone else's clear decisions into a structured and firm format.

Glucks was quite happily subservient to anyone of higher authority and incapable, almost terrified, of making decisions without guidance from above.

Glucks was in awe of Eicke who was everything he was not.

He had no influence with Eicke in his capacity as a staff officer. Eicke did not need help in making his decisions. He made them on his own.

Eicke did however value Gluck's opinions when it came to the selection and supervision of personnel.

Glucks was also good at acting as a brick wall between the camp commandants and his boss. If they had a problem or complaint for the boss, Glucks acted as a barrier and simply instructed them to follow their orders and solve their own problems within the confines of those orders.

Eicke valued this service highly and he repeatedly supported his deputy without qualification whenever a confrontation arose between Glucks and a camp commandant.

In nineteen thirty-nine when SS-Gruppenfuhrer Eicke was transferred to combat duty, he recommended Glucks for his replacement.

Reichsfuhrer Heinrich Himmler had never been overly confident in Gluck's abilities but when both Pohl and Eicke supported Glucks for the job, he heard them out.

Eicke assured Himmler that the whole camp structure for training and administration was now complete, written in stone and solidly in place. All that was now required of the head of CCI was someone to act as a caretaker who would supervise and make no changes within the systems that were now in place.

It was a job made for one such as Glucks, he argued.

Himmler accepted their recommendation and Glucks got the job.

Glucks was ambitious, but he did not feel particularly qualified for, or confident in his ability to succeed as the head of CCI.

He could not turn it down of course and he believed that it would only be a short term appointment in any event.

He was certain that he would only be left in the position temporarily until a suitable candidate for the position was found.

In point of fact, Glucks's appointment made no real difference to the day-to-day operation of the camps.

Glucks had never, ever questioned even one of Eicke's orders or instructions. He had simply put them into force and now that he was in charge he did not, even for a second consider changing a single one of them, even if it became perfectly clear to him that they might need changing or updating; unless of course he was instructed to do so by the Reichsfuhrer, at which time the change or instruction was entrenched and enforced immediately; verbatim.

Any suggestion of change coming from one of the camp commandants were either turned down outright or put '*under consideration*' with the full intention of burying it as deep as possible.

If Glucks had been in awe of Eicke, he was absolutely petrified of Himmler.

He dreaded the very thought of receiving a telephone call from the Reichsfuhrer.

If received, such a call left him utterly nonplussed.

He was similarly affected by a Himmler request for a report

or a written recommendation of any kind.

An order to report to the Reichsfuhrer in person left him in an absolute state of paranoia for days before the appointment.

He actively avoided making any request that might lead to a discussion with Himmler for fear of a refusal or of his causing any hint of displeasure.

If a report came in from a camp commander over some occurrence, however serious it might be, he was completely unconcerned providing that he could be certain that it would never reach the ears of the Reichsfuhrer.

With the Reichsfuhrer looking over his shoulder the words *'low profile'*, which had occasionally been used to describe Glucks performance previous to this time, instantly became the rule.

Basically liberated from supervision, camp commandants now had a free hand, as long as they did not suggest changes, rock the boat or cause problems in any way, and needless to say a few additional rows of brick had been added to that wall ensuring that complaints or problems from camp commanders never went upstairs.

Glucks was a double-sided coin for commandants.

They couldn't suggest changes to their new boss, but on the other hand they were left alone with a free hand to run their camps and having a boss who would bury their overzealousness, provided no negative feedback was allowed to slip out through the camp gates and make its way back to Himmler.

It isn't hard to see why this situation would not bode well for the future living conditions of the camp's inmates.

CHAPTER ELEVEN

- Breakfast –

Muller, who had met Richard Glucks on previous occasions, was not surprised to find that he and his two associates were to be seated at the head table for breakfast in the hotel dining room surrounded by the Gruppenfuhrer and his immediate aides.

Glucks liked his comforts and did not travel lightly there were a total of three tables set to one side of the big room for the sole use of Glucks and his entourage.

After the introductions had been made, Muller, who was seated on Glucks's right hand, opened the conversation.

Muller was confident enough in his relationship with Himmler to treat Glucks with the respect due his rank; however, he was not, unlike some of the men seated at the three tables, attempting to gain favour with the Gruppenfuhrer.

"I understand Herr Gruppenfuhrer, that your camp system is expanding rapidly and you are looking for a good deal of new staff."

The rotund Glucks, who was obviously enjoying his meal and would much rather be discussing some other topic, lifted his hand and used his fork as a pointer to indicate the man seated on the other side of Muller, an SS-Hauptsturmfuhrer and obviously an aid to the Gruppenfuhrer.

"Meier there looks after that kind of thing…"

His eyes shifted to his aid.

"Meier, answer Muller's questions will you."

Without waiting for a response Glucks turned his attention back to his dish and began to dig in again with gusto.

Glucks's aide, Meier, who Muller had earlier noticed eyeing in turn both Wilhelm and Konrad, who were seated to his right, shifted slightly to meet Muller's eyes.

"I was enquiring as to camp expansion and if you were

having trouble getting sufficient staff to meet your needs?"

The aide, who was obviously far more interested in the topic than Glucks, nodded.

"Yes, we are growing, it's true.

The Fuhrer's three successful military campaigns have vastly expanded the Reich and given rise to the need for several more and much larger containment facilities.

A transit camp at Westerberg in the Netherlands, an interment camp in Le Vernet France, Breendonk camp in Belgium, Ravensbruck, the woman's labour camp, and Hinzert, a sub-camp and collection point here in Germany, as well as the upgrading and expanding to meet our growing local needs and then there is of course, Poland.

In Poland alone, we've built Soldau, a transit and labour camp and Stutthof, another labour camp, Poznan, a combination concentration, detention and transit camp, as well as carried out the construction of Auschwitz and there will certainly be more to come.

Why do you ask?"

Muller managed a conspiratorial smile before responding.

"I was noticing that you appeared to be sizing up my two companions...and I thought I should save us all some time by making it clear that the Reichsfuhrer has specific plans for these two young officers.

Unfortunately they are spoken for.

Von Stauffer is a new *aide de camp* on the Herr Reichsfuhrer's personal staff and Hauptsturmfuhrer Kauffmann will shortly be taking up a new post under SS-Oberfuhrer, Dr. George Ebner, Chief, Main Health Department; Office of Race and Settlement, head of the *Lebensborn* program.

Kauffmann leaves for Norway in a few weeks. He will be assuming the responsibility of overseeing the expansion of the Reichsfuhrer's pet project into our recently acquired Nordic territories."

The aide nodded sagely at receiving this news and Wilhelm sitting right next to the man and who had been carefully following the conversation, immediately became pensive.

A handsome, unmarried, young and seemingly socially astute - knows what fork to use at least, practicing medical doctor from what sounds like a good family who will, with any luck, find himself sitting out the remainder of the war in Norway - now this is looking promising!

I need to find some time to talk privately with Konrad and do a little digging methinks.

* * * * *

- KWG –

The *'Kaiser Wilhelm Gesellschaft'* (KWG) or (Kaiser Wilhelm Society (KWS) was founded in Berlin in nineteen eleven under the patronage of Kaiser Wilhelm II.

It was financed by both the public and Private sectors and its aim was the establishment of pure research institutes which would be additional and separate from the existing university system.

The idea was to set up non-teaching research only establishments for outstanding scientists in order that the top researchers in specific fields would be able to pursue their research projects free from the accompanying teaching obligations, which would normally encumber those scientists if they attempted their research within the confines of a standard university setting.

The concept was based upon other similar entities which had been set up elsewhere in the world.

A prime example of these earlier organizations was the French *'Institut Pasteur'* in Paris.

The resulting research units initiated in Germany by the KWG played a great part in making that country a world leader in scientific accomplishment prior to the Nazis rise to power.

* * * * *

- Institute of Chemistry –

The Kaiser Wilhelm Institute of Physical Chemistry and

Electrochemistry opened its doors in nineteen-twelve.

It was the first of two Institutes to be located in the Dahlem district of Berlin.

This research centre consisted of three self-contained departments. The founding director Fritz Haber headed the Inorganic and Physical Chemistry department. Richard Willstatter headed the Organic Department and Otto Hahn and Lise Meitner headed the Radioactivity Department which was subdivided into two sections, one for chemistry and the other for physics.

In nineteen fifteen, for his clarification of the structure of chlorophyll, Willstatter became the first of many scientists supported by the KWG to win the Nobel Prize.

Fritz Haber early years at the institute were mainly directed toward research on ammonia.

He was awarded the Nobel Prize for chemistry in nineteen-nineteen for synthesizing ammonia which proved to be of great importance in the fields of fertilizer and explosives production.

During the Great War he used the expertise of the institute to support the German military with the result that the majority of their effort went toward developing poison gases to be used against the enemy.

He became known as the *'Father of Chemical Warfare'* for his development and deployment work involving chlorine and other poisonous gasses.

When the Nazi party came to power in nineteen thirty-three there was a purging of the civil service of non-Aryans and the result of new laws brought about the loss of a quarter of the staff as they were of Jewish stock.

Haber himself was Jewish, but he was exempted from dismissal due to his unquestionable co-operation with the military during the Great War.

Haber refused to fire his staff as directed, choosing to resign his position.

The Nazi doctrine offered no option, they cleaned house of the Jews and appointed a staunch Nazi supporter in Haber's place.

In nineteen thirty-eight and thirty-nine chemical experiments were carried out by Otto Hahn and Fritz Strassmann which, with the aid of physical interpretation of Lise Meitner, resulted in the discovery of nuclear fission.

This colossal discovery took precedent over all other work and Hahn directed the institute's entire efforts toward nuclear research, becoming part of the *'Uranium Project'*, a military research program into the possible technical applications of nuclear fission as a source of energy and for use in weapons development.

* * * * *

- Institute of Physics –

The Kaiser Wilhelm Institute of Physics was founded in the Schoneberg area of Berlin in nineteen-seventeen. Initially it served as a receiving point for funds directed toward research into the field of Physics and was based in the home of its director, Dr. Albert Einstein.

In nineteen thirty-seven, with the aid of funding from the American Rockefeller Foundation, it moved into a large complex located in the Dahlem district of Berlin.

Einstein was lecturing in the USA when Hitler came to power in nineteen thirty-three and being Jewish and never a man to miss the obvious; he decided not to go back to his position at the University of Berlin.

Instead he gave up his German citizenship and stayed in the States, and eventually became a US citizen.

The Nazis quickly moved to downplay Einstein's theories, brushing them aside as just another example or Jewish idiocy.

Peter Debye, a Dutchman, took over Einstein's position as the head of the institute in thirty-three and remained in charge until nineteen-forty.

The most striking piece of equipment at the new institute was located in the massive circular tower, nicknamed the *'Lightening Tower'* which literally towered over the large building that housed the massive complex.

It had been constructed on the west side of the building and housed a high voltage generator which was later developed into a particle accelerator for nuclear experiments.

The uniqueness of the apparatus located inside the tower made it inevitable that the military would eventually take control of the institute and that came to pass later under Werner Heisenberg and Otto Hahn in their determination to built a German atomic bomb.

* * * * *

- Institute of Anthropology, Human Heredity & Eugenics–

Founded in nineteen twenty-seven in Berlin, both the Kaiser Wilhelm Institute of Psychiatry and the Kaiser Wilhelm Institute of Anthropology, Human Heredity and Eugenics (KWI-A) had been financially supported during their construction and throughout the lean years of the Great Depression.

The Rockefeller Foundation had faithfully funded and helped to developed Germany's ongoing eugenics programs from its inception.

The first director of the KWI-A was Dr. Eugen Fischer.

He held that position until nineteen forty-two.

Fischer was an Anthropologist and worked primarily in the area of race eugenics.

Fischer authored a study in nineteen thirteen whose theme was a study of the *'Mischlinge'* (racially mixed) children who were the product of Dutch men coupling with the Hottentot women of the German Second Reich *(German South-western Africa).*

His paper strongly opposed what he referred to as, *'racial mixing'* and held forth that *'Negro Blood'* was of lesser value and that mixing it with *'White Blood'* would serve to eventually destroy all traces of European culture.

Fischer was absolutely delighted when the Nazis came to power in thirty-three and they welcomed him into their propaganda machine with open arms.

Fischer immediately adapted his institutes' activities to fit hand in glove with the Nazi party's anti-Semitic policies, taught courses for Himmler's SS doctors, served as a judge at Berlin's Hereditary Health Court and provided hundreds of opinions on the paternity *'Racial Purity'* of individuals, so called *'Bastard Studies'*, with regard to the German/Jewish offspring or *'Mischlinge'* children.

He was strongly supported by and coordinated his work with, one of leaders of the American eugenics movement, Charles Davenport, a Harvard graduate with a PhD in biology and a prominent US eugenicist and biologist.

Davenport was a leader in his science and had become one of the most prominent scientists in the field. He had gone so far as to take an active part in the sterilization of approximately sixty thousand so called *'unfit'* Americans.

In eighteen ninety-eight Davenport became director of the Cold Spring Harbour Laboratory in New York where he founded the Eugenic Records Office in nineteen-ten.

It was here that he began to study heredity.

Written in nineteen-eleven, his book entitled, *'Heredity in Relation to Eugenics'* was used as a textbook for many years.

In nineteen-twelve Charles Davenport was elected to the National Academy of Sciences.

In nineteen twenty-five Davenport founded the International Federation of Eugenics Organizations (IFEO).

Within this organization, the German, Eugen Fisher was chosen as Chairman of the Commission on Bastardization and Miscegenation (*The mixing of different racial groups through marriage, cohabitation, sexual relations and procreation*), in nineteen twenty-seven.

Davenport's dream was the founding of what would become the *'World Institute for Miscegenations'*. He was at this time working on drawing up a world map of the *'Mixed Rare Areas'* and he introduced his masterpiece to the meeting of the IFEO which was held in Munich in nineteen twenty-eight.

Holding an absolutely fanatic belief in his determination to develop a comprehensive and quantitative approach to the scientific study of human miscegenation, Davenport, together with the aid of his assistant Morris Steggerda, published their research in a book titled '*Race Crossing in Jamaica*' which was intended to scientifically support the position that biological and cultural degradation was a direct result of interbreeding between white and black populations.

Openly supporting and serving to strengthen the Nazi stance on eugenics from the moment they came into power, Eugen Fischer joined the Nazi party in nineteen-forty.

He devoted himself to the direction of programs strongly identified with the Nazi agenda, primarily the study of twins, sterilization methods, and euthanasia techniques.

CHAPTER TWELVE

- Camp Visit –

Wilhelm, Konrad and Muller shared a vehicle on the way to the camp, climbing into the third vehicle in a line of four staff cars that were to make up the convoy being used to travel from the Hotel to the Dachau site.

Once the vehicles had begun to move, Muller, who was sitting between the other two SS officers in the centre of the back seat, turned to Wilhelm who was seated on his left.

Before speaking, he glanced briefly at their driver to ensure that the NCO behind the wheel was concentrating his full attention on the road and not surreptitiously eavesdropping on their conversation.

Satisfied that that was the case, he nevertheless kept his voice low.

"Based on our discussions yesterday on the train, I gathered that neither you nor Konrad are particularly interested in joining the camps as part of the SS-Totenkopf compliment."

Wilhelm nodded his agreement and before Muller continued he turned toward Konrad who also tipped his head to indicate he concurred.

"Well I'm fairly certain that Maier, who is under the gun and desperate to reach his recruitment levels will, despite my warning to him, endeavour to solicit one or both of you for the Totenkopf.

I know he will not succeed with his efforts for the simple reason that you are under the direct protection of the Reichsfuhrer.

However, I see no sense in putting you into the position of having to parry his thrusts for the rest of the day and I have a means to avoid such pestering in mind, if either of you is interested."

Konrad responded first.

"Yes, please."

Wilhelm wasn't far behind.

"By all means."

Muller nodded.

"You understand of course that the Reichsfuhrer sent you along on this little expedition in order for you to gain a basic overview of what the camps are about and how they are administered, and that what I am about to suggest to you must in no way interfere with accomplishing that goal."

Now a captive audience, both men nodded and Muller continued.

"As I did with his predecessor, I have accompanied Glucks on several of these camp inspection tours.

Glucks, unlike Eicke, prefers to have his aides do the overall camp inspection while he spends the bulk of his visit in the Officers Mess.

If he holds true, he will send Meier and other aides off to do the actual inspection. Since I am here as the eyes and ears of the Reichsfuhrer, I am obligated to accompany that party.

I could arrange for the two of you to spend your time with Gluck's smaller group.

Glucks will do a short trip by car, which will be enough to give you both a basic idea of the camp and then he will settle into the mess and remain there until our group rejoins him.

Glucks likes a good audience and during his quick trip of the camp he tends to avoid areas he finds unsettling.

Once you reach the mess he will hold court in his usual fashion and I'm sure if you're prepared to listen to what he has to say, he will be a good host.

If you choose to pursue this course of action, I warn you to avoid any discussion pertaining to the camp unless he raises it himself. Such discussion tends to make him nervous, so stick to other topics.

If you do that it should make your visit to Dachau reasonably informative and a good deal more enjoyable than it would have been had you joined Meier's group."

The cavalcade of staff cars moving down the narrow country road was nearing the camp and the extent of its exterior walls and fences was coming into view.

By this time, definitely curious, Wilhelm was gazing intently ahead through the windshield.

His first impression was one of surprise at the sheer size of it.

Based on what little he knew about prisons, he had been prepared for something much smaller.

"I had no idea the camps were so large!"

A stiff smile formed on Muller's lips.

"Yes, well at this point in the war we find ourselves having to ramp things up considerably when it comes to internment facilities.

The more territory we take the more dissidents we find ourselves forced to deal with.

The camp situation has reached the saturation point and as we continue to absorb 'lebensraum' in preparation for our German pure-blood resettlement programs, we know the expansion of our current internment capacity will be mandatory.

Although we are doing our best, due to serious overcrowding, the conditions within the camps are not ideal.

The Fuhrer has given the SS the responsibility for dealing with this problem and we will accomplish our assigned task, but we don't see it as particularly advantageous to have the German people share in our burden.

The conditions within the camps are no longer given any press and you would both be well advised to keep that in mind when you have finished your little tour.

What goes on in the camps remains in the camps and there is to be no discussions outside of the SS family in relation to it."

The motorcade had entered an area boxed in by fences on both sides of the roadway and the main gate to Dachau had now come into view.

It was an impressive edifice; even from this distance it radiated a sense of functional German-designed structure and permanence.

The main gate consisted of a large, solid, barn-type door of wood construction.

It was approximately twenty-four feet wide and framed in a substantial arch which had been formed out of large cut blocks of stone.

The two supporting columns for the arch had been assembled out of the same stone and were solid looking sentinels, each approximately six feet wide.

The one on the right had a man door set into it.

Approximately eight feet in front of the left supporting column there was a stout-looking one-man cement pillbox, an example of the *Moll System* of guard-bunkers which were strategically spread around the camp.

This structure was arrayed with several business-like and menacing-looking firing slots.

Poised atop the stone arch, in the center of the cut-stone gate frame was a large stylized bronze German eagle. It held a wreath-enclosed swastika within its claws.

It was an impressive rendering, wings spread wide and at least eight feet wide.

Wilhelm had a hard time taking his eyes from it.

The motorcade came to a halt in front of the closed gate and an SS-Totenkopf NCO carrying an MP-38 machine gun approached the lead car.

As the man leaned down to speak to the driver, Konrad spoke, his voice pitched low within the confines of the vehicle.

"It was my understanding that these camps were constructed for the temporary housing of political dissents.

This looks very different from what I'd imagined.

I expected something less permanent.

This looks like it was built to last for some time."

Muller nodded and shifted back into his seat.

"Yes, well as I said earlier, with the taking of new territory we have had to revalue our needs. SS-Gruppenfuhrer Eicke took the problem on and he has done a fantastic job in organizing the reconstruction and administration processes needed for the camps.

Generally, the main function of the camps now is the housing and administration of a labour force rather than the temporary incarceration and intended re-education of dissidents.

What you are about to see today is an impressive accomplishment and it's all been completed by using inmate labour.

Dachau has evolved to become the training centre for all the new '*Totenkopf*' staff that will be needed for the future expansion of the camp system in the conquered territories and is now being used as the model for the entire organization.

The fact that you are forbidden to discuss what you see and hear here today, outside of the SS-family, is another good reason why you should concentrate your visit on the efficiency of Dachau, and you will best accomplish that by spending your time with Glucks rather than tromping about the camp with me.

This is a labour camp, not a holiday camp and little will be gained by your viewing the mundane activities involved in its effective day to day operation.

The Totenkopf are doing good work here under difficult conditions and the experience you two take away today should reflect that, so that if the topic of camps should come up later, you will be able to answer honestly and in good conscience as to your firsthand impression of our astounding success with this program."

* * * * *

- German Medical Researchers –

Looking back at it, one has to wonder where on earth the Nazis come up with their view on '*racial purity*' and how did an entire nation either actively leap on board with the program or choose to ignore what it could mean?

Take Doctors.

In Germany as well as in the rest of the world, these were the people who took the 'Hippocratic Oath'.

A close look at some of the histories of a few of the German Doctors who, during the rise of Hitler and his Party, joined and served the Nazis may help to make it easier for us to understand how it all came about.

* * * * *

The 4th Reich

- Otmar Freiherr von Verschuer –

Otmar Freiherr von Verschuer, a physician, anthropologist and fervent geneticist, once a member of the nationalist paramilitary Freikorps unit of veterans of the Great War and one who typified the great number of German academics interested in National *'regeneration'*, had in nineteen twenty-seven recommended the forced sterilization of Germany's *'mentally and morally subnormal'*.

Von Verschuer joined the Nazi Party in nineteen-forty. On joining the KWI-A Department of Human Genetics in nineteen twenty-seven he took up the position of director under the leadership of Eugen Fischer, and a short time later shifted to acting as director of the division specializing in the research of twins.

In nineteen thirty-five, von Verschuer, in addition to his responsibility for KWI-A duties, took on the added accountability of advancing the work of the *'Institute fur Erbbiologie and Rassenhygiene'* (Frankfurt Institute for Genetic Biology and Racial Hygiene) by taking charge of the overall supervision of the sterilization effort for the city of Frankfurt.

* * * * *

- Dr. Julius Hallervorden –

Dr. Julius Hallervorden, a respected German neuro-pathologist became head of the neuropathology Department of the *Institute for Brain Research* in nineteen thirty-eight.

While holding this position he received hundreds of human brains for examination.

Initially these brains, many of them those of children, were harvested as a result of the opportunity provided by the Nazis now entrenched *'euthanasia'* programs.

A member of the Nazi party and not at all hesitant to get his hands dirty, Hallervorden was well aware of the origins of the brains he examined and on at least one juncture he personally removed them from the heads of recently *euthanized* patients.

On one occasion he was overheard describing the value of these brains to a colleague as *"wonderful material…feeble minded, malformations, and early infantile disease".*

In wartime Germany approximately one hundred and twenty thousand handicapped adults and children were lawfully euthanized.

The Nazi programme of active euthanasia provided quick access to a veritable fountain of pathologic materials.

Hallervorden felt strongly that it would be a wasteful sin not to make use of, for the purposes of medical research, the specimens now being made readily available in such great numbers.

He was anything but *'a voice in the wilderness',* among his medical research colleagues when he articulated this belief.

* * * * *

- Dr. Fritz Lenz –

Dr. Fritz Lenz was a medically trained geneticist.

Born in eighteen eighty-seven in Pflugrade Pomerania in nineteen-nine he began a study of medicine and philosophy, first at the University of Berlin and then at that of Freiburg.

Early on he became enthused with the philosophy teachings of Heinrich Rickart in regard to the origins of *'good and evil'*; reaching the conclusion that applied practical racial hygiene could, over time, eliminate evil.

He met Alfred Ploetz, an early pioneer in the field of racial hygiene and began to devote himself to the subject and while in university at Freiburg he attended lectures given by Eugen Fischer.

Fischer was very impressed with the young student and the two of them joined together to found a Freiburg branch of the *'Society for Racial Hygiene'.*

By nineteen-seventeen Lenz envisioned a future Germany's territorial expansion into the east.

In this eventuality, he foresaw the Slavs as an undesirable and substandard racial element that could easily become an obvious threat to the presence of the occupying Germans, and who, if not checked, could eventually *'overrun the superior (German) Volk'*.

The close relationship between Lenz and Fischer blossomed and in collaboration with the geneticist Erwin Baur, led to the publication in nineteen twenty-one of the first of what was eventually to be a massive two volume work.

This first book was entitled *'Grundiss der Menschlichen Erblichkeitslehre und Rassenhygiene'* (Outline of Human Genetics and Racial Hygiene).

The publication was well received by the scientific community, not only in Germany but on a worldwide basis and went on to strongly influence the German biomedical thinking of the time.

In nineteen twenty-three a prisoner severing his sentence in the fortress of Landsberg found time to read this publication.

This man was at the time writing a book of his own.

His name was Adolf Hitler, and his resulting publication *'Mein Kampf'* drew heavily on the material espoused within Linz's collaborative work.

If anyone wonders where Hitler and the Nazi party got their strong views on racial purity, they need look no further.

Arguably the most brilliant scientific minds of the age, not only in Germany but throughout the world, were deeply involved in researching the new field of eugenics and were convinced of the need to cleanse mankind of inferior genes.

These scientists firmly believed that only those human beings with *'hereditary valuable traits'* should be allowed to propagate.

In *Mein Kampf* Hitler fortified his position on the need for Germany's development of a pure, superior or *'Aryan'* race by pointing to what the science of the day was telling the world.

The new fields of eugenics and racial hygiene had, from the early nineteen hundreds, produced a mountain of unchallenged scientific proof of such need.

These were not ideas plucked from thin air, nor a matter of guesswork. They were concepts based on the best and most modern scientific concepts of eugenics and racial hygiene; concepts that were no way unique to Germany but strongly held throughout Europe, Great Britain, her Empire and in most of the new world.

These men tenaciously believed that for the sake of future European mankind, racial cross-breeding had be eradicated.

In nineteen twenty-three Linz received the first chair in eugenics in Munich.

In nineteen thirty-two Lenz and his collaborators published their second book which was then combined with the first and published under the title *'Human Heredity Theory and Racial Hygiene'* in nineteen thirty-six.

Lenz had specialized in the field of the transmission of hereditary human diseases and racial health. His publications and his theory of recognizing *'race as a value principle'* placed him and his colleagues at the top of the heap among the world's racial theorists.

It just so happened that their positions served to support and justify the Nazi ideology, specifically in relation to the superiority of the *'Nordic race'* and the necessity of eliminating the inferior strains of humanity.

In nineteen thirty-three Lenz had moved to Berlin where he established the first specific department devoted to eugenics at the Institute of Anthropology, Human Heredity and Eugenics.

When the Nuremberg laws of nineteen thirty-five were promulgated Lenz stated the following"

"As important as the external features for their evaluation is the lineage of individuals, a blond Jew is also a Jew. Yes, there are Jews who have most of the external features of the Nordic race, but who nevertheless display Jewish mental tendencies. The legislation of the National Socialist state therefore properly defines a Jew not by external race characteristics, but by descent."

Lenz joined the Nazi party in nineteen thirty-seven.

* * * * *

- Dr. Robert Ritter –

Dr. Robert Ritter was born in nineteen-one at Aschen, in North-Rhine Westphalia, the westernmost city of Germany, situated on its borders with Belgium and the Netherlands.

He was a psychologist and physician and received his doctorate in educational physiology at the University of Munich in nineteen twenty-seven and was awarded his doctorate in medicine at the University of Heidelberg in nineteen-thirty.

After graduation he worked as a child physiologist and specialized in juvenile delinquency.

In nineteen thirty-six Ritter was appointed to head the newly created Eugenic and Population Research Station of the Reich Health and Sanitation Office.

While he held this post, he worked closely with Eva Juatin, a trained nurse who went on to become an anthropologist and psychologist in her own right.

This team specialized in the research into the makeup, both biological and eugenic, with the view to assessing the general value of the '*Gypsy*' (Roma) race as a whole.

With eager determination Ritter and his group threw themselves into their research.

They took physical measurements, blood samples and amassed detailed genealogies of German '*Roma*' residing in jails, camps, and in their own natural surroundings.

By nineteen-forty Ritter had reached his conclusion as to the value of the '*Roma* peoples'.

He had without question determined that they were a '*primitive*' people, incapable to leading a normal civilized lifestyle.

His research had clearly demonstrated that almost all Gypsies were the product of tainted blood and that this was true of any '*Gypsy*' who had at least one grandparent of full '*Roma blood*' or if at least two grandparents were of partial '*Roma blood*'.

In part, his progress report forwarded to his Nazi masters in nineteen-forty read:

"*The gypsy question can only be solved when the main body of asocial and good-for-nothing Gypsy individuals of mixed blood is collected together in large labour camps and kept working there, and when the further breeding of this population is stopped once*

89

Patrick Laughy

and for all".

His government supplied research money was increased immediately.

* * * * *

- Dr. Ernst Rudin –

Dr. Ernst Rudin, born in St. Gallen, Switzerland in eighteen seventy-four was a psychiatrist, geneticist and eugenicist who is still considered to this day by many to be the *'Father of Psychiatric Genealogy'*.

Rudin began his career in psychiatry in Munich Germany and influenced by his brother-in-law Allred Ploetz, concluded that achieving racial purity was the answer to saving the human race from a from obvious decline.

Early in his career he urged that preventative coercive measures be taken to prevent the reproduction of the mentally ill.

He began researching racial hygiene and Social Darwinism, after which he developed the concept of *'empirical genetic prognoses'* of mental disorders.

He published his initial results in a paper on the genetics of schizophrenia in nineteen-sixteen and was president of the International Federation of Eugenic Organizations.

He was a recognized world leader of the eugenics movement whose mandate was to remove *'inferior'* individuals from society, through segregation or sterilization, with the aim of producing a *'better'* German race.

In nineteen-sixteen he established the field of *'Psychiatric Hereditary Biology'* or what was referred to as *'Psychiatric Genetics'* during the nineteen-thirties.

Rudin became director of the Genealogical-Demographic Department at the German Institute for Psychiatric Research in Munich, in nineteen-seventeen.

Over time he amassed a large collection of patient genealogies and based on their study, concluded that mental disorders were genetic and could be predicted and therein prevented by way of sterilization.

In nineteen thirty-three Rudin was chosen by Hitler's Reich Ministry to lead the German racial purity program.

Dr. Rudin went to work drafting and preparing the Nazi Sterilization Laws, which were initially aimed at the sterilization of all schizophrenics, manic-depressives and alcoholics.

The widespread euthanasia programs soon introduced at German psychiatric hospitals were a natural progression.

Rudin spoke out publicly in support of the Nazi Party's actions bringing about what he referred to as his *more than thirty-year-old dream a reality* through the imposition of *racial Hygiene* upon the German people.

* * * * *

- Dr. Ernst Wentzler –

Dr. Ernst Wentzler ran a Paediatric Clinic in Berlin and was recognized in Germany as one of the best in his field.

He treated the children of many of the Nazi Hierarchy, developed methods to treat premature infants and children with birth defects, and invented a life saving incubator know as the *'Wentzler warmer'*.

Wentzler also supported the euthanasia of incurably ill babies and children, and served as one of the primary coordinators of the paediatric *'euthanasia'* program, evaluating incoming forms and unhesitatingly pronouncing judgement on whether a child would live or die.

* * * * *

- Medical Professionals –

In the German environment of the day it was very, very, easy to understand how medical professionals, those who needed financial backing and support for their continued research could succumb to the wonder of the Nazi Party's rise to power and as well to those everyday Germans who were not in the scientific field, who could easily accept and support what the highly effective German propaganda machine was pumping out in a steady flow…the pounding spirit of nationalistic fervour.

This was a New Germany and the Nazis could and would build a better Germany, build a better German, cleanse the Fatherland of misfits and subhumans and make Germany's future one of a race of pure and strong '*Aryans*'.

CHAPTER THIRTEEN

- Prospective Brother-in-law –

As predicted by Muller, Glucks sent part of his staff off, under the supervision of Meier, to carry out the required in-depth inspection of the camp while he and his party took a short motorized tour of the various areas within the confines of the fences.

Muller's suggestion that Wilhelm and Konrad accompany the SS-Brigadefuhrer and the camp Commandant while he tagged along with Meier's group was agreeably received by Glucks without comment, although Wilhelm caught what he took to be a flicker of distinct displeasure in Meier's features as he, with his group in tow, split off from the others to head out on foot.

Muller, who had been watching the two of them closely, managed a surreptitious wink delivered in Wilhelm's direction as he left them to join Meier's party.

Wilhelm and Konrad were directed into Gluck's car to ride with him while the others in their group climbed into a following vehicle and the two cars began to move.

It soon became obvious that Glucks was no stranger to this placement into the position of acting as a tour guide.

He seemed to enjoy having a captive audience in the two young SS offers as he leaned comfortably back into the rear seat of the open staff car and spoke with avid pride and gestured often while they drove around the camp.

It reminded Wilhelm of some sort of victory parade.

The man was obviously in his element and the tour was informative from the prospective of the gleaning of a general overview of the massive facility.

Glucks eagerly pointed out various building and facilities as they passed by them.

They began with a sighting of the Commandant's villa

which was substantial and located in a picturesque setting, surrounded by a densely forested area, well away from the remainder of the camp's buildings.

From there they moved on to view the *'Kommandantur'* (Headquarters) building, which had originally been the office building used for the administration of the old armaments factory on the site.

They saw the railhead where trains arrived at the camp, the kennels housing the crowd-control dogs, the *'gate building'* at the center of which was the *'Jourhaus Gate'* through which newly arriving prisoners entered the camp.

The gate itself, of wrought iron construction, held the motto *'Arbeit Macht Frie'* (Work makes you free) and opened into the *'Appellplatz'*, the roll call site of the Prisoner compound.

Through the gate Wilhelm could see the massive L-shaped *'SS Kaserne'* (SS barracks building).

With the same sense of pride Glucks pointed out the housing provided for the officers of the *'Totenkopf'* staff, the sports field for SS staff, the heat plant, the angora rabbit barn, the bakery, the workshops, the SS hospital, the large herb garden and finally the small building containing the crematorium, at the time of which he made the observation that the camp, like a small city, was self-contained and offered inmates everything they required.

Wilhelm had never seen the inside of a prison before and had no experience to rely on for comparison with what he had now been shown.

He'd never had any difficulty in accepting that there were bound to be people who had to be locked up for the protection of the state and this seemed to be a well organized and constructed facility, designed to fulfill that requirement.

After his tour, he honestly felt that Dachau was both an efficient and effective incarceration facility, which appeared more than adequate to manage its mandate.

* * * * *

- U-Boat War –

The first sea-going U-boat, U-27 was launched in nineteen thirty-six. Early in the war the available fleet of U-boats had a number of important successes.

The sinking of the passenger liner *SS Athenia* by U-30 on September third of nineteen thirty-nine, just two days after war had been declared was the first U-boat strike made in the war of the Atlantic.

Hitler, who was at this point in time, still of the opinion that he would be successful at getting both the French and British to reach a diplomatic solution to the declaration of war rather than choose to actively seek military confrontation with Germany over the Nazi invasion of Poland, had forbidden the sinking of commercial ships.

However, for whatever reason, U-30 sank her.

She was the first ship out of the total tonnage of sixty-five thousand U-boats would sink in the first week of the war.

On September of nineteen thirty-nine, the aircraft carrier *HMS Ark Royal* narrowly avoided being struck by two torpedoes fired by U-30 and in the same month the aircraft carrier *HMS Courageous* was sunk by U-29.

On the first of October nineteen thirty-nine, Donitz became Rear Admiral and Commander of the Submarines.

On October fourteenth, nineteen thirty-nine U-47 managed to penetrate unseen into Scapa Flow, the base for the British Grand Fleet, and once inside she successfully sank the battleship HMS Royal Oak.

These early sub successes caught the British with their pants down from both a practical and propaganda perspective.

The last of these incidences had forced the *Home Fleet* to move from *Scapa Flow*, which had always been considered by the Admiralty to be a secure harbour, into a series of temporary anchorages primarily around the coast of Scotland.

Two facts became obvious to all.

Firstly, the British intention of holding the German surface fleet captive in the North Sea with the use of its own surface fleet and preventing the Germans from moving into the Atlantic was no longer practical due to the successful U-boat attacks.

Secondly, if the Germans intended to practice *'unrestricted submarine warfare'* in this war as they had done in the Great War, which was certainly indicated by the sinking of the *SS Athenia*, then the island nation of Brattain was in a very great deal of trouble with regard to maintaining the supply line from the new world that it relied on for its very survival.

By nineteen thirty-nine a newer U-boat design model boasting more powerful engines and a greater fuel carrying capacity, the Type VII B, became available.

The designs of the U-boats themselves, achieved between the wars, was proving effective but there were definite problems with the torpedo designs.

There were many reports of successful firings that had failed to explode upon impact.

Initially these were ignored as unsubstantiated but the reports steadily increased to the point where they had to be addressed.

After all, once a torpedo had been fired, the wake it set off provided a direct path back to the U-boat which had done the firing.

A prime example of how serious the problem was can be found in an examination of the sinking of the *HMS Royal Oak* at *Scapa Flow*.

This particular patrol by U-47 had been carefully planned before she'd left Kiel.

She was on a secret mission to slip into *Scapa Flow* and attack the Home Fleet while it was at anchor.

Once U-47 had managed to get into the anchorage - no easy task - her skipper, Otto Prien, ordered an immediate attack. The ship's log clearly describes what transpired thereafter.

In discussions held with Donitz prior to the trip a decision had been reached that U-47 was to carry only G7 E electric torpedoes.

These traveled more slowly than the compressed air driven G7 A torpedo, but had the advantage over the air driven model in that it left no telltale wake when it was fired.

Prien had positioned U-47 between the silhouettes of two

large ships. At a distance of three thousand meters they appeared to be sitting ducks.

He fired four torpedoes simultaneously, two from the bow and two from the rear tubes.

Only three of the four torpedoes successfully fired. The fourth never left the tube due to a firing mechanism failure.

Only one of the torpedoes struck.

It raised no alarm on the ship and did little damage. The other two never made it to their targets.

U-47 then swung around and fired off a single torpedo from a rear tube. It also failed to reach its target.

Prien swung his U-boat around again and utilizing the three bow tubes that were functional and had been reloaded with torpedoes, he fired three more toward *HMS Royal Oak*.

By this time the distance from his target was down to only fifteen hundred meters.

A miss was unthinkable.

One torpedo struck *Royal Oak* in the stern and it exploded and it has been surmised that the warhead of at least one and perhaps both of the other two were set off by the first blast.

The result was a huge explosion that rocked the Battleship soundly and caused her to sink.

It was of course a huge victory for the Nazis.

However the fact is that Prien had to fire a total of seven torpedoes in order to have one or perhaps two actually explode on contact.

This was not at a moving ship at sea, but at an anchored stationary target the size of a battleship which was lying at anchor only a short fifteen hundred meters away from the U-boat.

Submarines carrying unreliable torpedoes were not only impotent but could quickly become deathtraps.

Work on new torpedo designs began immediately.

Testing of the new and redesigned models was intense and thorough.

* * * * *

Patrick Laughy

- Lebensborn Project Expansion –

From the inception of Himmler's SS, those recruited for the elite service had been carefully selected from both a physical and genetic point of view.

To be accepted into the SS the men had to be excellent physical specimens who exhibited the qualities of a true German as decreed by the Nazi Party and had to be able to trace their ancestry back to seventeen-fifty to confirm they were the product of pure Aryan bloodlines.

In short order Himmler began to see his men as the source for selection of the breeding stock of the future German Reich.

Created by Himmler in December of nineteen thirty-five, the Lebensborn Project had been initiated by the Reichsfuhrer as the fist step in an evolving programme to attempt to increase the sagging birth rate of what the Nazi Party had determined as pure German Aryan bloodlines.

In a letter to SS members written on September nineteen thirty-six Himmler stated:

"The Organization "Lebensborn e. V." serves the SS leaders in the selection and adoption of qualified children. This organization "Lebensborn e. V." is under my personal direction, is part of the race and settlement central bureau of the SS, and has the following obligations:

1. Support racially, biologically, and hereditarily valuable families with many children.

2. Place and care for racially and biologically and hereditarily valuable pregnant women, who, after thorough examination of their and the progenitor's families by the race and settlement central bureau of the SS, can be expected to produce equally valuable children.

3. Care for the children.

4. Care for the children's mothers.

It is the honourable duty of all leaders of the central bureau to become members of the organization "Lebensborn e. V.". The application for admission must be filed prior to 23 September 1936."

Under the watchful eyes and personal control of Dr. Ebner, who had been appointed Oberfuhrer of the Lebensborn Project because Himmler considered him an expert on matters of *'racial hygiene'* and who the Reichsfuhrer had personally chosen to be an SS lecturer on the *'Problems of Racial Selection'* for all SS recruits, the first Lebensborn home, *'Heim Hochland '*was opened in nineteen thirty-six in Steinhoering, a small village close to Munich.

During his tenure at *'Heim Hochland'*, Ebner oversaw the births of over three thousand children.

By nineteen thirty-nine there were eight thousand members in *Lebensborn e. V.,* of which thirty-five hundred were SS leaders.

The Lebensborn office was part of the *'SS Rasse und Siedlungshauptamt'* (SS office of Race and Settlement) until nineteen thirty-eight at which time it was transferred to *'Hauptamt Personlicher Stab Reichsfuhrer-SS'* (Personal Staff of the Reich Leader SS) which was directly supervised by Himmler.

Those directly responsible to Himmler for the program as designated leaders of the Lebensborn e.V. were SS-Standartenfuhrer Max Sollmann and SS-Oberfuhrer Dr. Gregor Ebner.

This initial programme, designed to take the first step toward the *'cleansing'* of Germany of impure blood, directed the SS to provide maternity homes and financial assistance to the wives of SS members and all unmarried mothers who were pregnant and considered to be biologically fit and racially pure for a minimum of three generations as designated by Himmler's predetermined racial standards necessary for the production of the future Aryan race.

Initially Himmler publicly advocated the concept of actively soliciting single racially pure young German women to couple with members of the SS and produce children out of wedlock.

The product of these liaisons would then become wards of the state to be raised by SS staff at the homes, until they could be placed for adoption by those of good German stock.

They would then be raised in adoptive German homes as proper Germans and thereby over time propagate Aryan traits throughout the expanding New Reich.

There was an understandable backlash over this suggestion by the citizens of a Christian Germany and Himmler quickly and publicly backed off from it, but privately, he continued to support such a concept.

He actively encouraged his men to impregnate any willing pure-German girl they could and directed that any pregnant racially pure, Aryan female, whether married or not was to be warmly welcomed into the SS run Lebensborn *'birth houses'* now operating throughout Germany.

The SS was now also running orphanages and adoption services.

By nineteen forty, seventy percent of those giving birth under the care of the SS Lebensborn program were unmarried and plans for the expansion of the programme into the newly occupied areas now under the control of the Reich had begun to be formulated.

CHAPTER FOURTEEN

- A Target for Cupid –

Pleading the need to make notes on the visit, Wilhelm finally connived to get Konrad alone after they had spent a half hour in the mess listening to Glucks, the Camp Commandant and his senior staff share war stories.

Wilhelm managed to find a quiet table at the far end of the mess where they could have some privacy and as soon as one of the white-coated stewards had set a large pitcher of beer before them he began to probe.

"So Konrad, you're off to Norway soon. Are you pleased with your new assignment?"

Concentrating on pouring their glasses full, Kaufmann waited until he had completed the task before he replied.

He set the pitcher down and then raised his glass in salute, and Wilhelm smiled and lifted his own to meet it.

"Yes…Yes I am."

Wilhelm set his glass down and wiped his mouth with the back of his hand and then let his eyes meet Konrad's.

"Your girl is going with you then?"

"No actually…apparently she didn't share my sense of adventure.

Either that or she simply wasn't ready to leave the nest.

I knew that she was very close with her parents, but I expected that she was ready to marry and leave home.

We parted as friends and it was probably for the best anyway."

He's on the rebound and he's leaving Germany for Norway. He's ripe for the plucking.

Wilhelm pursed his lips and nodded.

"Well that's too bad. I remember you were saying that you wanted to settle down and have a family."

Konrad frowned over the top of his glass.

'Yes, I am ready to start a family and my parents have been on my back about it for several months now.

I thought Lise was the girl for me, but…well it's good that I found it out now and not after I'd married her I guess."

"For sure! Well I'm sure you'll find some nice Norwegian girl."

Konrad let out a short, lifeless chortle.

"Nope, my Mother and Father wouldn't like that one bit.

If I do get married it will have to be to some well-bred German girl of good station, I'm afraid.

I'll just have to settle for waiting until I can get some leave and trust in my mother to set me up with someone new when that time comes."

Thank you God!

"Say, speaking of Mothers and Fathers. I was wondering if you could help me with a little problem my family is trying to deal with."

"Sure, I'd be happy to help, if I can."

"My little sister Gabriella is about to graduate from a nursing program and I was wondering if you could steer me in the right direction.

My parents are worried you see….afraid that she will end up in some military hospital, continually faced with dealing with those suffering from horrific injuries.

Do you think there would be a possibility that she would have a chance at getting into something within the Lebensborn program instead?"

Konrad features grew more serious.

"Wow, yes…yes for sure. She could work with me. In the next month I have to put together a skeleton staff to take to Norway …

Oh, perhaps Norway wouldn't work. She's pretty young isn't she?"

In some ways my friend…but she's an old hand in others.

"She's twenty-two.

Mature beyond her years in some respects, definitely

outgoing and adventurous.

Norway sounds like a wonderful solution to securing a positive start for her nursing career and the Lebensborn programmed would be great.

She loves babies. It would be right up her alley. She'll jump at the chance to join your team and I have to tell you that I would feel very secure about her wellbeing in a new setting if she were working under your watchful eyes.

I really appreciate the offer and I know my parents will be much relived by this solution to our problem."

* * * * *

- Hans Michael Frank –

Hans Frank was born in Karlsruhe Germany on May twenty-third, nineteen hundred. He joined the German army at the age of seventeen, during the Great War.

Like many other veterans, he served in the Freikorps after the end of the war.

In nineteen-nineteen, as one of its founding members, he joined the German Worker's Party which was to evolve into the *'Nationalsozialistische Deutsche Arbeiter-Partei'* (National Socialist German Workers' Party) or the more generally used term of *NAZI* Party, which was an abbreviation of the first word of its full name.

Frank studied law and became a lawyer in nineteen twenty-six and at that time became the personal legal advisor to Adolf Hitler who was by then the party leader.

From the beginning Frank was a staunch supporter of the Nazi party and all its platforms. His view on the roll of a judge in the New Reich was:

'to safeguard the concrete order of the racial community, to eliminate dangerous elements, to prosecute all acts harmful to the community, and to arbitrate in disagreements between members of the community. The National Socialist ideology, especially as expressed in the Party programme and in the speeches of our

Leader, is the basis for interpreting legal sources.'

In September of nineteen thirty-nine, Hans Frank was assigned as Chief of Administration to the German military administration of occupied Poland under Gerd von Rundstedt.

On October twenty-sixth of that year he was given the rank of *SS-Obergruppenfuher* (SS-Lieutenant General) and assigned as *'Generalgouverneur fur die besetzten polnischen Gebiete'* (Governor-General of the occupied Polish territories) in control of the Central Government of the area of Poland not directly incorporated into Germany, a land mass of approximately ninety thousand square kilometres out of the total one hundred and eighty-seven that Germany had gained during the invasion.

* * * * *

- Ausserordentliche Befriedungsaktion –

The AB-Aktion or *'Ausserordentliche Befriedungsaktion'* (Extraordinary Operation of Pacification) was part of the larger *'Generalplan Ost'* (Master Plan East) which was a secret Nazi plan for the German colonization of Central and Eastern Europe and it was specifically designed for use in Poland, a country populated by a people who the Nazi Party experts considered as subhuman and whose only purpose in life within the New Reich would be as a source of slave labour.

The initial research for this plan, which was part of Hitler's overall plan for his envisioned *'New Order'*, which envisaged a German expansion to the east in order to provide *'Lebensraum'* (Living Space) for a future and much larger German Fatherland, commenced some time before the Nazis actually made their move to invade Poland.

There were a substantial number of citizens living within the borders of pre-war Poland who were of German extraction.

Working in cooperation with these German expatriates, the German police and Gestapo were able to prepare special lists *'Sonderfahndungsbuch Polen'* of Poles who were to be considered as *'enemies of the Reich'*.

Polish citizens to be targeted by the lists were generally termed '*the Intelligentsia*', those who were seen by the researchers as representative of the Polish government administration, culture and life in the region to be occupied by the Germans.

Specifically to be considered as '*the enemies of the Reich*' were: '*anyone with a middle school or higher education, teachers, priests, doctors, dentists, veterinarians, veteran military officers, bureaucrats, members of the Polish administration, police, medium and large businessmen and merchants, medium and large landowners, writers, journalists and newspaper editors and all persons who during the interwar period had belonged to any of the Polish cultural and patriotic organizations*'.

Hitler had ordered that after the invasion of Poland, the people on these lists were to be removed from the general population.

This action was considered to be mandatory in nature by those formulating the plan because they felt it would go a long way toward ensuring the nipping-in the-bud of any Polish resistance movement and hold any such organized action to a minimum during the impending attack on France, something that was of great concern at the time.

The idea was considered to be of such import that its implementation was even discussed openly with Soviet officials at a series of secret pre-war Gestapo-NKVD conferences.

In addition to the lists prepared before the invasion of Poland, further lists were prepared after the occupation by the Gestapo who, in late nineteen thirty-nine and early nineteen-forty, briefly arrested and interrogated the majority of university professors, intellectuals, writers, politicians, teachers and other members of the elite of Polish society.

On May sixteenth nineteen-forty, satisfied that current lists contained all the names of any Poles who might be of danger to the '*New Reich*', the Governor-General of the occupied Polish territories, SS-Obergruppenfuher Hans Frank, accepted the '*Ausserordentliche Befriedungsaktion*' and authorized the activation of the plan.

In the weeks that followed, the German police, Gestapo, SD,

and units of the Wehrmacht arrested approximately thirty thousand Poles within the major cities.

The prisoners were interned in prisons located in Warsaw, Krakow, Radom, Kielce, Nowy Sacz, Tarnow, Lublin and Wisnicz, where they were subjected to interrogation by Nazi officials.

Once they had been thoroughly interrogated most were sent to concentration camps.

Sachsenhausen, Mauthausen and the newly constructed camp at Auschwitz were the primary recipients.

About thirty-five hundred were summarily executed by the *'Einsatzcommando'* (SS paramilitary death squads) and the *'Volksdeutscher Selbstschutz Polen',* which were paramilitary organizations formed from members of the German minority in Poland; at mass murder sites in Palmiry near Warsaw; Firlej, and Wincentynow near Radom and in the Blizyn forest near Skarzysko-Kamienna.

Entirely on board with the concept, the Russians, who had helped to carve up the Polish nation, promptly and enthusiastically executed twenty-two thousand Polish military officers who had surrendered to them in the areas under their control.

CHAPTER FIFTEEN

- A Family Matter –

Count von Stauffer set the phone receiver in its cradle and helped himself to a cigarette from the box on his desk and then lit it with the matching silver lighter and inhaled deeply before setting the lighter down and leaning back in his comfortably padded leather chair.

He was deep in thought as he exhaled.

The three calls had brought a real sense of relief.

The first, long distance from Munich, had come from Wilhelm shortly after noon and had given him real hope in finding a viable method of dealing with the Gabriella situation.

She would be away from Berlin, working with babies, not in some military hospital struggling within the depressing atmosphere of having to deal with an endless supply of torn bodies and in a real sense, still doing her part by playing a positive role in the creation of the New Germany.

He could think of no reason not to trust Wilhelm's judgement of Hauptsturmfuhrer, Doctor Konrad Kauffmann and based on his son's description it he seemed like a good match, should the two, as predicted by Wilhelm, become romantically attached.

However, to be on the safe side, he had then put through a call to long time family friend SS-Sturmbannfuhrer, Doctor Baron Heinrich von Kliest, at the Kaiser Wilhelm Institute of Anthropology, Human Heredity and Eugenics.

Wilhelm had indicated that Kauffmann had studied under Heinrich, and the Count knew that if he asked he would an honest evaluation of the young man's abilities and personality from the Baron.

Heinrich's description of Kauffmann, although delivered from a completely different perspective, had served to generally support Wilhelm's earlier assessment.

A brilliant and very serious young man, very much wrapped up in his work. A future that would most likely revolve around medical research, once the required period of practical field experience had been garnered.

Honest, good natured, earnest, compassionate, of good family and possessing sound morals.

It was almost too good to be true and after thanking Heinrich and finishing the call, the Count actually found himself feeling a good deal of the stress related to the matter, which had been building over the past couple of days, beginning to slip away.

This could really work, not only from the point of view of settling Gabriella down but also as a potential catch with regard to the long term goals of Operation Fatherland.

The Baron's assessment was that Kauffmann was brilliant and interested in research. He could well play a very large part in the overall plan.

The third call, one he had placed to Erika at their Berlin residence, had immediately followed the second.

He knew that while his wife would certainly take both Wilhelm's and the Baron's assessment of the potential husband under consideration, she would nonetheless want to personally undertake a far more detailed investigation into the young man's background, before she would throw her support behind the plan.

The Count wanted to ensure he had all his ducks in a row before his scheduled meeting with his youngest daughter, meaning that Erika would only have a few hours to vet Kauffmann to her satisfaction and get back to him with her approval, before his critical meeting with Gabriella.

* * * * *

- Schnorchel –

When Germany defeated the Netherlands in nineteen-forty, part of the booty they gleaned while overrunning the country was the capture of two of the Dutch O-21 series submarines, O-25 and O-26.

These two subs were fitted with an operating device which the Dutch had named a *Snuiver* (Sniffer).

These devices had been designed by Jan Jacob Wichers and in the initial stages had been simple appendages consisting of an arrangement of pipes which the navy had been experimenting with since nineteen thirty-eight.

The concept had been previously considered by the British as early as the Great War when a manager at a Shipbuilding and Engineering Company in Greenock Scotland had come up with a like system and it had been patented by a British firm and offered to the Royal Navy.

At the time the British had considered it to be impractical.

In nineteen twenty-six Captain Pericle Ferretti of the Italian Navy ran tests of a fitting with similar purpose but it met a similar fate to that of the Scottish fitting.

The original diesel submarines had been designed to operate primarily on the surface and to utilize their ability to dive only as a means to evade surface ships or for stealth during daylight attacks.

When they dived they relied on electric motors to manoeuvre. These electric motors relied on batteries for power and could only be used for short periods before draining their power source.

The batteries could only be recharged while operating under diesel power on the surface.

The invention of ASDIC sonar by the British and its effectiveness against submerged subs quickly brought about its expanded use in surface ships that were escorting convoys.

By nineteen-forty the success of the British ASDIC determined that the German submarines found it much safer to travel on the surface at night, and they did so, but it was very risky to remain on the surface during the day.

Increasingly, when they made that choice, they found themselves risking being spotted by surface ships that were, by this time, likely using new ship-board radar systems.

In order to avoid the risk of being spotted by the long range radar in daylight hours, German sub commanders progressively found themselves being forced to operate underwater, in both daylight and night time conditions, running on their electric motors which offered only low speeds and very limited endurance.

With the capture of the two Dutch submarines the Kriegsmarine submarine engineers and designers, very conscious of the restrictive circumstances now facing their operational U-boats, took a serious look at adopting and improving upon the *Snuiver* system, which they coined a 'Schnorchel', both with a view to eventually managing to take in fresh air for the crew while a sub was submerged as well as a potential method or allowing a sub to run its diesels to charge its batteries while submerged.

If these aims could be realized the effectiveness of the submarines and a reduction in the risks they faced during their war patrols would be vastly improved.

* * * * *

- New Bases –

During the spring and summer of nineteen-forty, in a short span of time, a matter of weeks, the military forces of Nazi Germany overran Norway, France and the Low Countries.

From the point of view of the Kriegsmarine, this successful invasion provided the answer to a very serious logistical problem.

Instantly the restriction placed upon the German navy, that of having all their home ports confined to the Baltic, was eliminated in that they now found themselves inheriting control of a large number of ports which had previously been situated within the newly conquered lands.

This was a wonderful windfall, especially for the U-boats. It was however, a two sided coin.

While moving their fleets to take advantage of the availability of these new ports would negate the restrictions their previous Baltic homeports had placed on range and wear and tear on their ships, they would also bring any of the newly positioned fleets within range of bombers launched from British bases.

The Germans began to quickly move their fleets into these new ports and in consideration of the increased danger to these fleets that would be on offer from British bombers, the Nazis began immediate steps to limit that threat.

Huge reinforced concrete bunker-like U-boat pens were immediately designed for these new facilities.

The large labour force required for this massive program was to be supplied courtesy of the SS, who planned to employ approximately fifteen thousand prisoners of war and concentration camp inmates for the task.

CHAPTER SIXTEEN

- A New Start –

It was four-thirty before the Count had finished his appointments for the day and an excited Eric was able rejoin him in his office.

The two of them were bent over Karl von Stauffer's massive desk where Eric had again spread out some of the super-submarine engineering diagrams and was enthusiastically going over the specifications with his father.

Both were smoking and a blue haze had formed above the desk as Eric ran his finger over the large sheet on top of the pile.

"They were originally designed as mine-layers - that's why they're so large. I can't tell you how excited I am about being able to command the first one commissioned.

When will it be finished?"

The Count was pleased by his son's exuberance over the prospect of his knew command and he couldn't resist a smile as he responded.

"It will be ready for sea trials next week; you will be leaving for Kiel tomorrow morning to join your crew who are already at the 'F. Krupp Germaniawerft A.G. shipyard' (Germania Shipyard) where the entire production run for this series of large U-boats is being built.

Keels for all four of the U-boats we are concerned with have already been laid there. One will be completed approximately every nine months.

Each U-boat is being constructed in twenty large component sections elsewhere and then transported to the *'Germaniawerft'* where they will be assembled into the finished product.

The trials for this first sub, which you will command, have been scheduled to begin on Monday September thirtieth, which gives you only four days before you will find yourself back at sea again."

* * * * *

Gabriella wheeled her sleek sports car into the parking lot behind her Father's office building and revved the powerful engine before switching it off.

She was carefully arranging her talking points in her mind, as she checked her makeup in the rear-view mirror, applying a little lipstick.

For her entire life she had been able to manipulate her father and she was relatively confident that she could manage to do so again at the scheduled meeting.

It was obvious that he was displeased with her activities of late, and she could even admit to herself that there was probably good reason for at least part of that.

But, if she presented her case well to him, apologised and indicated a desire to tone things down…

* * * **

Before she spoke, Ursula reached over and took her Mother's hand.

The two of them were riding in the back of the Count's staff car which he had sent to pick them up from home and bring them to his office in time for the meeting with Gabriella.

"It will be fine Mother, please stop fussing."

Erika's eyebrows arched as she turned to face her daughter. She kept her voice low as she responded.

"Well you know how your father is with Gabriella. She's had no trouble at all in winding him around her little finger…she's been able to do it since the day she was born."

The countess swivelled her head slightly to check that the driver was not following the conversation.

Satisfied that he was intent on his driving, she continued.

"We as a family can not put up with this foolishness any longer and your Father had better be prepared to take firm action. I made it quite clear to Karl that the rest of the family would be there to see to it that Gabriella isn't able to worm her way out of this with him again.

Wilhelm is off to Munich on some business or other but the rest of us will join to ensure that Gabriella understands just how serious things have become and immediately agrees to the suggestions that we have decided upon.

A new start in Norway with a Doctor and from a very good family with old money, I swear to God, if she lets this slip away I will have nothing more to do with her…"

Ursula let out a soft sigh and squeezed the Countesses fingers gently.

"It will be fine Mother, Gabriella is no ones fool. She'll see that we are right in this. She's just young and a little immature and has been enjoying herself a little too much."

The colour drained out of Erika's face.

"…enjoying herself… enjoying herself…really Ursula, sometimes I just don't know what this world is coming too. You young people seem to have lost all the social graces and don't seem capable of exercising even a trace of common sense anymore."

This time Ursula bit back the sigh.

Well my darling little sister, like it or not, I think your wild days are about over.

You'd better be prepared for a solid front, because mother isn't going to let go this time!

* * * * *

The Count glanced at his watch and then up at Eric.

"You'd better wrap these documents up…and I'd better open up the windows and get some fresh air in here; your mother isn't going to like all this smoke."

Eric removed the paperweights he'd used to hold the drawings open on the desk and let them roll back up before scooping them up in his arms and carrying them over to the credenza behind his father's desk.

He placed the bundle on top.

Karl von Stauffer had no more than flipped the latch to facilitate the opening of the first window when his intercom buzzed.

He pushed the window open wide before crossing to his desk and pressing the button down.

The sound of his secretary's voice flooded the room.

"Your daughter is here Herr General…oh and the Countess and Ursula have just arrived as well."

* * * * *

- The German Economy –

The fact that the German economic situation during the period of Hitler's rise to power in Germany was dismal played a large part in the Nazis successful rise to power.

When campaigning for the Nazi Party, Hitler made it clear that if elected his Party would reject the terms of the Treaty of Versailles outright.

The Treaty had been implemented by the allies against Germany after Germany's defeat in the Great War and it provided for crippling financial war reparations to be paid to the winning side.

The provisions of this hated document had led, in part, to hyper-inflation in the country during the mid nineteen-twenties.

When the great stock market crash of nineteen twenty-nine occurred it sparked the Great depression which devastated economies throughout the world.

It hit a financially weakened Germany especially hard sending unemployment rates throughout the Reich through the roof.

* * * * *

- Early Financial Support for the Nazis –

Given the deplorable economic circumstances facing Germany in the *'dirty thirties'* it was not surprising that many of the financial and industrial barons of Germany eagerly joined together in support of the rise of the Nazi Party.

What was somewhat surprising however, was the support the Party received from some members of these same groups who resided outside Germany.

For example, it's hard to imagine that Hitler's fledgling Party would have ever received financial and/or industrial support from the United States of America.

But it did.

And that help was to come from major players in their field.

Morgan, Rockefeller, DuPont, General Electric Company, Standard Oil, National City Bank, Chase Bank, Warburg Manhattan Bank, Kuhn, Loeb and Company, General Motors and Ford…to name just a few.

Perhaps this surprising interest in the creation of a Hitler controlled Germany by the Wall Street elite and the resulting influx of support by major U.S. firms, can be explained by the fact that business and financial ventures are often large in scale and include worldwide endeavours, with branch plants in other countries.

And, of course, it must also be remembered that the Germany Hitler was elected to lead was, at the time, a democracy and additionally, that Germany was a world leader in many industrial sectors.

History records that those initial steps toward bringing Hitler to power in Germany, by supporters in the United States, were initiated at the home of banker Baron Kurt von Schroeder on January fourth of nineteen thirty-three.

The Baron was born into an old established banking family in Hamburg in eighteen eighty-nine, attended the University of Bonn and jointed the *'Reichswehr'* during the Great War, where he served as a Captain on the General Staff.

It is of interest to note that an earlier member of his family had changed his name to Schroder and set up a banking firm known as J Henry Schroder of London England and later also that of Henry Schroder Banking Corporation of New York U.S.A..

At the end of the Great War, Baron von Schroder joined a German banking firm and in nineteen twenty-eight became a member of the German People's Party which subsequently morphed into the *'National Socialist German Workers party'* (NAZI).

He joined the *'Freundeskreis der Wirtschaft'* (the Circle of Friends of the Economy) during the same time period. This group provided Hitler and the Party with considerable financial support throughout the horrific world financial struggles of the Great Depression of the early nineteen-thirties.

Von Schroeder resided in Cologne, Germany and was a member of the Nazi Party.

He was the same von Schroeder who hosted the infamous meeting between Franz von Papen and Hitler which directly led to the Fuhrer's assumption of the position of Chancellorship of Germany.

* * * * *

- Hitler the Economist –

In his early political life Adolf Hitler regarded economic issues as relatively unimportant.

In nineteen twenty-two he proclaimed that:

'world history teaches us that no people has become great through its economy but that a people can very well perish thereby' and that *'the economy is of secondary importance'.*

Hitler felt that all economic considerations were of a purely material nature and as an idealist saw no need to give them serious deliberation.

He deplored the financial management of Germany's current and recent leaders, accusing them of having *'subjugated the nation to materialism'* by relying on peaceful economic development rather the historically proven policy of national economic expansion through war.

Under his leadership the Nazi Party took the position that

'human events are historically guided by a small number of exceptional individuals who follow a set of high ideals'.

This approach to economic planning destined that while in power the Nazis would never pursue any specific economic programme.

Hitler considered the Party's lack of a firm economic programme for Germany not as a weakness, but as strength, publicly stating:

'The basic feature of our economic theory is that we have no theory at all.'

Between the year's nineteen thirty-three and nineteen thirty-nine Germany's total revenue was sixty-two billion marks.

Expenditures were one hundred and one billion, leaving a thirty-eight billion mark national debt.

As time went on, Hitler, not atypically, was not easy to nail down when it came to an economic commitment for Germany. He tended to vacillate on economic measures and terms.

He publicly stated:

'We are socialists; we are enemies of today's capitalistic economic system'

'Socialism! That is an unfortunate word altogether. What does socialism really mean? If people have something to eat and their pleasures, then they have their socialism.'

'Socialism has nothing to do with Marxian Socialism. Marxism is anti-property, true Socialism is not.'

'I absolutely insist on protecting private property. We must encourage private initiative.'

'The government should have the power to regulate the use of private property for the good of the nation.'

* * * * *

- Nazi Pre-war Economy –

In nineteen thirty-three Hitler appointed Horace Greeley Hjalmar Schacht to the presidency of the Reichsbank and then as the German Minister of Economics in nineteen thirty-four.

Prior to his birth, both of Schacht's parents had spent a good deal of time in the United States before settling in Germany

Schacht was born in Prussia on January twenty-second, eighteen seventy-seven.

He studied medicine, philology and political science prior to completing a thesis on mercantilism and receiving a doctorate in economics in eighteen ninety-nine.

Schacht joined the Dresdner Bank in nineteen three and in nineteen five, took part of a business trip to the U.S. with board member of his bank and had occasion when there to meet the American banker J.P. Morgan as well a President Theodore Roosevelt.

Schacht joined the freemasons and was made a deputy director of the Bank in nineteen-eight and held that position until nineteen-fifteen when he took up an appointment with the committee of direction of the German National Bank.

In the Great War he was assigned to the staff of General von Lumm, the Banking Commissioner for Occupied Belgium, whose mandate was the organization of financing of Germany's purchases in Belgium.

While in that position it was discovered that Schacht had been channelling the note remittances for nearly five hundred million franks of Belgian national bonds destined to pay for requisitions through his old employer, the Dresdner Bank and was dismissed from his position.

In nineteen-eighteen he co-founded the '*German Democratic Party*'.

Schacht returned to the Dresdner Bank briefly and then moved through positions at various other banks during nineteen twenty-three. He applied for the position as the head of the Reichsbank during that time but his application was rejected.

Disappointed but undaunted, he applied for the position of currency commissioner for the Weimar Republic and was accepted for this lesser post.

During his tenancy in the position he took part in the introduction of the *'Rentenmark'*, a new form of currency whose value was based upon a mortgage held of all the properties in

Germany.

In his new position, he took part in drafting the somewhat successful policies used in the battle to attempt to reduce Germany's hyperinflation and stabilize the German mark with the result that both the President and Chancellor of Germany requested that he accept the Presidency of the Reichsbank.

In nineteen twenty-six Schacht left the small *'German Democratic Party'* and although he did not become a member, began to support the NSDAP (NAZI) Party.

Schacht was becoming disillusioned with the government of the Weimar Republic.

His disillusionment was not a variation in his general economic philosophy but rather, was brought about by his dislike of their new inclusion of socialist party members in the government benches and the costs to the state of the resulting make-work projects.

He saw them as undermining the government's recently initiated anti-inflation efforts.

Fed up, he resigned his position as President of the Reichsbank on March seventh, nineteen-thirty,

In the period from nineteen-thirty to nineteen thirty-two, he continued his political shift to the right and after meeting Hitler began to actively raise funds for the fledgling Nazi party.

Schacht had always been a strong supporter of the idea that Germany should be working hard to retake its place on the international stage and at the time he observed that *'as the powers became more involved in their own economic problems in nineteen thirty-one and two, a strong government, based on a broad national movement, could use the existing conditions to regain Germany's sovereignty and equality as a world power.'*

And it got better.

Schacht had become convinced that if the German Government were to ever have a chance to commence a wholesale re-industrialization and rearmament in spite of the restrictions imposed by The Versailles Treaty, it would have to be accomplished during a historical period lacking clear international consensus among the Great Powers of the world.

Music to Hitler's ears!

The Nazis won more than a third of the seats in the German election of July nineteen, thirty-two and it was then that Schacht, in conjunction with Wilhelm Keppler, organized a petition to circulate among the German leaders of industry requesting that President Hindenburg appoint Hitler as Chancellor of Germany.

Hitler took power in January of nineteen thirty-three and it was no surprise to anyone when he re-appointed his old comrade Schacht to the position of President of the Reichsbank on the seventeenth of March of that same year, nor when he appointed him as his Minister of Economics in thirty-four.

Schacht remained high in Hitler's esteem for some time.

He initiated public works programs and supported the building of the autobahn as measures to deal with the unemployment crisis, something that was, at the time, mimicked by the President of the U.S. with his *'New Deal'* and introduced Germany's *'New Plan'* in an attempt to reach economic *'autarky'* (economic self reliance) to cut imports in September of thirty-four in an attempt to work at reducing Germany's massive foreign currency deficit which the Nazi's had in-herited when they became government.

He successfully negotiated several contracts with Eastern European and South American counties for much needed raw materials with the provision that payment would be made in German Reichsmarks rather than the currency of the county contracted, thereby ensuring the German deficit would not grow any larger than it already had.

Schacht also created an innovative method for dealing with the deficit situation through the use of *'mefo bills'* (promissory notes) which could be used for deferred payment of domestic industrial armament purchases.

Unfortunately for Schacht, he spoke out against what he viewed as *'unlawful activities'* against Germany's minority Jewish population in a speech he made in August of nineteen thirty-five.

Not a particularly sensible thing to do in nineteen thirty-five Germany under the Nazis rule.

It distanced him from previous support provided from those

within Hitler's inner circle and when, during the economic crisis of nineteen thirty-five - thirty-six, Schacht chose to join forces with Price Commissioner, Carl Goerdeler in leading the minority *'free market'* faction in the German Government, which urged Hitler to reduce military spending, repeal protectionist policies and shrink state interference in the economy, he found himself up against a faction lead by *'des Grossdeutschen Reiches* himself', Herman Goering.

Goering had, as had most of his cohorts in Hitler's inner circle, become jealous of the esteem Hitler had for the banker and the Reichsmarschall began an immediate campaign aimed at Schacht's fall from grace.

It was not a fight Schacht was likely to win,

Just months later, Hitler, who had always tended to favour creating an atmosphere of competition and infighting between his immediate underlings, appointed Goering *'Plenipotentiary for the Four Year Plan'* and gave him broad powers that, with full intention, strongly intruded into the area of Schacht's authority.

With a programme of continual backroom backstabbing Goering was successful in forcing Schacht to resign as Minister of Economics by nineteen thirty-seven.

Hitler made Schacht an honorary member in the Nazi Party and awarded him the *'Golden Swastika'* in January of thirty-seven and he retained his position at the Reichsbank for several more years, but his influence with the Nazi leadership was largely over.

In eventually putting his support behind Goering, Hitler had stepped in to remove the in-house government and party arguments around the conflicting recommendations he was receiving from both sides of the discussion on the economy.

He did this decisively in a manner he rarely used. He put it into writing.

Hitler was convinced that the world was headed for an inevitable and earth-shattering struggle between the forces of *'Judeo-Bolshevism'* and *'German National Socialism'*.

The *'Four year Plan Memorandum'* originated from his office and was disseminated to those concerned and whose names appeared above his signature.

Part of this memo read:

'Since the outbreak of the French Revolution, the world has been moving with ever increasing speed toward a new conflict, the most extreme solution of which is called Bolshevism whose essence and aim, however are solely the elimination of those strata of mankind which have hitherto provided the leadership and their replacement by worldwide Jewry. No state will be able to withdraw or even remain at a distance for this historical conflict. It is not the aim of this memorandum to prophesy the time when the untenable situation in Europe will become an open crisis. I would only want, in these lines, to set down my conviction that this crisis cannot and will not fail to arrive and that it is Germany's duty to secure her own existence by every means in face of this catastrophe, and to protect herself against it, and that from this compulsion there arises a series of conclusions relating to the most important tasks that our people have even been set. For a victory of Bolshevism over Germany would not lead to a Versailles treaty, but to the final destruction, indeed the annihilation of the German People...I consider it necessary for the Reichstag to pass the following two laws.: 1) A law providing the death penalty for economic sabotage and 2) A law making the whole of Jewry liable for all damage inflicted by individual specimens of this community of criminals upon the German economy, and thus upon the German people.''

Hitler demanded that Germany develop the world's *'first army'* in terms of fighting ability within the confines of a four year plan, stating that *'the extent of the military development of our resources cannot be too large, nor its pace too swift'* and that the role of the economy was simply to support *'Germany's self-assertion and the extension of her Lebensraum'*.

He addressed his decision to end the infighting that existed within the Party as it related to the economy in the following words:

'...given the magnitude of the coming struggle the concerns expressed by members of the 'free market' faction that the current level of military spending was bankrupting Germany was irrelevant. However well balanced the general pattern of a

nation's life ought to be, there must at particular times be certain disturbances of the balance at the expense of other less vital tasks. If we do not succeed in building the German army as rapidly as possible to the rank of premier army in the world...then Germany will be lost. The nation does not live for the economy, for economic leaders or for economic or financial theories; on the contrary, it is finance and the economy, economic leaders and theories, which all owe unqualified service in this struggle for the self-assertion of our nation!'

Hitler had taken his stand on the future German economy.

After the nineteen-thirty-six crises within the membership of the Reichstag and Hitler's decision to intervene, the German industrialists were increasing left out of economic decision-making as the German state began to dominate in all decisions relating to the economy.

CHAPTER SEVENTEEN

- A New Command –

Enthused by the prospect of returning to U-boats and excited at the potential of taking command of the first commissioned super-sub, Eric had taken an early train for Kiel, leaving at just before six in the morning and reaching the port city shortly after noon.

His first thoughts upon awakening that morning had been taken up with the anticipation of the upcoming trip; however, by the time he'd boarded the train he found himself thinking back to the family dinner of the night before when Gabriella had been pigeonholed and effectively chastised by the others involved, himself included.

His outlook on life was liberal enough in nature to cause him to readily understand and personally lean to at least a partial acceptance of his sister's recent activities, which in many ways mirrored his own preferred social life, but he had no hesitation with regard to the positions he had taken during the discussion around the table.

Despite that fact he considered himself a modern man from the perspective of, to what extent a young adult should be free to practices questionable activities in the personal expression of the enjoyment of their youth and his solid love for his sister, it had not been at all difficult for him to press firmly for a change in her current behaviour. She was a female after all.

In the early stages of the discussion he had been quick to express that he was in favour of the right of personal choice for young German adults.

However he had immediately stated that there could be no doubt that Gabriela had gone over the line of what could be considered as acceptable and was on a destructive course that required correction.

Surprisingly, it had not been a long nor particularly grievous discussion.

Gabriella had been uncharacteristically receptive and Eric had wondered what had been said by his parents behind the scenes that had brought about such contrition in his flamboyant young sister.

He had been prepared for and dreading a real fracas but was pleasantly surprised to find the whole thing over in less than an hour.

Not only had the discussion been of short term but tempers had been controlled and if Gabriella had not definitively agreed to accept the entire package sight unseen, she had expressed, with what had seemed to him at the time a sincere interest in the concept of extending an invitation to Konrad to join the family for dinner three days hence on Saturday evening.

She would make her decision after she had met the man.

It was a reasonable demand and there was an obvious sense of relief all round after that simple commitment had been expressed.

Although Eric was unable to put his finger on exactly why, he found himself leaving the gathering confident that this plan for Gabriella's future stood an excellent chance of success.

He was inordinately pleased by that thought.

He liked Konrad very much and saw him as a good match for his extroverted sister.

As he neared Bahnhof Kiel, Eric's thoughts shifted away from the previous evening and jumped to a string of delightful remembrances covering the experiences of his earlier liaison with the young, wildly delicious, blond twins he'd been forced to leave behind earlier when he'd been transferred to Berlin.

He had every hope of picking up on that blissful association where they had left off now that he would be stationed back in town.

His pulse quickened at the very thought of it.

As he left the train station at Kiel and inhaled his first lungful of crisp air he registered the tangy taste of salt water being carried on the breeze blowing in off the Baltic and his step quickened with anticipation.

The family held a good sized block of shares in Krupp and at Eric's urging his father had arranged to have him met and picked up by the Germaniawerft A.G. dockyard manager and taken directly to the fabricating facility.

His forecasts were great and he couldn't recall a time when he had ever been more pleased at his future prospects.

* * * * *

- Initial Wartime Economy –

Because Germany had been preparing for war for six years, the outbreak of the war had initially required little change in the Nazi's economic policies.

While other governments drawn into the conflagration were forced to increase taxes significantly in order to fund their involvement in the conflict, Germany required no significant changes.

As the war progressed successfully from the German perspective, and new lands were placed under either direct or indirect Nazi control, raw materials and agricultural products needed by Germany were removed from these territories and the payment received for what was then transported to Germany was determined by the Germans not the sellers.

Needless to say, the costs to the Reich were ridiculously low.

A massive quantity of goods flowed into the Fatherland from the lands conquered in the west.

At one point, entirely two-thirds of all French railway rolling stock spent most of its time carrying goods into Germany.

Large amounts of foreign state capital were also removed and shipped to Germany to be used as forced investment into German industry.

The first samplings of the use of forced or slave labour was also explored with what the Nazis felt was admirable success.

* * * * *

Patrick Laughy

- Nazi Plunder –

The Nazi rape of controlled, conquered and occupied territories mirrored most historic endeavours undertaken by Germans in that it was practical, well organized and efficient.

The concept of converting windfall property and valuables of any kind to the benefit of the state began as soon as the Nazi Party came to power.

Initially this was a domestic operation.

In a general sense, both the savings and property of those judged unworthy of German citizenship and who were then placed within the concentration camps, plus that of those Jews who had successfully migrated out of Germany in the early days of the new German Reich, were forfeited to the state.

Once German expansion had begun, organized looting of the European countries overrun by the Nazis was a given.

But this was not to be considered by the Nazis as looting in that their plans were cloaked within the admirable intent of simply making certain that the enemy's art and culture was to be sheltered from the ravishes of war.

It was for this reason that after the declaration of war in nineteen thirty-nine the Nazis revived the Great War concept of *'Kunstschutz'* (Art Protection).

This was the German term used for the worldwide principle of preserving the cultural heritage and artworks of an enemy country during armed conflict.

An example of this type of art preservation was the Goebbels massive inventory of French artworks.

Count Franz Wolff-Metternich headed the *'Kunstschutz'* in France after the occupation of that country.

He immediately began to strip the French museums of their valuable collections.

This was to be the first example of how the Nazis would systematically plunder the valuable cultural property from every territory they overran.

In nineteen-forty the *'Einsatzstab Reichsleiter Rosenberg fur die Besetzten Gebiete'* (The Reichsleiter Rosenberg Institute in the occupied Territories) or ERR was formed.

The first operating unit of this organization, *'Dienststelle Western'*, was the western branch under the control of Kurt von Behr.

It was headquartered in Paris and was mandated to cover the occupied areas of France, Belgium and the Netherlands.

Its original order was to collect Jewish and Freemasonic books and documents, either for destruction or removal to Germany for further study.

In nineteen-forty, *'Reichsmarschall'* Herman Goering, who headed the ERR decreed that the organization change its mandate and ordered that in future it was to seize all *'Jewish'* art collections and valuables.

All such seizures were to be immediately forwarded to the *'Museum Jeu de Paume'* in Paris where they would be examined by art historians, who would see them properly inventoried before onward shipment to Germany.

Goering further ordered that upon reaching Germany, art treasures were to be divided between himself and Hitler.

Patrick Laughy

-Part Two-

CHAPTER EIGHTEEN

- A Time for Diplomacy –

Eric was riding high.

For the duration of his current posting, his father, Count Karl von Stauffer, had arranged to rent a small six bedroom house for Eric in one of Kiel's better areas.

According to his father, the house, one of several owned by the Krupp family, came fully furnished and with a small staff and would certainly be more than sufficient for his needs.

After a quick tour of the *'Germaniawerft A.G.'* factory, where he was pleased to find the second of the super-subs already undergoing construction, three of the twenty sections having already arrived on site, Eric attended an obligatory late lunch hosted by the plant manager.

An increasingly overcast sky had darkened threateningly by the time he could reasonably excuse himself. His assigned driver then drove him the short distance to the dockyard area where he got his first look at his new, yet to be commissioned, U-boat.

It was dark by the time Eric finished a brief, cursory inspection of the massive craft and returned to the waiting car.

His Krupp driver then dropped him off at the rental house where an excited, but by now mentally exhausted, Eric, quickly introduced himself to his staff of two, cook/housekeeper and maid, then unpacked and got himself settled in.

By this point in his day he had been pumped on adrenalin for more hours than he could remember and now that he had seen his new U-boat with his own eyes he had reached the stage where he was able to shift his mind to other thoughts.

After all, a man had his priorities. He had to breath, eat and consider other things.

His new combination housekeeper and cook was obviously disappointed when after a call to the twins he informed her, while taking pains to make the best possible use of his boyish smile, that he would be eating out and would in all probability not be able to make his way home until very late.

* * * * *

- September Twenty-Sixth, Nineteen-Forty –

- Embargo –

On this date the United States of America fulfilled its earlier-expressed intention to impose an embargo on all shipments of scrap iron and steel to Japan.

The consideration of such a move was far from a surprise to the Japanese but the implementation of the embargo may well have been, for them, the straw that broke the camel's back.

* * * * *

- Joachim von Ribbentrop –

Ulrich Friedrich Wilhelm Joachim Ribbentrop was born on April thirtieth, eighteen ninety-three in Wesel, Rhenish Prussia.

His father was a career army officer.

Joachim spent his early formative years gleaning an irregular education at private schools in both Switzerland and Germany.

Between nineteen-four and nineteen-eight he attended school in Metz where he studied French.

He did not do well in school, being described by one of his teachers as *'stupid, full of vanity and very pushy'*.

In nineteen-eight his father was cashiered from the German army after repeatedly making disparaging remarks about the alleged homosexuality of then Kaiser, Wilhelm II.

As a young man Ribbentrop spent periods of time living in London, France and Grenoble.

By nineteen-eight he had formulated a plan for his future. He'd decided to immigrate to Tanganyika, German East Africa, where he intended to seek his fortune as a planter.

He was by this point, fluent in both English and French.

In nineteen-nine, while on holidays in Switzerland he met and fell in love with a wealthy young Canadian socialite, Catherine Bell.

Miss Bell was a member of a Montreal banking family, and Joachim decided to forget his earlier plans for seeking success in Tanganyika as a farmer, in favour of immigrating to Canada and marrying well.

With this in mind, he arrived in Montreal in nineteen-ten.

Upon his arrival he first worked at the Molsons Bank and then for M. P. and J.T. Davis who worked on the Quebec bridge reconstruction.

His next move for employment was to the National Transcontinental Railway which was in the process of constructing a line from Moncton to Winnipeg.

By nineteen-fourteen, Bell had dropped out of the picture and Joachim made the decision to move to the United States, where he worked both in New York and Boston, as a journalist.

He contracted tuberculosis while in the States and returned to Germany long enough to recover before returning to Canada to set up a small wine and champagne import business in Ottawa.

At the outbreak of the Great War, Canada, as part of the British Empire went to war against Germany. Finding himself persona-non-gratis, Ribbentrop headed across the border into the U.S, which was at that time, neutral.

He sailed from New Jersey for Rotterdam on the Holland-American liner *The Potsdam* on August fifteenth, nineteen-fourteen and from there made his way back to Germany, where he promptly enlisted in the 12th Hussar Regiment.

Joachim served on both the Eastern and Western fronts.

He was awarded the Iron Cross and received his commission in nineteen-eighteen after which he was transferred to Istanbul as a staff officer.

It was while he was in Turkey that he met and became friends with Franz von Papen, a German staff officer destined to become a right-wing politician. As luck would have it von Papen was later to serve as Chancellor of Germany in nineteen thirty-two and as Vice Chancellor under Hitler from nineteen thirty-three to thirty-four.

Ribbentrop liked the good life and he had not wavered from his earlier intention of marrying well.

He met the daughter of a well-to-do Wiesbaden champagne producer, in nineteen-eighteen and married her in nineteen-twenty. From that point on he spent his time travelling Europe as a wine salesman.

In nineteen twenty-five, Joachim, always the social climber, managed to convince his aunt, Gertrud von Ribbentrop, to adopt him thereby allowing him to legally add *'von'* to his name.

In nineteen twenty-eight, von Ribbentrop managed to wangle an introduction to Adolf Hitler.

He was introduced by Count Wolf-Heinrich von Helldorf, an old 12th Hussars comrade, as a businessman with foreign connections, who *'gets the same price for German champagne as others get for French champagne'*.

Eyeing his future as always, Joachim and his wife joined the Nazi party on May the first, nineteen, thirty-two and began his political career by way of offering to act as a secret emissary between his old friend and now Chancellor, Franz von Papen and Adolf Hitler.

The offer was not taken up initially but by the time six months had passed in December of thirty-two, von Papen found himself in a tenuous position after being ousted from the office of

Chancellor by General Kurt von Schleicher.

Things had changed.

Political intrigues in Germany had reached a pinnacle by this point in time and von Papen and various friends of President von Hindenburg now found themselves aligned and trying desperately to find ways to negotiate with Hitler with a view to replacing the von Schleicher government.

In his political career, von Papen was running out of options and in desperation he called Ribbentrop to accept Joachim's earlier offer to act as a go-between between himself and Hitler.

Suddenly, an exuberant von Ribbentrop found himself playing in the big leagues.

Pompous and self-centered, Joachim had suddenly been elevated to the political level where he felt he belonged.

Ecstatic with his good fortune, he immediately went to work.

On January twenty-second, nineteen thirty-three, von Ribbentrop hosted a dinner at his posh residence in the exclusive Dahlem district of Berlin.

Those in attendance included State Secretary Meissner, President Hindenburg's son Oskar, Hitler, Goering and Frick.

Taking great care to offer no affront to the political icons seated around his table, von Ribbentrop worked hard at being the perfect host while struggling to keep his mouth shut and maintain a low profile during the discussions.

At the time von Papen was filled with the pressure of a personal vendetta against von Schleicher, who he held singularly responsible for his ouster from the Chancellorship.

He desperately wanted his old job back.

As the meal progressed it became apparent to von Papen that he was not going be successful in accomplishing both the removal of von Schleicher from the post of Chancellor, and his own reinstatement to the position as he had hoped when he had initially sat down at the table.

While Hitler was eager to help him dump von Schleicher, it quickly became obvious to all in attendance that he wanted the Chancellorship for himself.

Hitler was, however, prepared to toss the deposed Chancellor a bone.

Hitler offered von Papen the position of Vice Chancellor on the understanding that von Papen would actively back his own bid for the Chancellorship.

Von Papen's hatred of von Schleicher was so strong that once it had been fortified by the force of Hitler and his entourage's arguments, the man seemed to lose all perspective.

Soundly brow-beaten by Hitler and his supporters, von Papen eventually agreed to abandon his own demand to be returned to the Chancellorship and instead made the decision to accept the Vice Chancellorship under Hitler once the von Schleicher's government had been removed.

In order to accomplish that, he would also agree to throw his support, and the influence he had with President von Hindenburg, behind Hitler's move to take over the job.

The deal was struck.

A jubilant Hitler had gotten everything he had hoped for from von Papen and he moved on to his next challenge.

He and Oskar von Hindenburg retired for a private meeting which lasted for over an hour.

Oskar came out of that one-on-one meeting a changed man, prepared to actively throw his support behind Hitler and determined to convince his father to accept Hitler's move to step into the German Chancellorship. In good part, as a result of the dinner and discussion which had been arranged and hosted by Joachim von Ribbentrop, Adolf Hitler was appointed Chancellor of Germany on January thirtieth, nineteen thirty-three. In that one evening, von Ribbentrop had endeared himself to the Nazi leader and therein earned himself a position within Hitler's inner circle. He had also seen Hitler's forceful personality in action close-up and had instantly become a committed admirer of the strength of the man and his vision for a future Germany.

From that day forward von Ribbentrop became emotionally dependent on Hitler's favour to the extent that thereafter, he would quickly drop into the depths of depression and exhibit signs of psychosomatic illness whenever Hitler expressed even the slightest disappointment with something he had done.

In nineteen thirty-three, at Hitler's order von Ribbentrop was given the honorary rank of *SS-Standartenfuhrer* (Colonel).

Joachim had now been elevated to the exotic heights of membership within the elite inner circle that surrounded and fed off Adolf Hitler.

The infighting and on-going struggles for power and position among the members of that group, which was aided and abetted by a leader who firmly believed that competition among his underlings was a positive force, were legendary.

Although to different degrees, each member of the inner circle was both self-serving and ever-striving to improve his personal lot.

Alliances between members did occasionally form, but only as a net benefit for those involved and normally for only short periods of time.

Each member of the inner circle worked tirelessly to enhance, and jealously protected, his position with Hitler.

While there was a certain degree of respect publically extended to each other among these ambitious men, there was no love lost between those of this group as each individual fought to protect and expand the weight and authority of his own position.

Any long-term member, who for whatever reason suddenly fell out of favour with the Fuhrer, was very quickly ostracized by those still basking in the Hitler's glow.

Any new member was, of necessity, treated with the respect required; however, that respect was most certainly routinely delivered with a jaundiced and assessing eye.

From the first day of his arrival as a member of the top echelon of those who surrounded and directly served Hitler, Joachim von Ribbentrop was, with the exception of The Fuhrer, strongly disliked by the entire assemblage he had joined.

Perhaps Joseph Goebbels best expressed their feelings when he derisively noted in his diary: *'Von Ribbentrop bought his name, he married his money and he swindled his way into office'.*

Of all those who clung to Hitler's coattails, von

Ribbentrop was perhaps the one who most strongly relied on the direct sup-
port offered by the Fuhrer's good favour to maintain his newfound position within the Nazi Reich. He would certainly not find any sincere support among his peers. Joachim recognized this fact and in order to ensure the goodwill of his, to him, God-like leader, he began to accept, adopt and mimic Hitler's every thought and statement as pure gospel.

As a result, the previously apolitical von Ribbentrop, who had eagerly done business financing with Jewish bankers in the past, became an absolute follower and supporter of Hitler.

Seemingly overnight he became a fanatical Nazi and a raucous anti-Semite.

Hitler, when he came to power, did not have much faith in the ability, commitment and enthusiasm of the German Foreign Office he inherited.

He was a new broom and he had little confidence in the abilities of the professional diplomats who were currently under the control of Germany's Foreign Minister, Konstantin von Neurath.

Hitler doubted that they were equipped to properly carry out the policies and aims of the new Nazi government.

It was for this reason that he named Ribbentrop *Special Commissioner for Disarmament* in April of nineteen thirty-four.

This appointment meant that von Ribbentrop and his small staff now had responsibilities that firmly overlapped those of the German Foreign Office.

As was often the case with the dictator, he had created a system wherein two entities under his command would be forced to vie for control.

CHAPTER NINETEEN

- Treading Carefully –

The idea of creating and maintaining a secret organization that, in order to succeed, had to grow to massive proportions while resting painfully close to the paranoid and controlling eye of a Nazi-governed Third Reich, seemed inconceivable.

In order to improve the odds for success for *'Operation Fatherland'*, Count Karl von Stauffer had, in conjunction with his planning team, spent a great deal of time in seeking ways to protect and camouflage every move they made.

From the inception of *'Operation Fatherland'* the Count had accepted and understood that he would, of necessity, find himself having to perform a balancing act, poised on the edge of a razorblade stretched across a precipice, as he repeatedly played off one of these ambitious and dangerous men who made up the new Nazi regime against another.

To begin their planning, the team made a careful study of the personal strengths and weaknesses of all the newly-raised leaders who held positions of power within the *'New German Reich'*.

Hitler and each of the members of his inner circle were placed under a microscope and their personal folders grew very thick before that microscope was removed.

It had been determined that in order for *'Fatherland'* to succeed, parts of its operation could safely withstand direct scrutiny from the government, but the overall set of goals and aims had to remain compartmentalized and conducted in secret.

The long term scale of the operation was huge, many of the various components required to fulfill its needs were, in themselves, massive endeavours.

He and his associates planned and executed each individual step in the ongoing process very carefully, knowing that the risk of challenge was ever apparent and that there was an absolute necessity to use subterfuge to disguise and shelter in depth every new project.

They went to great lengths to make good use of the old adage *'you can't see the forest for the trees'*.

Compartmentalization of each individual project helped to reduce the risk of a security breach.

Under the Count's forceful control this principle grew from that of simple Project-Compartmentalization to one of Compartmentalization of the Compartmentalization itself, individual components being constructed by small groups at diverse locations

Early on in the organization and under his personal guidance, only those with a *'need to know'* in each segment of any given project were apprised of anything more than the job they individually needed to accomplish.

To date, all had gone well but as the Count had anticipated the Super-Sub project was to be the first big test of his ability to make use of his dossiers on the leaders of the Reich in and attempt to create the *'trees'* which would hide the *'forest'*.

With that in mind, his first appointment scheduled in this endeavour was to see the top of the heap.

It was with the Fuhrer, Adolf Hitler, and it was set at eleven in the morning, the Nazi leader's first available opening in his calendar for that business day.

* * * * *

- Martin Bormann –

The son of a postal worker, Martin Bormann was born on the seventeenth of June, nineteen-hundred, at Wegeleben, in the Kingdom of Prussia.

Bormann was a school dropout who spent his early years employed on a farm in Mecklenburg, northern Germany.

He joined the military in the final days of the Great War, assigned to an artillery regiment in the final days of the war and he saw no frontline action.

After the war Bormann returned to Mecklenburg and took up a position as an estate manager.

As chance would have it the estate he'd chosen had a connection to the *'Freikorps'*. He immediately became involved in their activities which consisted mainly of the intimidation of trade union organizers and occasional assassinations.

On March seventeenth, nineteen twenty-four Bormann was sentenced to a year in prison for the part he played in the murder of an informer who had passed on information to the French occupational troops in the Ruhr District regarding *'Freikorps'* sabotage operations which had taken place there.

In nineteen twenty-seven Bormann joined the Nazi Party.

He became a region's press officer and business manager for the Nazis in twenty-eight.

At this time Bormann became engaged to a nineteen year old whose father, Manor Walter Buch, served as chairman of the *'Nazi Party Court'*.

It was as a result of his engagement that Bormann found himself being introduced to the party leader, Adolf Hitler a short time later.

On July first nineteen thirty-three Bormann was appointed to serve as the personal secretary to Rudolf Hess, the Deputy Leader of the Nazi party.

In September, nineteen twenty-nine Bormann married the girl and Hitler, who had been asked to serve as a witness to the ceremony, agreed to participate.

October tenth, nineteen thirty-three marked a turning point in Bormann's career.

On that date he was appointed *'Reichsleiter'* (Reich Leader) of the Nazi Party and a month later he became a member of the *'Reichstag'* (The legislative body of Germany).

The stocky, relatively homely, bureaucrat had now become a ghostly figure, moving unobtrusively around the other Nazi leaders.

While certainly not considered a part of the Fuhrer's inner circle, he floated about on the periphery of the inner circle of those who clung tightly to Hitler's coattails.

Ambitious, but both patient and wily, Martin Bormann was initially satisfied with that amount of success.

He did however plan to take steps to better position himself with The Fuhrer.

He would bide his time.

Bormann commissioned the building of the *'Kehisteinhaus'* (Eagle's Nest), a chalet-style structure to be erected on a sub-peak of one of the mountains above Berchtesgaden, Hitler's home.

The roads, tunnels and elevator shaft needed to complete the project cost a king's ransom and it took thirteen months to build.

It was presented to Hitler as a gift on his fiftieth birthday.

While the building was going on, Bormann managed to convince Hitler to allow him to take charge of his personal finances, offering to relieve the busy Fuhrer of any concerns over his personal wealth.

Hitler accepted the offer and Martin did not fail to please.

Bormann took charge of royalties coming in from the sales of Hitler's book *'Mein Kampf'*, arranged for the German State to obligate itself to pay Hitler royalties for the use of his image on German stamps (all stamps issued by Germany were already mandated to carry Hitler's picture), and set up the *'Adolf-Hitler-Spende der Deutschen Wirtschaft'* (Adolf Hitler Fund of German Trade and Industry), which, under any other circumstances but a dictatorship would have been classed as the bald-faced extortion directed at German industrialists.

* * * * *

- Joachim –

Joachim von Ribbentrop now had Hitler's ear and he wasn't at all hesitant to take advantage of that fact.

He began to use his new position in the power structure to meticulously sink wedges into the muscle, authority and effectiveness of the Foreign Office, actively working to undercut Neurath's official influence and enhance his own foreign-policy profile with The Fuhrer.

His new status provided him with the authority to view all diplomatic correspondence relating to disarmament and by abusing this power, he managed to go through all incoming diplomatic messages, disarmament related or not.

While doing so, he would blatantly cherry-pick, removing whatever communications appealed to him and promptly, and without notice to Neurath, takes these directly to Hitler.

He would then arrange for a written reply under Hitler's signature without Neurath's input, effectively taking the Foreign Minister and his office completely out of the loop on many matters of serious importance to the future of the Reich.

With Hitler's support, he also initiated diplomatic missions on his own and without pre-consultation with the official German Foreign Office.

For example, Hitler wanted to sign a Franco-German non-aggression pact in order to ensure he would have time for full rearmament before having to face France militarily.

The Fuhrer expressed impatience and was openly dissatisfied with the pace of these ongoing negotiations being conducted between the officials of the two countries Foreign Offices.

Von Ribbentrop promptly arrived in France to personally meet with the French Foreign Minister, Louis Barthou and bluntly suggested that Barthou should put a stop to the endless negotiating and instead visit Hitler immediately to sign a non-aggression pact.

In the first instance Neurath found he was unable to seriously consider von Ribbentrop as a significant contender to the official German Foreign Office.

After all, the man's written communications, be they in whatever language: French, English, or even German, were full of grammatical and spelling mistakes, a fact that he did not find at all surprising when authored by one who had no formal training whatsoever in diplomacy.

Privately he viewed this new upstart, unschooled diplomat with decided contempt.

Aware of von Ribbentrop's shortcomings and convinced that the man was his own worst enemy and would soon implode, Neurath arranged that one of Ribbentrop's aides *'make no corrections in any document originating from Ribbentrop'.*

He was sure that this ill-mannered nonentity would shortly become the author his own demise.

These little sojourns of von Ribbentrop into the foreign affairs of Germany continued however, with no seeming ill effect.

As they expanded, the behind the scenes struggle began to heat up between the Foreign Office and von Ribbentrop.

In August of nineteen thirty-four Joachim founded an organization within the Nazi Party first called *'Buro Ribbentrop'* and later adopting the name *'Dienststelle Ribbentrop'*.

In so doing it was his aim to overtly provide increased stature for his own form of diplomacy and openly offer it as an alternative to that of the *'other'* German Foreign Ministry.

Openly flaunting his plan von Ribbentrop, with Hitler's support, opened up an office in Berlin on Wilhelmstrasse, directly across the street from the official offices of the German Foreign Ministry.

His now expanded staff held no trained diplomats. It consisted instead of a group of *'ex-Hitlerjugend'* members, right-leaning businessmen and disgruntled journalists.

These men were all ambitious Nazi Party members in their own right who, under Ribbentrop's lead, endeavoured to conduct a foreign policy which was more often than not contrary to that of that of the official Foreign Ministry.

Keeping in mind that von Ribbentrop had no original ideas, but simply drew his inspiration from his personal conversations with Hitler, it is not surprising that The Fuhrer was pleased with the activities of his new protégé.

An example of how this process worked in reality would be to conduct an overview of how it played out as a result of Hitler's pre-war, strong hope and belief that he would be successful in achieving an alliance with Britain before he had to take on Russia in his move for lebensraum for the future Reich.

Hitler considered this to be a necessity if he was to avoid having to fight a two-front war.

Ribbentrop knew Hitler wanted to form an anti-Soviet alliance with Britain, and that The Fuhrer considered the British to be obvious allies in any future war against bolshevism.

Realistically speaking, this was a very unlikely scenario.

Be that as it may it soon became the overriding policy of the new von Ribbentrop, quasi Foreign Office.

Joachim made numerous trips to Britain, and upon his return from each, he fed Hitler's need to confirm his personal beliefs by informing the Fuhrer that the majority of the British people longed for an alliance with Germany.

An example of one of these trips, conducted in November of nineteen thirty-four wherein von Ribbentrop met with Sir Austen Chamberlain, Lord Cecil, George Bernard Shaw and Lord Lothian saw Joachim, upon his return, present Hitler with a sunny picture indeed.

Based on these meetings with already pro-German Englishmen and relying strongly on the individual positions expressed by Lord Lothian, von Ribbentrop informed Hitler that all elements of British society wished for closer ties with Germany.

Not surprisingly, the report he received form Joachim not only delighted, but was soundly applauded by The Fuhrer.

Contrast this with the intelligence and information on the matter that Hitler was being steadily provided from the German Foreign Office. The latter strongly indicated that an alliance between Germany and England could not likely be achieved in the foreseeable future and it was certainly deemed unachievable at this time.

Hitler's response to the receipt of this diverse information was to comment that Ribbentrop was the only person who told him *the truth about the world abroad*, and Herr von Ribbentrop's influence with Hitler increased after each trip.

The Fuhrer considered Ribbentrop's personality and his open disdain for the diplomatic niceties as a good fit for what he saw as the need for a new German Foreign service that would reflect the necessary, relentless dynamism required to further the beliefs and polices of the New Nazi regime.

Von Ribbentrop's policy of *give the man what he wants* was working beautifully.

And what was Joachim's reward?

Hitler promptly appointed him *'Reich Minister Ambassador-Plenipotentiary at Large'*.

The German Foreign Office was not impressed, but then in a Hitler-controlled Germany, common sense, something diplomats are known for, came to the fore and they bit the bullet publicly and kept their collective mouths clamped resoundingly shut.

Patrick Laughy

CHAPTER TWENTY

- Start at the Top -

When he arrived at the appointed time for his scheduled meeting with The Fuhrer at the new, Albert Speer designed, Reich Chancellery, Count Karl von Stauffer was asked to take a seat in the waiting room attached to Hitler's huge, four hundred square meter, Chancellor's work-study.

Moments later the door to the Fuhrer's personal office opened and Martin Bormann emerged.

Von Stauffer, who had been careful to remain as distant as possible from Hitler's close associates, had met Bormann, who at the time had been part of a much larger group, only once.

The encounter had been brief, little more than an introduction. However at that time, the single passing contact had left him with the impression that there was more to this, seemingly obscure bureaucrat than met the eye.

As was his practice, the Count had, after that initial meeting, opened a file on Bormann and endeavoured to find out as much as possible about the man.

His research had provided him with all the information at hand but surprisingly, it hadn't really provided a great deal of insight into what lay below the surface. The man's behaviour was rather shadow-like and was hard to categorize in any normal sense.

The Count recalled that he had been left somewhat uneasy after carefully reading the completed file. The exercise had been like trying to fit a square peg into one of the expected round holes that had been filled by the other Hitler hangers-on.

He recalled having shut the file and staring at the folder for some time before determining he could not be sure of how the new arrival on the scene, Martin Bormann, fit into the picture in relation to Hitler's day to day activities. He'd decided to keep his eyes and ears open and, should the occasion arise, take care in any required future contact with the man.

As Bormann made his way across the waiting room von Stauffer's attention shifted away from him when a secretary advised that the Fuhrer would see him now.

The Count nodded and got up and began to walk toward the doorway leading to Hitler's study and as he moved he shifted his gaze back to Bormann and found that the other man had briefly stopped moving and turned to study him carefully with piercing eyes,

Von Stauffer thought he caught a momentary flash of hostility in those eyes before they softened.

He gave no outward indication of that recognition; instead he forced himself to smile pleasantly and nod to Bormann before turning his head back toward the now open door and entering The Fuhrer's office.

* * * * *

- Albert Speer -

Berthold Konrad Hermann Albert Speer was born in Mannheim in south-western Germany on March nineteenth, nineteen-five.

In nineteen-eighteen the family took up permanent residence in what had previously been their summer home at Heidelberg.

Albert was a good student and an avid sportsman, involving himself in team sports and enthusiastically participating in outdoor activities, primarily hiking, skiing and mountaineering.

As a youth Speer had decided he wanted to become a mathematician. His father dissuaded him from such a course and instead pressed for his son to follow in the footsteps of himself and Albert's grandfather by taking up a career in architecture.

Albert was living in a time when a German boy was subordinate to and did not question the advice of his father.

He gracefully agreed to take up the path suggested.

In nineteen twenty-two, the tall, lanky, physically-fit Speer fell in love with and began courting his future wife Margarete

Weber, the daughter of a minor but successful businessman.

Albert's extremely social-conscious mother, who felt the girl's family were of inferior stock, disapproved of the relationship and did her best to break it up.

However mothers did not have the range of authority that fathers held over a German boy in those times and perhaps more importantly, a young man in love is not easily swayed from his chosen path.

Albert began his post-secondary studies in nineteen twenty-three at a time when the German economy was suffering from a period of hyperinflation.

As there was not a great deal of unattached money available to the Speer family, he joined the student body of one of the lesser institutions of advanced learning, the University of Karlsruhe.

In nineteen twenty-four when the family's financial situation had improved he left Karlsruhe to continue his architectural studies at the more expensive, acclaimed and reputable, Technical University of Munich.

The family's fortunes continued to improve with the result that Albert was able to change institutions yet again in nineteen twenty-five, this time moving to the Technical University of Berlin and thereby availing him of the opportunity to study under the much admired, Heinrich Tesssenow.

Tessenow was a popular, well known and respected architect during the period of the Weimar Republic as well as a recognized urban planner and University Professor at the Technical University of Berlin.

Albert, enthralled at being mentored by Tessenow, studied hard and when he successfully passed his exams in nineteen twenty-seven, Tessenow took him on as his personal assistant.

For a young architect of such tender years to have accomplished so much by the age of twenty-two was unheard of.

Speer was absolutely thrilled.

He now took over some of the instruction for the architectural courses offered by the university and was able to continue with his post-graduate studies under the tutorship of Tessenow.

Seemingly apolitical during his formative years, Speer, at the urging of some of his students, attended a Berlin Nazi rally in December of nineteen-thirty.

His attendance was to fundamentally change his life.

The party leader spoke and Albert was swept up in both Hitler's performance and his ideas for a New Germany.

He left the rally, by and large, enthralled by the whole presentation and unquestionably in awe of the Nazi leader.

Over the next few months he found himself unable to shake the impression Hitler had made on him and as a result he joined the Nazi party on the first of March, nineteen thirty-one.

The fact that Speer was the only party member living in the Wannsee suburb of Berlin who owned his own car was to be auspicious in that he promptly found himself appointed as the head of the Party's Motorist association for that segment of Berlin.

As such he reported to the Party's leader for the West End, Karl Hanke.

As chance would have it, Hanke had just rented a villa in the area and when he found out that Albert was an architect, he immediately gave him a commission to renovate the villa.

No fee was mentioned by Hanke to be forthcoming with regard to recompense for this newly assigned task but Speer, who was extremely eager to do his part for the Nazi cause, made the decision to consider the commission as part of the cost of his initiation into the exciting Nazi organization.

Hanke was most pleased with the result of Speer's work and began to sing the young architect's praises with party members.

The poor financial situation throughout Germany brought about belt-tightening at the university and in nineteen thirty-one Speer lost his position as Tessenow's assistant.

Albert returned to Mannheim in the hope that he could make use of his father's contacts to pick up some architectural commissions.

The depression had firmly settled in and there was no work to be had. Eventually Speer settled in to labour for his father by managing properties the family owned.

Germany was about to go to the polls in a general election

and in July of nineteen thirty-two, just prior to leaving for a planned holiday, Speer and his wife travelled to Berlin to assist in the pre-election organizing for the Nazi Party.

Goebbels was in the process of overseeing the renovation of the Party's Berlin headquarters at this time, and Hanke, who was still singing Albert's praises over the job he'd done on his villa, suggested to Goebbels that Speer would be a good choice as architect for the project.

Goebbels agreed and Albert was delighted to receive the commission. The planned vacation was dropped and Speer immediately went to work on the project.

Once the job had been completed, the Speer's returned to Mannheim and remained there until Hitler took office in January of nineteen thirty-three.

Shortly after the Nazis came to power, Hanke contacted Speer and ordered him to return to Berlin immediately.

Joseph Goebbels, the newly appointed Minister of Propaganda, who had been pleased with Speer's earlier work on the renovation of the Berlin Party Office, had some work for him.

Albert was absolutely thrilled and upon his arrival in Berlin he was taken directly to Goebbels who promptly commissioned him to renovate his Ministry's building located on Wilhelmplatz.

It was the beginning of Speer's acceptance into the party framework and he went on to design the nineteen thirty-three May Day commemoration ceremony in Berlin.

During this period Speer developed a good working relationship with Hanke who was still functioning in the position of and aide to Goebbels and now held the position as the Propaganda Minister's *State Secretary*.

Albert happened to be in Hanke's office one day and noticed the plans for the upcoming Berlin rally spread out on Hanke's desk.

Unimpressed with what he saw, Speer made a disparaging remark about the designs and Hanke suggested that he attempt to create an improved design.

Albert took up the challenge.

A short while later he produced his vision for the rally which strongly relied on the use of a large number of massive Party flags.

Hanke was impressed with the new rendition provided by Speer and took the designs directly to Goebbels, who was delighted by them and promptly passed them directly on to Hitler.

Hitler, who at the time was unaware of the originator of the plans, was enthusiastic about the visual effect that would be created by using the concepts as detailed.

He congratulated Goebbels and decreed that the design was to be implemented without further changes.

Albert Speer was very excited when Hanke advised him that his design was going to be used for the rally.

Delighted, he took a copy to show his mentor, professor Tessenow, expecting praise but instead received a dismissive response.

After viewing the designs carefully, Tessenow commented: *'Do you think you have created something? It showy, that's all.'*

Speer was temporarily disheartened by the response, but was surrounded by positive support from the party members responsible for the rally; he quickly dismissed Tessenow's negativity as unrealistic.

The rally proved to be a striking success and some of the congratulations for its design trickled down from Goebbels who had taken the credit for it, to Speer, who was more than pleased to settle for the crumbs he received from the Propaganda Minister.

Over time, word of who was really responsible for the planning for the rally, got out to others and as a consequence the planners of the nineteen thirty-three Nuremberg Nazi Party Rally approached Speer and asked him to submit designs for his vision of the upcoming massive party gathering.

Albert did as he was asked and once produced, his plans went successfully up the line of command until they reached the desk of the Deputy Party Leader, Rudolf Hess.

The importance of the success of the first, nationally staged, Nazi Party Rally was lost on no one and neither Hess nor anyone below him was prepared to make the final decision as to its design.

Albert Speer was about to meet Adolf Hitler.

Hess called Speer in and directed him to gather up the plans and take them directly to Hitler's apartment for The Fuhrer's personal approval.

By the time Albert reached the Party Leader's apartment his heart was racing and he was sweating bullets.

Hitler was in the process of cleaning a pistol at his desk when Speer entered.

Without speaking the Fuhrer placed the gun aside and an intimidated Albert, silently laid sheet after sheet of designs out before him on his desk.

Hitler examined each sheet briefly, approving them one after another.

He did so without ever looking up at Speer and then he promptly returned to the cleaning of the pistol as Albert, who understood that he had been dismissed, rapidly gathered up the designs and left.

Shortly thereafter Albert Speer was appointed to the position of *'Nazi Party Commissioner for the Artistic and Technical Presentation of Party Rallies and Demonstrations'*.

Speer was also assigned to act as the Party's liaison, to the Berlin building trades for Paul Troost's renovation to the old Chancellery.

Troost was a successful architect who had come to reject the old standards of the highly ornamental styles of his early years and now projected a lean new approach to architecture; one devoid of ornamentation, a style combining Spartan-traditionalism with elements of modernism.

Hitler considered Troost a mentor and highly respected the aging architect.

Although Troost was not a leader in his field when the Nazis came to power, Hitler had, in the early years, chosen him as his foremost architect and Troost's neo-classical style had then become the basis for the official architecture of the Third Reich.

Therefore Alfred Speer had now moved into what was, career-wise, very good company indeed.

When he came to power Hitler had inherited the Chancellor's apartment that was situated in the old Chancellery and which was now being renovated by Troost.

Hitler took a very personal interest in the work, taking time out of his schedule to routinely visit the scene of the renovations every day.

Upon his arrival at the site he would discuss the progress of the overall renovation with Speer and the building supervisor. Over time a relationship began to build between Hitler and Albert and one day Hitler casually invited Speer to join him for lunch.

Albert, who was still in awe of The Fuhrer, was left almost speechless and couldn't believe his good fortune.

Hitler did not like to eat alone.

He was always joined at his meals by invited members of his inner circle, those who he felt, at any given time, to be deserving of his company.

The majority of those close to Hitler actively vied for these invitations and sought out Hitler's attention when they were in attendance.

The lunch that Speer had been invited too was no exception.

To the consternation of those of the inner circle who had been invited to lunch with The Fuhrer on that particular day, during the meal Hitler demonstrated considerable interest in this young new interloper.

By the time lunch was over it had become obvious to the regulars that their portentous inner circle had just grown to include Albert Speer.

For some time Hitler had been searching for a young architect he felt would be capable of carrying out his architectural dreams for the 'New Germany'.

He had recently come to the conclusion that Albert Speer might be the man for that job.

From that time on Speer was expected to visit Hitler each morning for a walk or a chat during which he was to provide consultation on architectural matters, act as a sounding board and to share in and discuss Hitler's on-going ideas for projects within the Nazi Reich.

The strength of the relationship grew and Albert now joined, on a daily basis, those of the inner circle who were privileged to be invited to join The Fuhrer for his late dinners.

These meals regularly led to subsequent entertainment and conversation shared with Hitler, a prize which the hangers-on rated as well above that of a luncheon invitation.

It seemed to Speer that he had overnight morphed from an unknown to a star.

When Troost died on January the twenty-first, nineteen thirty-four Hitler appointed Albert to head of the *'Chief Office of Construction'*.

His first commission was the massive *'Zeppelinfeld'* stadium (Nuremberg Parade Grounds).

This huge project was to be designed to hold three hundred and forty thousand people.

Speer decided to surround the construction with one hundred and thirty anti-aircraft searchlights. These, when turned on at night, when most of the ceremonies were scheduled to be held, would create the prospect of a *'cathedral of light'* surrounding the entire installation.

Hitler was very pleased with the design and quickly set Speer to work designing many more official Nazi buildings.

Speer was in seventh heaven.

In his early designs he determined that Hitler's vision of a Nazi Third Reich that *'would last for one thousand years'* meant that all of these major building should be constructed in such a way that they would, even after suffering through the ravages of time, leave an aesthetically pleasing set of ruins.

These ruins would then endure for thousands of years into the future as a testament to the greatness of the Third Reich as had the ruins of the ancient Romans and Greeks.

Hitler adopted this concept without question and ordered that all the major buildings constructed in the future were to be built in strict accord with that aim.

When the initial designs for the Berlin Olympic Stadium for the nineteen thirty-six Summer Olympics were presented to Hitler by another architect, Hitler immediately rejected them as too modern and promptly turned the further development of the project over to Albert.

Speer went to work and modified the designs by adding a

stone exterior.

Speer was also commissioned to design the German Pavilion for the nineteen thirty-seven International Exposition in Paris and in that year Hitler appointed him to the position of *'General Building Inspector for the Reich Capital'* with the rank of undersecretary of state in the Reich government.

This made Albert a member of the Reichstag and therein answerable only to Hitler.

He ordered Speer to immediately begin the designs for the rebuilding of Berlin which, as the capital of a newly-expanded German Reich, was to become a world-renowned centerpiece constructed on a scale to reflect the supremacy and wonder the Nazi Party.

This newly envisioned and renovated city was then to be renamed *'Germania'*.

The plans for this new city, created by Speer with Hitler's direction and input, were massive in scale.

When Speer's father was given the opportunity to view the model of what was planned for the core of the perceived future German capital city of *'Germania'* he said to his son: *'You've all gone completely insane'*.

In January of thirty-eight Hitler instructed Speer to build a new Reich Chancellery as the current building did not properly reflect the importance of the *'New Germany'*.

The Fuhrer wished to have this massive structure completed in time for his next New Year's reception for diplomats which was to be held on January tenth of nineteen thirty-nine.

He wanted something that would show the representatives sent to Germany from the rest of the world exactly how rich, prosperous and strong, the *'New Germany'* under the Nazis had become.

Despite the massive size of the undertaking and the short time frame given for completion, Speer eagerly agreed to take on the project.

Given a blank cheque by Hitler, Albert managed to pull it off, employing thousands of workers around the clock for nine months, once the humongous construction site had been cleared of existing buildings.

The amazing structure included a *'Marble Gallery'* that stretched for one hundred and forty-six meters in length, almost twice as long as the *'Hall of Mirrors'* in the Palace of Versailles.

The edifice was built with the intent that any ambassador or VIP who wished to visit the Fuhrer would have no option but to walk the full length of the Marble-faced hall to reach his office.

Hitler was busy with other things and he removed himself from the project once he'd assigned it to Speer and when Alfred turned it over to his Fuhrer two days ahead of schedule, Hitler was so impressed with it that he awarded Speer the Nazi prized *'Golden Party Badge'*.

When viewing the structure at Speer's invitation on a later occasion, his old mentor, Tessenow, was less impressed.

He suggested to Speer that he should have perhaps taken nine years to complete the construction, rather than nine months.

This was the second time he'd failed to please his old master, but by this point in time Alfred wasn't particularly concerned about criticism from that source, after all not many people had been given the privilege of having the *'Golden Party Badge'* personally awarded to them by Adolf Hitler.

Albert Speer was riding on a cloud.

He was to state later to his biographer-to-be, Gitta Seremy, how he felt when Hitler shifted his attention away from peace toward war, something that would naturally bring about an interruption in the building plans for the new 'Germania', but which he nevertheless strongly supported:

'Of course I was perfectly aware that (Hitler) sought world domination. (At the time) I asked for nothing better. That was the whole point of my buildings. They would have looked grotesque if Hitler had sat still in Germany. All I wanted was for this great man to dominate the globe.'

At the commencement of war Speer placed his department at the dispose of the Wehrmacht.

When Hitler heard of this reaction, he promptly advised Speer that it was not for him to decide how his workers should be used, but Speer chose to ignore him.

Albert Speer was living a dream.

Hitler was delighted with the young architect, referring to him as a *'kindred spirit'*, for whom he maintained *'the warmest human feelings'*.

Albert had reached the top overnight, his rapid rise within the Nazi party and his close proximity to Hitler determined that he received a virtual torrent of commissions from both the Nazi government and the top ranking party members.

Albert continued along with the planning and designing of new structures intended for both Berlin and Nuremberg and he oversaw construction of buildings for the military, but he could not be convinced to retract his imposed restriction on peacetime construction projects while Germany was at war.

CHAPTER TWENTY-ONE

- An Ounce of Prevention –

As had been requested by The Fuhrer at their first meeting, Hitler's office received regular reports from the Count on the progress of the most important scientific breakthroughs and the development of any outstanding new weapons.

These reports, which Hitler had ordered sent addressed personally to him and marked *'Personal and confidential'*, normally comprised numerous pages.

Any individual discovery of sufficient merit listed therein would be supplemented by an enclosed package which contained additional information on the topic.

In the first instance Count von Stauffer had no idea how much of the information he regularly forwarded to the Fuhrer had been personally studied by the man.

Initially he'd suspected that someone on Hitler's staff would likely vet the material once it was received and then provide The Fuhrer with whatever material they felt would interest him.

Over time Karl had come to realize that his original take on how Hitler would have the material vetted before he saw it had been flawed.

He'd come to this conclusion after receiving literally hundreds of short, succinct and well-structured queries from Hitler's office with regard to many of the on-going projects overseen by the Count.

These questions always arrived in Hitler's own handwriting on his personal note paper and above the Fuhrer's signature. Responses to each enquiry were sent in envelopes contained within the regular reports forwarded to Hitler's office.

Clearly the man was reading and giving consideration to most, if not all the material the Count forwarded to him.

The two men had thereby regularly communicated with each

other since that meeting, but they had not spoken since by phone, nor had they met face to face.

Hitler had made it clear that he wanted their relationship to be one of arms-length and that he had neither the time nor inclination to immerse himself in the day-to-day administration of the many projects.

All he wanted was an overview of what new discoveries were being made, and as exhibited by one of his personal notes, *'Interesting - if this new explosive could be produced in sufficient quantities, it would have many practical applications - keep me informed'.*

On this occasion when the Count entered his office, Hitler was seated at his massive desk with his head bent down. He appeared to be reading some documents resting in front of him as von Stauffer approached the massive desk.

Karl snapped his heels together and saluted and Hitler looked up at him and impatiently waved his hand in the general direction of one the two richly upholstered armchairs that bracketed each end his desk.

He waited for Karl to sit and then he swivelled slightly in order to directly face the Count and raised his right hand to sweep back some stray strands of hair, which had draped over his right eye, before he bobbed his head slightly.

"Herr General, you wished to speak with me."

Karl nodded and chose his words carefully.

"When you asked me to take up my position, you instructed that I was to come to you if, while I was fulfilling my duty to carry out your instructions, I was in any way obstructed by someone in authority."

Hitler leaned back in his chair slightly, his piercing eyes probing. He seemed to consider the words for a few seconds and then nodded curtly.

"And now there has been such an occurrence?"

Karl shook his head.

"No, Mein Fuhrer, but I am anticipating one and I'm hoping that you will nip it in the bud before certain people have time to take a stand that will later require them to further obstruct me in order to save face."

Hitler didn't react immediately but after a few moments his features softened slightly. Eyes suddenly sparkling, he nodded his understanding.

"I see. You do good work Herr General. I find that I am required to spend little of my time interacting with you in order to get excellent results."

He raised his hands from the surface of the desk and rubbed them slowly together then continued.

"Those were words of praise my good Count. I can not say the same for many of those who surround me; they are for the most part prima donnas you see…"

Von Stauffer made no comment and Hitler's features grew more serious.

"Well you have enough on your plate; you do not need any undue interference. Perhaps you could explain what it is you wish me to do.

Karl sucked in a deep breath and delivered his carefully rehearsed speech.

"It is the Super-U-boat development programme. You will recall that these new craft have been designed for several varied applications, all of which are highly classified."

The Count paused, watching for a positive reaction, which was immediately forthcoming.

"Yes…massive U-boats, which I will use for mine laying and the transportation of large numbers of men and equipment to foreign shores among other things. "

Von Stauffer nodded.

"The first of the crafts is about to begin its sea trials and naturally this means a compliment of U-boat personal was needed. I have been able to keep the programme secret up to this point but with the assignment of the crew, the existence of something out of the ordinary being constructed has come to the attention of the Kriegsmarine.

This is a new and experimental design. It has not reached the stage where is can reasonably become part of a combat mission of any kind. It is my desire to keep the programme secret and under my personal control until such time as you see fit to make use of it.

I do not want this highly advanced and very specialized unit to become common knowledge at this time, and have therefore, under your personal authority, ordered the crew compliment seconded to my project without supplying any further specific information to the Kriegsmarine.

I have received the crew from the navy but there is now an indication of building pressure from the Kriegsmarine for more information as to why this large crew had to be seconded and exactly what it will be sailing.

I would appreciate it if you could see your way clear to speak to the Admiral and order him to put a stop to any further inquiries into the issue of the seconded seamen. I would then ask you to speak to Herr Himmler and advise him that he should expect from me, and honour a request for a compliment of SS to act under my orders. I would then use these men to take up the responsibility for the physical security for the programme now that the first U-boat of this class is in the water. They would continue to fulfil that need until such time as you wish to make operational use of it and the additional craft the programme is scheduled to produce.

The SS belong to you personally mien Fuhrer, and with them in the picture the Kriegsmarine will have no option but to cap any further interest in this programme until you see fit to bring them on board."

* * * * *

Count Karl von Stauffer's next scheduled appointment was with Heinrich Himmler.

Hitler had placed two calls while Karl was still in his office.

The first was to the Admiral. His instructions were short. Any request received by the Kriegsmarine from the offices of Count von Stauffer was in future to be considered as coming directly from the Fuhrer himself and was to be immediately facilitated without question or explanation.

The second call had been to the Reichsfuhrer.

Karl thanked the Fuhrer and returned to his waiting car. He

instructed his driver to take him directly to the office of the Reichsfuhrer.

Upon his arrival Himmler welcomed Karl von Stauffer warmly and the Count had no difficulty in achieving a secondment of SS personnel for the purpose of providing security for the new and secret Super-U-Boat programme.

Himmler, always eager to expand his empire, had expressed delight in being able to facilitate any request which would place him, with Hitler's support, into the position of extending his authority over another arm of the German military.

* * * * *

- Ambassador - Plenipotentiary –

In his new capacity and at a time when the British strongly favoured appeasement when it came to any dealings with Germany, Joachim von Ribbentrop managed to successfully bumble his way through the negotiations needed for the Anglo-American Naval Agreement in nineteen thirty-five, achieving the result that Hitler had been hoping for.

Hitler was extremely pleased with Ribbentrop for bringing the agreement off.

The Fuhrer saw this agreement as the first step in drawing the British into a full alliance with Germany.

Still working toward this desired alliance, he instructed von Ribbentrop to turn his attention to seeking the return of Germany's former African colonies which had been lost as part of the Treaty of Versailles.

In fact, Hitler did not particularly want the colonies back but he felt that the demand for such a return could be used as a negotiating ploy wherein Germany would later agree to formally renounce such claim in exchange for the sought after alliance with the British.

With this in mind Hitler appointed Joachim to the position of Ambassador to the United Kingdom in August of nineteen thirty-six.

The 4th Reich

Von Ribbentrop took up his post in October of that year.

The German Foreign office was appalled at the appointment.

In that same year Joachim was able to complete ongoing negotiations with the Japanese to bring about the signing of the Anti-Comintern Pact (anti-communist pact) with Japan.

Von Ribbentrop was anything but a diplomat.

His term as Ambassador to the United Kingdom was fraught with diplomatic gaffs which only served to reinforce the contempt in which the British Foreign office already held him.

Von Ribbentrop was never happy to be too far from Hitler. He knew he had little support from those that made up The Fuhrer's inner circle and as a result the new ambassador spent far more of his time in Germany than he did in England.

Because Joachim was rarely in London, the British Foreign Office found it difficult to accomplish any serious negotiations with him and often gave up any attempt to conduct policy with Germany as a result of von Ribbentrop's rare availability.

On one occasion when meeting the king, von Ribbentrop actually gave the Nazi extended stiff-armed salute and almost struck the monarch who was, at the time, in the process of extending his arm in offer of an expected handshake.

Ribbentrop had no basic understanding of the limited role the monarch played in governmental affairs of Great Britain. He actually believed that the new King, Edward VIII, could dictate British foreign policy.

Ribbentrop had spent a good deal of time cultivating Edward prior to his ascendancy to the throne and was convinced that the new English King was a friend who was strongly pro-German and unquestionably supportive of the aims and policies of Hitler and the Nazi Party.

As an example of how ill-informed Ribbentrop was in relation to the realities of British life, during the Edward VIII abdication crisis of December nineteen thirty-six, Joachim informed Hitler that the crisis had resulted from a conspiracy to depose Edward which had been initiated by anti-German, Jewish-Masonic reactionaries and that civil war would soon break out between the King's supporters and those of the British Prime

Minister, Stanley Baldwin.

The fact that von Ribbentrop was ill-chosen for his positron as ambassador was not lost on the other members of Hitler's inner circle.

As Joachim alienated more and more segments of British society it was finally Goering, who had the courage to speak up to Hitler about it, bluntly calling von Ribbentrop a *'stupid ass'*.

Hitler dismissed the comment, with the response that *'after all, he knows quite a lot of important people in England'*, to which Goering replied *'Mein Fuhrer, that may be right, but the bad thing is, they know him'*.

As time went on, von Ribbentrop, who was never able to grasp the fact that the British had no intention of forming an alliance with Germany but were instead determined to maintain a policy of appeasement, became exasperated with his unsuccessful struggle to achieve the alliance.

He began to fear that his failure to bring it about was going to cost him Hitler's favour and from that point on he blamed England for destroying his bond with The Fuhrer.

By nineteen thirty-seven Joachim had convinced himself that the British government was conspiring to destroy his influence with Hitler and he had become a bitter Anglophobe.

He shifted his diplomatic thrust away from achieving an alliance with the British and turned instead to trying to save face with Hitler by forcing the British diplomats to push on Germany's behalf for a return of the German colonies.

He seemed to be spinning his wheels and became seriously depressed during this period and at the time authored two very anti-British reports to Hitler.

The first of these was presented to The Fuhrer on January second, nineteen thirty-eight. In it Ribbentrop stated that *'England is our most dangerous enemy'*, and counselled Hitler to scuttle the idea of securing a British alliance and instead advised him to seek an alliance between Germany, Italy and Japan with the eventual aim of securing the destruction of the British Empire.

In nineteen thirty-eight Hitler stepped into the ongoing battle that was now openly raging between the German Foreign Office and von Ribbentrop's separate show.

He dumped Neurath and on February fourth replaced him by Ribbentrop, appointing Joachim as the new German Foreign Minister.

In his new position Ribbentrop's sole concern revolved around attempts to convince other states to either take up positions of military alliance with Germany at best, or to provide stated positions of neutrality at worst; this in preparation for the upcoming world war which he saw as both necessary and inevitable if Germany was going to reach its proper potential on the world stage.

As a part of this new and now official Foreign Office policy, von Ribbentrop took aim at setting up a realignment of Germany's policy with regard to the Far East.

He saw Japan as a possible future ally for Germany and immediately moved to reverse the previous Foreign Office policy of favouring China in the region to one of throwing Germany's full support behind the Japanese expansionist plans for the area.

His first step was to convince Hitler to recognize the puppet state of Manchuria which the Japanese had overrun and to publicly renounce all German claims regarding her former colonies in the Pacific, all of which were currently held by Japan.

Within sixty days of taking up his new position von Ribbentrop had cut off all German arms shipments to China and recalled the many Germany military advisors from that country.

When it looked as though some of the officers imbedded with the Chinese army might rebel and choose to ignore Ribbentrop by remaining with the Chinese, the new Foreign Minister, furious at such an affront, announced that the families of those currently posted to China who did not immediately return home would be sent to concentration camps.

The Military personal came home.

Hitler was less concerned about the Asian situation than he was about the home front.

His attention was centered on the orderly advancement of his own plans for expansion of German territory within Europe and he left it to von Ribbentrop to negotiate with Japan while he turned his personal attention to take advantage of the British policy of appeasement by concentrating his diplomatic efforts on a push for his plan to amass additional *'lebensraum'* for the *'New German Reich'*.

Von Ribbentrop's assessment of the world situation with respect to the balance of overall military power was overshadowed by his eschewed sense of a natural German superiority and his view of Hitler and the Nazi party as the embodiment of a new world messiah. He had the finesse of a street brawler and would have eagerly pushed an, as yet decidedly unready, German military into a world war without a second thought.

While Hitler liked Joachim's assertive, autocratic approach to negotiations he had to take notice of the fact that his military advisors strongly held the belief that it would take several years to create a force of arms that would allow for a superiority of German armaments and manpower that would dictate a readiness for war.

They had made it abundantly clear to their new leader that Germany was not yet ready for the war that Hitler considered inevitable.

While he was of the opinion that his advisors were far too conservative, he accepted the proposition that they did need some time to build up the pitiful German military machine.

Hitler knew the British and French did not want war and would avoid it at any cost. It was his intention to use that knowledge to his advantage. He had nothing to lose and was prepared to sabre-rattle for all it was worth while he impatiently awaited the build-up of his fighting capability.

With that in mind his immediate sights and his propaganda machine shifted toward the destruction of Czechoslovakia.

He instructed his State Secretary, Baron Ernst Weizsacker, to begin negotiations with the British with that aim in mind.

Von Weizsacker, who was not impressed with von Ribbentrop's approach to the Czechoslovakian problem, which was that of a military invasion he believed would lead to a world war spoke against any such approach.

Instead he pushed for a diplomatic solution to the problem and it was an approach that Hitler reluctantly warmed to.

If he could gain territory for Germany without having to resort to a contest of arms, as von Weizsacker believed was probable, then it would be foolish not to take that step.

While von Weizsacker wasn't any more prepared than the rest of his peers in the Foreign Office to openly challenge his new boss von Ribbentrop, he was able to bring Hitler onside with his own plan for a non-antagonistic diplomatic solution to the quandary rather than risk the chance of the creation of a need for a potentially dangerous military engagement.

Hitler promptly sidelined Joachim in the negotiations and left it to von Weizsacker to work out the details which led to a private arrangement prior to the September fifteenth nineteen thirty-eight Anglo/German summit held at Hitler's home in Berchtesgaden.

Joachim privately hoped that the summit would bring about a war by October first of nineteen thirty-eight.

The joint agreement set up with the British by Baron Ernst Weizsacker allowed for a separate, private meeting to be held at the summit. This special meeting would include only Hitler, British Prime Minister Chamberlain and the translator.

This one-on-one meeting was designed to specifically exclude the hawkish von Ribbentrop from the discussions.

An openly brooding Joachim, who had personally considered the so called German/Czechoslovakia Sudetenland dispute as a simple excuse for the intended German military intervention leading to the destruction of Czechoslovakian, roved unhappily around the fringes of the conference.

The resulting *'Munich Agreement'* reached between the two leaders was viewed by von Ribbentrop as a disaster.

At the time he expressed his feelings to the head of Hitler's Press Office: *'first-class stupidity...all it means is that we have to fight the English in a year, when they will be better armed...It would have been much better if war had come now.'*

* * * * *

- Munich Agreement –

The '*Munich Agreement*' resulted from the appointment of the British as mediators in the dispute and on-going clash between Germany and Czechoslovakia over the so-called suppression of the German-speaking minority on the Czech side of the border.

The British reviewed the matter and came up with what they determined a fair and unbiased solution.

In reality it was anything but.

The agreement was signed on September thirtieth, nineteen thirty-eight by Adolf Hitler for Germany, Neville Chamberlain for the United Kingdom, Benito Mussolini for Italy and Edouard Daladier for France.

It authorized the annexation by Germany of the disputed area, now to be renamed the '*Sudetenland*'.

This agreement had been reached among the major powers of Europe, those of Germany, France, the United Kingdom and Italy, without the presence or inclusion of any member of the Czechoslovakian government.

The area annexed to Germany included the majority of Czechoslovakia's border defences which had been built against a possible German invasion, many of its banks and a good deal of its heavy industry.

The loss of this territory was of enormous strategic importance to Czechoslovakia.

CHAPTER TWENTY-TWO

- A South American Investment –

Count Karl von Stauffer's next appointment for the day was with his lawyer.

He had lunch at home with Erika before being driven to that meeting.

The prestigious Berlin legal firm of *'Von Hauptmann and Sons'* had been responsible for representing the legal maters of the von Stauffer family for over two hundred years.

Karl's appointment was with the current senior partner, Hans von Hauptmann who received him cordially at the door leading to his private office and offered him a drink form the sideboard and a good cigar before they settled into one of the four antique overstuffed-armchairs that nestled in a corner of the large room.

The chairs bracketed a highly polished mahogany table that fronted the cheerily burning logs nestled inside the deep marble-faced fireplace.

Old friends, the two men talked in a leisurely manner about family and generalities until they had finished their first drink and a good portion of their cigars before Karl brought up the purpose of his visit.

"Hans, I'd like you act for me in a land purchase I wish to make in Brazil. It is with regard to the corporation you formed for my associates and me earlier, an add-on to the mining operation we are setting up. Would it be possible for you to co-ordinate the purchase though a Brazilian legal firm located in Porto Alegre?"

He proffered a card which von Hauptmann accepted and studied briefly.

The Lawyer exhaled a cloud of smoke as he replied.

"Yes I'm sure we could manage that. As it happens we've done several acquisitions in Brazil through this particular firm and have a good relationship with them. You have some ties with them?"

Karl smiled and nodded. Yes, their senior council is an in-law of a distant branch of the family, actually. They will act as my representatives there until such time as I can make other arrangements."

The lawyer smiled.

"And this would be in addition to the land the corporation is expecting then, a von Stauffer trust family purchase?"

Karl nodded.

"That's correct. As you are aware, the immediate family will hold a large block of the stock in the new corporation and I expect it will be a very successful operation over the long term.

It seemed to me prudent that the family have a physical presence there and it is my intention to set up an estate nearby for that purpose.

I have distant family in the area of *'Rio Grande do Sul'* who will assist the Brazilian lawyers in the selection of a suitable property near the proposed mine site and through them I have made some initial inquiries and found that there are large areas available for purchase in the valleys adjacent to the coastal property the mining corporation is in the process of obtaining.

I thought it would be a good idea to buy up an adjoining good-sized parcel before development starts as a mine this large will no doubt send surrounding land prices soaring as a community springs up around it to house and support the local workers needed."

Hans smiled.

"Seems like a good idea. I'll get on to the Brazilian firm straight away and ask them to stay in contact with your family there. I assume time is of the essence?"

Karl nodded.

"Brazil is a backward country compared to Germany. In consideration of that fact and the degree of secrecy with which our current negotiations with the government have been experiencing, I would say that we have a few months yet before the plan for the mining operation will become common knowledge in the country let alone in the area in question, which is quite remote.

If we could make our purchase say, within the next forty-five days or so, we should be in a position to get in on the ground floor. Once that has been accomplished I would further request that you have the Brazilian firm in coordination with my relatives to act on your behalf to arrange for the onsite construction of a suitable domicile, plans for which are already being worked on and are to be forwarded for my consideration within the next sixty days."

* * * * *

- After Munich –

Despite the fact that Hitler had been strongly advised that Germany was not ready for war and the ability of Germany to achieve a diplomatic success with the signing of the Munich agreement, The Fuhrer was frustrated with the situation.

Hitler was not comfortable with diplomatic negotiation. He was, by this point in time, teetering on the edge of megalomania and it was difficult for him to stand by while his explicit wishes were negotiated and bargained with others.

Having to go seeking for agreement amongst those of less knowledge and foresight than himself was degrading and humbling in the extreme.

The very audacity of having to justify his determinations to anyone else often left him enraged.

It was something that he no longer had to tolerate within the expanded German Reich and he found it both wearisome and exasperating that he should have to accept such foolishness when dealing with entities outside Germany.

Despite the rational reasons for his not being able to go to war to destroy Czechoslovakia, before and during the summit, Hitler had been torn inwardly between his strong desire to lash out to enforce his will by taking military action and the necessity of letting the diplomats negotiate a solution to the dispute.

The truth be known, The Fuhrer's wishes for the outcome of the Munich Agreement were not that different than von Ribbentrop's.

After the signing of the agreement, Hitler's disappointment in the outcome festered rapidly and he soon became extremely anti-British, claiming that Chamberlain had *'cheated'* him out of his desired war to *'annihilate'* Czechoslovakia.

Hitler was beginning to realize that despite his earlier belief that the United Kingdom was a natural partner for Germany in a path to share world domination, the foolish British had no intention of allying themselves with Germany, nor, under the current circumstances would they be prepared to remain neutral in the case of war.

For the first time he also began to question the British determination for appeasement at any cost.

It now appeared to him however, that it was obvious that the weak leadership of that country could still be mined with a view to further appeasement although there might well be a limit to how far they could be pushed.

That being the case he would forget achieving an agreement with them and instead test the current British commitment to appeasement for all it was worth.

This new philosophy on the part of Hitler was enough to draw von Ribbentrop, who shared Hitler's beliefs, back into the Fuhrer's good graces.

Britain suddenly became Germany's greatest enemy.

Early nineteen thirty-nine Hitler took his first step in pushing the boundaries of British appeasement.

He assigned von Ribbentrop the task of destroying the rump-state of Czecho-Slovakia (Czechoslovakia having been renamed in October of nineteen thirty-eight after the annexation to Germany of the Sudetenland).

Once again basking in Hitler's favour Joachim gleefully entered into the breech with his typical bullying tactics.

He ordered the German diplomats in Bratislava to make contact with Father Jozef Tiso, Premier of the Slovak regional government, with instructions to force him into declaring independence from Prague.

Tiso balked at the suggestion as such an act would jeopardize the autonomy he'd gained since October of thirty-eight and leave a militarily-inferior, independent Slovakia, open to annexation by Hungary.

Ribbentrop promptly make contact with the German Embassy in Budapest with instructions that they contact the Regent, Admiral Miklos Horthy, of Hungary with the suggestion that the Germans would be open to having more of Hungary restored to former borders (infringing on Slovakian territory as drawn after the Great War), and with that in mind the Hungarians should immediately begin concentrating their troops on their new northern border if they wished to achieve their demands for a return of the lost territory.

The pleasantly surprised Hungarians eagerly agreed and the build-up of troops began at once.

Ribbentrop then presented Tiso with the choice of either declaring the independence the German's had earlier demanded, with the further understanding that the newly formed state of Slovakia would then move into the German sphere of influence or having Hungary overrun and absorb all of Slovakia with German approval.

Tiso found himself between a rock and a hard place.

With little option if he wanted to save Slovakia from instant oblivion, he ordered the Slovak regional government to declare independence on March fourteenth, nineteen thirty-nine.

There was of course an immediate crisis in the Czecho-Slovak relations. This crisis was then used by Ribbentrop as a reason to step into the dispute with the declared intention of having Germany immediately mediate the crisis.

Talk about inviting the fox into the henhouse!

Ribbentrop promptly ordered Czecho-Slovak President, Emil Hacha, to Berlin to discuss his *'failure to keep order in his country'*.

Hacha was not in a position where he could safely afford to ignore the German command performance.

He headed for Berlin.

On March fourteenth and fifteenth nineteen thirty-nine Hacha, all but held hostage in the Nazi Reich Chancellery, was bullied by the Germans led by von Ribbentrop, into agreeing to have his country become a German Protectorate.

On March fifteenth nineteen thirty-nine German troops occupied the Czech area of Czecho-Slovakia, absorbing it into the *'Reich Protectorate of Bohemia and Moravia'*.

Elated, Ribbentrop instantly launched his next move.

He summoned the Lithuanian Foreign Minister; Juozas Utrbsys, to Berlin on March twentieth, nineteen thirty-nine and upon his arrival brazenly informed him by way of an ultimatum: *'If Lithuania did not immediately return Memelland to Germany'* (It had been lost to Germany by way of the Treaty of Versailles after the Great War*), 'the Luftwaffe would raze the large Lithuanian city of Kaunas to the ground'*.

On the twenty-third of March, Lithuania unsurprisingly reached the decision to return Memelland to Germany.

So far things were going very well for Joachim.

With Hitler's encouragement, von Ribbentrop was batting a thousand.

Without the loss of a single drop of German blood, The Fuhrer's plans for achieving lebensraum in the east were dropping into place like falling dominos.

Poland was next on Hitler's wish list.

He decided it should become yet another German protectorate.

Joachim began a series of negotiations with Polish diplomats, using the same bullying tactics that had, so far, served him well.

By March of nineteen thirty-nine the Poles, having watched the other victims submit to German demands, but made of sterner stuff, had determinedly rebuffed the German efforts on three separate occasions.

A disappointed and frustrated Hitler, urged on by von Ribbentrop, made the decision to place the destruction of Poland as the number one German Foreign Policy aim for thirty-nine.

Hitler decided to approach his goal piecemeal, still relying on the arguments of unfairness under the treaty of Versailles as an excuse for his territorial claims.

On March twenty-first he announced a demand for the *'Free*

City' of Danzig to be returned to the Reich and demanded that Germany be given free access to *'extra territorial'* roads across the Polish Corridor.

On the same day von Ribbentrop called in the Polish Ambassador, Jozef Lipski, and delivered a set of demands requiring the immediate release of Danzig to Germany. He did so in no uncertain terms, leaving the Ambassador with the clear impression that if this demand was not met, Germany would occupy the area by force.

The Poles took the threat seriously and on the twenty-third of March they ordered a partial mobilization of their armed forces and placed them on their highest state of alert.

Germany received an immediate diplomatic note of protest from the Poles over von Ribbentrop's astounding behaviour, reminding the Germans that *'Poland was an independent country and was not some sort of German protectorate which Ribbentrop could bully at will'*.

In response Ribbentrop offered a carrot with his usual large stick. It was delivered by way of the German Ambassador in Warsaw.

The message was simple.

If Poland agreed to the German demands, then Germany would ensure that Poland could jointly partition Slovakia with Hungary and receive German support for the immediate annexation of the Ukraine by Poland.

If Poland chose not to accept this offer to remedy the current situation, then she would be considered an enemy of the Reich.

On March twenty-sixth Ribbentrop once again called in and confronted the Polish Ambassador.

On this occasion he stormed at the man, suggesting that the Poles were attempting to threaten Germany by way of their troop mobilization and expressed absolute dismay for the Polish offer to do no more than, *'consider'* Germany's demand for *'extra territorial'* road access through the Polish corridor.

At the end of this session a frustrated Ribbentrop shrieked vehemently that if the Poles dared to enter Danzig in a further attempt at intimidation, *'Germany would go to war to destroy*

Poland'.

When word of this meeting was leaked to the Polish press it led to anti-German riots throughout the country.

The Nazi Party Headquarters in the ethnically diverse town of Lininco was attacked by a mob and destroyed.

The Polish government dug in their heels.

They refused to be intimidated, making it clear on March twenty-eighth that any attempt by the Germans to unilaterally change Danzig's *'Free City'* status would be considered by Poland to be an act of war.

Up to this period in time, Great Britain, dreading the thought of another major war and operating under its policy of appeasement toward Germany, had expressed sympathy with Hitler's territorial demands.

They justified their taking of this position by expressing a degree of remorse over the measure of harshness against Germany that had been demanded by the French after the Great War, as expressed by some of the, in English hindsight, unjust terms of the Treaty of Versailles to which the United Kingdom had been a reluctant signatory.

Before von Ribbentrop had come into the picture, the British government actually believed Hitler's claim that it was only the Sudetenland that he wanted returned to Germany and that he sincerely wanted peace and had no desire to dominate Europe.

Von Ribbentrop's brief and dismal term as German Ambassador to Great Britain and his performance during the month of March as Germany's Foreign Minister had done a great deal to bring about a rising tide of dismay within the United Kingdom.

There was now a serious and growing pressure from within the British Isles for a change in the British position visa-vie Germany. The revolt against the appeasement policy had even spread to include a good number of the backbenchers within the English ruling party.

CHAPTER TWENTY-THREE

- A Father's Trust –

Karl von Stauffer was alone in his office. He glanced up at the clock on the wall and noted the time.

Four-thirty - Ursula would be arriving shortly.

The Count had been deliberating with himself for almost an hour since the conclusion of his meeting with Luftwaffe Major General, Gunter von Schmidt.

In his capacity as Transport co-ordinator for *'Operation Fatherland'* his old friend had requested a meeting earlier in the day and the Count had managed to squeeze into his full schedule a short one-on-one conference at a quiet restaurant near his office.

His mind drifted back to the conversation that had taken place in that small eatery.

In itself, Gunter's news had been positive.

The Luftwaffe officer had opened the discussion by explaining that the planned siphoning-off of a portion of booty that was being systematically removed from the recently conquered territories and transported to Germany had become more successful than anyone could have envisioned.

Pleased, the Count, keeping his voice low and taking time to determine that they were safe from inquisitive ears, nodded his head and smiled.

"That is excellent news Gunter."

The General shrugged his shoulders and then lifted his arms and rested his hands on the tabletop between them.

"Yes and somewhat surprising really when you consider the fact that Goring is treating Paris as his own personal candy store. I swear the man spends more time in France selecting artwork for his personal collection than he does here with his responsibilities in Germany."

He chuckled and paused to light a cigarette before

continuing.

"I'm sure you are aware of who it is the good Reichsmarschall has chosen to oversee the transport of these treasures. I have to wonder if you anticipated this when you selected me to oversee transport tasks for our own little endeavour."

Karl smiled and shook his head.

"No Gunter, I'm afraid I have no such crystal ball. However I'm sure you are just the man to assist the Reichsmarschall with his transportation needs."

"Yes and I have been able to add a considerable amount of treasure over and above that selected by the Reichsmarschall, to each transport from France to Germany that I set up for Herr Goring and I have had no difficulty in laying my hands on the necessary French railway rolling-stock when I act under his authority.

We do have a problem though and that's why I asked to see you."

The Count, fearing the worst, set his coffee cup down and leaned slightly forward over the table.

"What is it Gunter?"

"The operation is proving so successful that I'm running out of places to safely store *our portion* of the material. It occurred to me that there is a relatively easy way to deal with our storage problem but I'm concerned that it might put you and your family at personal risk and for that reason I hesitate to suggest it."

The Count's brow furrowed and he let his gaze move about the room surreptitiously again before responding.

"What have you in mind?"

"The amount of treasure being shipped out of our newly conquered territory is immense and safe storage for the majority of it, that which is not being grabbed by Goring for his own immediate use, is becoming a problem. It is not only a problem confronting our endeavours. It is also a problem for the greater Reich.

In order to handle everything that it being taken, Goring, who Hitler has directed to store the stuff that won't fit into the new

Munich *'House of Art'* until after the war, when some envisioned wildly-massive new Gallery can be built to exhibit it all, is scrambling to find space for it.

His answer to the problem is to use several of the larger Castles located within the Reich as storehouses. As well there are also plans in the works to use some defunct mine shafts for this purpose. Of course the conditions in these areas must be such that artwork can be safely stored. The environment within these temporary storage spaces has to meet designated criteria which ensure that no damage to the artwork will result even from an extended period of storage.

Many of the Castles so far inspected have been found to meet the criteria and we have begun to use them for this purpose. It occurred to me that in order for us to solve our own little personal problem, Castle von Stauffer might be added to the list of storage facilities. If that were done I would have no difficulty in arranging for all treasure trains coming into Germany from France to make a stop there. It would mean of course that in addition to what treasures are stored at Castle von Stauffer in the name of the Reich, all treasure destined for the use of 'Operation Fatherland' could also to be housed there.

From what I remember you certainly have the capacity to handle it all, but the concern would be that some petty buearaucrat might inspect for some reason and realize that what is being stored there amounts to far more than the official documents indicate and therein be of a constant danger to you and your family."

The Count leaned back and thought for a moment.

"The sub-basement wouldn't serve, probably too damp. But the basement itself would certainly fit the bill and it's a huge area. If we kept the two cargos stored in separate areas with our consignments behind a false wall and we had one of our own people as caretaker working under your auspices and mandate …yes I think it would serve our purposes very well and as you say, you would have complete authorization and every reason to order each train to stop and unload at least part of its consignment as it passed by. I think the risk of discovery would be minimal."

Relief flickered across the Luftwaffe General's features and he smiled.

"It is an ideal solution to the problem and if you are comfortable with it, I can probably find a reliable man for the job - an onsite curator we could trust."

Lost in thought for a few moments, Karl von Stauffer shook his head slowly.

"No need; I have someone in mind. It will enable me to kill two birds with one stone. Leave the selection of a curator with me, but put the project of adding Castle von Stauffer to Goring's accorded list of secure storage sites into motion.

I will get back to you on my choice for the position of conservator tomorrow."

* * * * *

- Shifting Policy –

Germany's limited aims and intentions that had been expressed over the years since the Great War, once considered by the British as reasonable steps for redress in view of the terms of the Versailles Treaty, were becoming less and less acceptable.

Even obstructed by the self-imposed blinders induced by way of a sincere determination to never allow a repeat of the horror and destruction of the Great War and despite the heartfelt belief that Germany had been treated too harshly by the terms of the treaty, the British government was beginning to see the light.

Germany's occupation of the Czech segment of Czecho-Slovakia clearly demonstrated that its claim to be simply interested in realigning the alleged wrongs of the Treaty of Versailles was simply a façade.

By mid March of thirty-nine a cascade of fraudulent claims on the part of the Romanians that their country was under threat of German attack flooded London.

Ribbentrop actively and honestly denied that Germany had any such intention.

Unfortunately for Joachim, this denial was couched in almost identical terms to those he'd used earlier when he'd denied that the German had any intention of invading the Czechs.

These new denials on the part of the German Foreign Minister seemed so hollow after what had occurred with the Czechs that they tended to strengthen rather than reduce the suggested threat to the Romanians.

In offering them in the manner he chose, von Ribbentrop insured that the Romanian claims would receive a greater acceptance as credible, much more than they would have without his denials.

In England eyes were opening, if slowly and painfully. Positions were shifting as many of those in parliament came to the realization that the concept of *'peace at any cost'* was not only suicidal when dealing with the Nazis, but if continued, would very likely lead to the total destruction of Europe as they knew it.

The suggestion that Germany might occupy Romania was of great concern to the British.

Romania had oil, something Germany had little of. You could not fight a modern war without a large supply of oil.

If Germany moved successfully on Romania they would no longer have to rely on imported oil which could be derailed by a British naval blockade if necessary in a time of war.

The United Kingdom had a very real concern should the Germans achieve a secure source of oil.

The only realistic chance for the British to keep Romanian oil out of German hands was to strengthen its position with the Polish who possessed the most powerful army among the East European countries.

The Poles themselves had no interest in seeing Germany overrun the Romanian oilfields either. They supported the status quo.

While the Poles were already aligned with them, the British felt it advisable to strengthen that alignment in order to offer the Poles a firm foundation for their stance on maintaining the current situation in Eastern Europe.

The idea was to shore up the Poles, who would then be in a better position to support her neighbours, specifically Romania, if the Germans determined to continue pushing her weight around.

With this goal in mind the British announced in the House of Commons that as of March thirty-first, the United Kingdom had reached an agreement with Poland to *'guarantee'* that countries independence.

This *'guarantee'* included the provision that Britain would be committed to go to war to defend Poland should that country be invaded.

In addition to this development, von Ribbentrop received information in early April of thirty-nine that the United Kingdom and Turkey had opened talks aimed at an alliance to keep Germany out of the Balkans.

During these negotiations the Turks informed the British Ambassador that they had information that the Italians were intent on making the claim that their sphere of influence must extend over the entire Mediterranean.

This was soon to be proposed in a united diplomatic front which would include a German demand for placing the Balkans under their political control.

The Turks suggested an Anglo-Soviet-Turkish alliance as the only reasonable method of checking further axis expansion into the region.

The Germans had successfully broken Turkey's diplomatic codes and were therefore immediately aware of the details and depth of the ongoing negotiations between the Turks and the British.

The Germans had no Ambassador in Turkey at this time due to the Turks refusal to accept von Ribbentrop's earlier choice, made in nineteen thirty-eight, of von Papen for the job.

In view of the current situation between Turkey and the British, Von Ribbentrop once again proposed von Papen for the position which was still unfilled and Turkey reluctantly accepted him in the dim hope that they could successfully prevent German expansionism through direct diplomacy with the Nazi government.

A pleased von Ribbentrop promptly had von Papen arrange for the Italian Foreign Minister to promise the Turks that any rumours of Italy's intention to push for the expansion of their sphere of influence over the Mediterranean were unfounded.

It isn't surprising that the Turkish government took that suggestion with a good deal more than a few grains of salt.

While this was going on, von Papen upset von Ribbentrop by attempting to bypass him as Foreign Minister by cutting him out of the loop band reporting directly to Hitler on the negotiations he had now opened with the Turks.

This resulted in an immediate falling out between the two, who had been good friends for over twenty years.

A frustrated Joachim immediately lashed out by viciously haranguing the Turkish Ambassador in Berlin in an attempt to force the Turks into an alliance with the Third Reich.

This undiplomatic action on the part of von Ribbentrop went a long way to cementing into place the resulting Anglo-Turkish alliance that was announced on May twelfth of nineteen thirty-nine.

Von Ribbentrop was rapidly running out of options when it came to lining up allies for Nazi Germany in Eastern Europe.

Seemingly displeased but undeterred by his recent failures, the German Foreign Minister suddenly shifted his sights to an unlikely target, that of Soviet Russia.

He began by convincing Hitler that Germany could achieve her goals of crushing Poland in the short term and counter the British moves in the long term by securing a diplomatic agreement with the Russians, something he knew the English were currently involved in attempting to achieve.

Hitler immediately saw a hidden benefit in such an agreement over and above that of destroying Poland and thwarting the English.

The Nazi leader realized that if a pact with the Russians could be achieved it would also put him in a better negotiating position with the British.

It would serve to give him time to deal with England before his intended operation to seek even more lebensraum for the New Reich in the east.

He gave his support to von Ribbentrop but suggested he move forward with care.

Still smarting from his recent failures, Joachim initially

stayed behind the scenes in the negotiations and uncharacteristically, demonstrated some patience.

He dispatched a member of the Foreign Office trade department, Dr. Julius Schnurre, to Moscow with instructions to seek an economic agreement between the two countries.

While these early negotiations with the Soviets were taking place Joachim spent his time attempting to set up anti-British bilateral agreements with other countries.

He was initially unable to convince the Japanese who had their own agenda at the time, but after telling Mussolini that Germany would not go to war for at least three years, he was successful with the Italians, who signed the *'Pact of Steel'* with the Germans on May twenty-second nineteen thirty-nine.

Negotiations with the Russians went much better than von Ribbentrop could have reasonably hoped and the Russians hinted that much more than a trade agreement might me possible.

On August twenty-third, nineteen thirty-nine the *'Treaty of Non-Aggression between Germany and the Soviet Union'* was signed in Moscow.

The propaganda rhetoric of decades between the two countries suddenly disappeared.

A pact between the Nazis and the Communists: who could have ever conceived of such a thing?

The world was shocked by the news and with good reason,

The tenuous balance of power in the region had suddenly shifted.

World War Two had moved onto the horizon for anyone who took the time to look.

CHAPTER TWENTY-FOUR

- A Change for Ursula –

The main office for the Hitler Youth League of German Maidens, the *'Bund Deutscher Madel'* (BDM) was situated not far from Ursula's father's Berlin office.

Ursula's position as assistant to the Bund Leader, Doctor Jutta Rudiger, required her to do a fair amount of traveling but whenever Ursula found herself in Berlin she would make the short walk to meet the Count at his office in the late afternoon at the end of his working day and then catch a ride home with him to the large and imposing Berlin family mansion.

Such was the case on Wednesday, September twenty-fifth, nineteen-forty.

Ever punctual, Ursula, wearing one of her standard, severely-cut black suits with a long sleeved white blouse that buttoned to her neck, arrived at her Father's office promptly at five.

When she was shown inside she immediately took note of the blue, cigarette-induced haze drifting lazily above her Father's large desk, his slightly hunched shoulders and the deep lines of concentration temporarily etched into his face.

These signs, all but the haze, quickly faded as soon as he looked up and recognized her but they had been in place long enough for her to register them.

He's been making some serious decisions and they may have something to do with me.

The Count was well aware of his eldest daughter's ability to perceive his moods and he smiled as he waved her into one of the chairs on the far side of his desk.

"Nothing too serious, but we do need to talk for a bit before we head for home."

Ursula settled primly into the chair.

"What is it Father, not Gabriella again is it?"

Karl von Stauffer chuckled and shook his head."

"No, not Gabriella - it's something for you actually. An opportunity has come up and I thought you might be interested in it.

I know that you are getting a little tired of your current job."

Ursula crossed her legs and smoothed her skirt into position before responding.

"And you have a new one in mind for me."

The Count nodded.

"Yes, something I think you might enjoy taking on."

He paused for a second and chose his words carefully before he next spoke.

"You've always expressed an interest in the family art. You've made an impressive job of cataloguing and evaluating our personal collection over the past ten years and seemed to have immensely enjoyed completing the task."

He let those words register for a moment, leaning back in his chair and then, once she'd nodded her head in agreement, he continued.

"How would you like to take on a similar job, albeit a considerably larger challenge by far, something in the same vein but demanding considerably more responsibility?"

Ursula had no idea where the conversation was going but she was seriously intrigued by the picture forming in her mind. While she was certainly not at the point of acquiescing to the suggestion without more detail, her father had definitely piqued her interest

"You want me to catalogue and evaluate someone's art collection?"

"It would be that and more."

Ursula arched her eyebrows inquisitively and the Count continued.

"You would be responsible for the duties of cataloguing and evaluating works of art of course, but this project would also entail acting as curator for the works, which would be placed entirely under your control. And we are not talking about a small private collection...no, this would be a massive collection and it would belong the German State.

Accepting this position would require you to make a very long-term commitment."

Ursula frowned.

"And you think I am qualified to do this work?"

The Count was both relieved and pleased at her obvious interest.

"Very definitely - you see the Fuhrer has determined that the treasure from our newly conquered territories is to be brought to Germany for storage until it can be properly housed in its own magnificent gallery and it seems that Castle von Stauffer is one of the storage sites that have been selected as a repository for this purpose.

The amassed collection to be deposited and held at the Castle will need to be under the watchful eye of a curator during its stay and diligence will be required in regard to the proper storage and care of the artworks in question until the intended national gallery has been constructed and is ready to receive them.

Now that we are at war, non-military buildings, such as the one intended for construction for the purpose of permanently housing these artworks, are on hold. These valuable treasures will therefore have to be stored indefinitely until that can be accomplished.

You would need to be in residence at the Castle of course and that being the case, there will not a great deal of time or opportunity for you to enjoy much of a social life..."

Ursula smiled and cut him off.

"Frankly I would see that as an advantage Father, not a hindrance. God knows I've had enough of our new German society over the past couple of years. The peace and quiet would be a very welcome change, I assure you.

And as to the work and the challenge it entails, well, you know I would love the idea of it. However, in the New Reich, I have to wonder a little at how this offer came about. I realize that my current job is one of some prominence for a woman but I'm well aware that my holding of it has more to do with the fact that I'm a von Stauffer and more importantly a female, a necessity in that it consists of working with nubile young girls; but something like this is certainly a different kettle of fish.

It seems to me such a lofty position under our new Nazi government would be considered as beyond the abilities of a mere woman, who's only stated purpose in life should be the production of children."

Picking up on the sarcasm, the Count managed a wry smile.

"You are more than qualified to fill this position and it is in the family interest that you take it on.

What happens in Castle von Stauffer for the remainder of this war is a family affair regardless of who governs Germany and I would not like to have to trust in a stranger to properly see to it that our interests are properly considered. I would however, have no hesitation in entrusting such a responsibility to you."

* * * * *

- Tripartite Pact –

On September twenty-seventh, nineteen-forty Hitler and von Ribbentrop's plan for the sourcing out of new allies and the German wish for the realignment of the Asian sphere of influence reached fruition with the signing, in Berlin, of the *'Tripartite Pact'*.

Germany would now reject China and instead adopt a policy of support for Japanese expansionism.

Signed by Hitler for Germany, the Foreign Minister, Galeazzo Ciano, for Italy and the Imperial Japanese Ambassador to Germany, Saburo Karusu for Japan, the parties agreed that *'for the next ten years they would stand by and cooperate with one another in their prime purpose to establish and maintain a new order of things to promote the mutual prosperity and welfare of the peoples concerned.'*

In the document the three governments specifically agreed to the following articles:

1. Japan recognizes and respects the leadership of Germany and Italy in the establishment of a new order in Europe.

2. Germany and Italy recognize and respect the leadership of Japan in establishment of a new order in Greater East Asia.

3. Japan, Germany and Italy agree to cooperate in their efforts on aforesaid lines. They further undertake to assist one another with all political, economic and military means if one of the Contracting Powers is attacked by a Power at present not involved in the European War or in the Japanese-Chinese conflict.

4. With a view to implementation the present pact, joint technical commissions, to be appointed by the respective Governments of Japan, Germany and Italy, will meet without delay.

5. Japan, Germany and Italy affirm that the above agreement affects in no way the political status existing at present between each of the three Contracting Powers and Soviet Russia.

6. The present pact shall become valid immediately upon signature and shall remain in force ten years from the date on which it becomes effective. In due time, before the expiration of said term, the High Contracting Parties shall, at the request of any one of the other, enter into negotiations for its renewal.

Von Ribbentrop had gone a long way toward improving his position with Hitler by pulling off recent agreements with both the Soviets and the Japanese. The Fuhrer has seen fit to forgive Joachim for his previous unsuccessful attempts to bring Spain into the Fascist Axis.

* * * * *

- October Nineteen-Forty –

- Battle of Britain –

The Germans have recognized that daylight bombing raids against the English can be very costly to them.

By October they have chosen to send very few daytime raids across the English Channel, and those they do send consist of fighter-bombers and fighter groups of Messerschmitt one-o-nines, the latter being faster than either the British Hurricane or Spitfire. These attacks are made at low level only, therein giving the British less warning of their approach from the sea.

The German night attacks of the Blitz continue, launched primarily against London but also reaching Birmingham, Manchester and Liverpool.

During this month Hitler orders high-altitude recognisance over-flights of the Soviet Union in preparation for his anticipated later move eastward.

These flights are used primary for spotting troop dispositions.

* * * * *

- Cutting British Supply Lines –

During October the U-boat patrols are riding high.

They sink three hundred and fifty-two thousand four hundred tons of British shipping out of the total of four hundred and forty-three thousand tons lost by the United Kingdom from ships destroyed while travelling across the Atlantic from North America.

Convoys are being protected by British warships, west to about twenty degrees or three hundred miles off the coastline of Ireland and conversely defended by Canadian warships for a distance of approximately the same number of miles when they begin their crossing from the east coast of Canada and sail for British ports.

Escort vessels are in short supply on both sides of the Atlantic however and as a result the few ships available for this duty are stretched pathetically thin.

The Germans are now applying new wolf-pack tactics with great success and have developed a new attack pattern wherein they fire their torpedoes while on the surface at night and from inside the target convoy itself.

These new approaches of attack methods are producing an effectiveness never seen before.

The radar currently being used by the British and Canadian ships is not advanced sufficiently to pick up the ships which offer only a wisp of profile when on the surface in the dark, and attempts to spot them with the naked eye are completely ineffective.

Listening devices utilized are not sophisticated enough to

single out a surfaced U-boat once it has slipped in amongst the bunched ships making up the main body of the convoy itself and by running on the surface during the attacks; subs are immune from detection by the ASDIC (Sonar) systems operated by the escorts.

The vast majority of these escorts are of the Corvette class and the Germans soon learn that any U-boat which is spotted on the surface during one of these night attacks has a very good chance, due to their superior surface-speed capability, of out-running any shadowing escort Corvette who attempts to give chase.

* * * * *

- More Diplomacy –

Pleased with the Nazi diplomatic achievements of the previous few weeks, Hitler turns his personal attention to expanding other avenues of diplomacy.

On the first of October nineteen-forty, the Germans strengthen their ties with the Finns who are trembling under the shadow of Soviet Russia.

The Nazis get the rights to purchase nickel from Finland in exchange for their agreement to supply arms to the Finns.

October fourth sees a second meeting between Hitler and Mussolini who favours his title of *'Il Duce'* (The Leader), at the Brenner Pass when their two personal trains congregate at railway station (1) on the border between Austria and Italy, between *'Gries am Brenner'*, in Austria and *'Colle Isarco'*, in Italy.

Hitler was about to personally pick up the, so far, stagnated negotiations with the Spanish leader, General Franco to complete an agreement calling for Spain's entry into the war on the side of the Axis powers; this to solve the problem of occupying Gibraltar in the Mediterranean to put pressure on the British regional fleet operations.

Among other things, the Fuhrer wanted to discuss some of the Spanish leader's territorial demands with Italy's Fascist dictator, prior to his upcoming meeting with Franco.

The talks took place in Mussolini's armoured train.

A jubilant Hitler opened by stating:

'The war is won! The rest is only a question of time.'

He dominated the talks and while acknowledging to Mussolini that the Luftwaffe was still fighting for air supremacy over the English Channel, he expressed confidence that in view of the fact that the British aircraft were being shot out of the air at a ratio of three to one, the battle would soon be won.

The Fuhrer exposed the belief that the English were only hanging on by a thread in the hope of assistance coming from either the Americans or the Russians, and possibly both.

If so Hitler stated, they were living in a dream world in that the newly achieved Tripartite Pact would serve to negate any such response from the Americans and the Nazi-Soviet Non-Aggression Pact in conjunction with the number of German divisions present in the east would guarantee no forthcoming aid from Soviet Russia.

Now was the time for him and Il Duce to provide the coup de grace for the British. It was time to occupy Gibraltar and remove the British Mediterranean threat.

He then shifted gears and began to express his frustration over the inability of von Ribbentrop to reach an agreement with the Spaniards to facilitate such an enterprise.

He began a harangue against Franco who was demanding four hundred thousand tons of grain and large supplies of fuel before he would even consider allying himself with the Axis powers.

Further, he told Mussolini that when discussions on such an agreement had been undertaken and Spain was asked when payment for these required supplies would be made to Germany a pompous Franco had the audacity to reply that this *'was a matter of confusing idealism with materialism'*.

Flushed and eyes sparkling with resentment, Hitler told the Italian dictator that he had been treated *'as if I were a little Jew who was haggling about the most sacred possession of mankind'*.

After his diatribe against Franco, The Fuhrer relaxed and the topic of conversation soon shifted to other matters of concern.

Hitler advised Mussolini to avoid commencing any new military campaigns until he was better positioned for them and offered German assistance for the Italian front in Africa.

A confident Il Duce declines the offer of German help.

The two men part on good terms.

Hitler's train then pulled out of the Brenner Pass and headed for the Fuhrer's home in Berchtesgaden.

CHAPTER TWENTY-FIVE

- Engagement in the Offing? –

Erika von Stauffer was extremely pleased.

This was her favourite part of the day.

She was sitting in a large beautifully upholstered armchair with her legs up on a matching footstool, alone in the large drawing room of the Berlin family mansion.

The chair she sat in faced the large marble-faced fireplace where several logs burned brightly, offering direct flow of warmth on a cool overcast day.

It was shortly after four in the afternoon.

The Countess lost herself in her thoughts as she sipped occasionally from the fine crystal glass that contained a liberal portion of her favourite dry sherry.

The small dinner party she'd arranged to provide the opportunity for Gabriella and the family to meet Dr. Konrad Kauffmann had gone very well indeed.

After the guests had left, an uncharacteristically reserved Gabriella had candidly admitted to the immediate family that she *was quite taken* with the handsome, well-mannered SS-officer.

Erika hadn't needed her daughter to verbally enlighten her on that particular fact. The exchange between the two, who had been seated next to each other at the table, had clearly bespoken of that.

Erika had paid a great deal of attention to the pair not only during the meal but over the cocktails, before dinner had been announced.

There had been notable sparks and distinct hints of mutual surprise, interest and appreciation between the couple from the inception of the introduction.

While experience taught that this type of reaction could be reasonably expected from Gabriella in the case of her meeting any handsome new man, Erika sincerely doubted that such a an obviously deep and sparkling response could have been the expected norm coming from the soft-spoken, polite and socially well-rounded young doctor.

As the evening had progressed the Countess, pleasantly surprised but mindful of the fact that the good start to the relationship on the part of her daughter could be a facade, had turned her considerable powers of observation toward making a determined effort to forming a true assessment of the depth of the mutual interest in each other that appeared to have formed.

Yes, well Wilhelm was definitely correct in his original assessment of the man.

He was most certainly a handsome fellow; in or out of uniform I'm sure.

Tall, a full head of jet-black hair framing strong, chiselled and well-balanced features harbouring a very stimulating five o'clock shadow, obviously an athletic and toned body, broad shouldered and narrow wasted.

No surprise that Gabriella had been taken with him.

My God, any woman would find this man required a least a second and then a third glance. A magnificent specimen, he would certainly be a catch for any woman.

What had been somewhat surprising to her, in consideration his of his laid back character, had been his ability to gain and hold Gabriella's interest throughout the entire dinner.

While socially reserved, as was to be expected of one of his breeding and background, Konrad had clearly and easily demonstrated his ability to speak with knowledge on any topic that had come up and had shown no sign of hesitancy to speak freely and with conviction on various topics.

The truth be known, he had in fact been the center of attention for a good part of the evening, without, in any way, seeming to dominate or hold forth.

Well educated, a doctor and apparently one of some repute, with a likely future in research.

The questions remaining were, did Gabriella only see him as yet another prospective bed partner, or was she actually considering him as husband material and additionally, why on earth was he still single?

Since that evening things appeared to have gone well and Erika had known better than to involve herself in any way in what appeared to be at first glance, a burgeoning relationship.

Gabriella had been acting the part of a proper young woman of her social class. There had been no indication of any other dalliances, something that had apparently been the norm prior to Konrad's arrival on the scene.

There was no indication that she was sleeping with him yet, although there was a great deal of touching and holding going on and the two of them had become inseparable of late.

If she were to guess at Gabriella's intentions she would have to lean toward a substantial change in her youngest daughter who had suddenly become very serious about her nursing studies and spent her free time at public functions, partnered with Konrad, that were of a nature very different than had been demonstrated in the past.

The party girl had morphed into a dazzling young socialite on the arm of the handsome young doctor.

Without rocking the boat, she'd kept her lines out and was still compiling intelligence on both the relationship and the good doctor himself.

The Countess felt confident in saying so far, so good.

* * * * *

- October Fifth, Nineteen-Forty –

- USA –

The U.S Naval Secretary Frank Knox publicly condemns the Tripartite Pact and announces a partial call up of the American naval reserve.

* * * * *

- October Sixth, Nineteen-Forty –

- Romania –

Ion Antonescu, an anti-Semitic, politically far-right Romanian career military officer has risen to political prominence in Romania.

He has aligned himself with the *'Fascist Nation Christian'* and *'Garda de fjer'* (Iron Guard) groups for much of the pre-war period.

The Iron Guard Party is a right wing ultra-nationalist, Fascist, anti-communist political party that is strongly tied to the Orthodox Christian faith. It is virulently anti-Semitic and a central plank in its platform is the demand that Romania adopt *'state antis-Semitism'*.

On the sixth of October Antonescu assumes command of the Iron Guard.

Hitler is pleased with this development.

* * * * *

- October Seventh, Nineteen-Forty –

The next day Nazi troops enter Romania with the excuse that the Germans are moving in to assist in the reorganization of the Romanian army.

Hitler's troops now secure the Romanian oil fields.

Just to help out a neighbour, mind.

* * * * *

On October seventh, the Germans order all those of Jewish decent living within the occupied territory of France to immediately register with the French authorities.

* * * * *

- October Ninth, Nineteen-Forty –

Patrick Laughy

- United Kingdom -

On this date Winston Churchill is chosen as the successor to Neville Chamberlain who has resigned his position at Prime Minister under pressure from those in parliament who feel that he had been too soft on the Germans.

Hitler is disappointed in the change. He had been able to con and browbeat the appeasing Chamberlain but he sees Churchill as a possible potent adversary and believes that under his leadership there is bound to be a hardening of the British political position visa-vie the European situation.

* * * * *

Between October ninth and the twentieth of that month Germany has been able to keep eleven U-boats on active operational patrols against British convoys in the North Atlantic.

They sink thirty-nine ships.

The British, under Churchill, begin to dismantle segments of their anti-invasion defences in favour of increasing their convoy escort capability.

* * * * *

With an eye on world opinion the Nazis run a plebiscite on the question of their occupancy of Luxemburg with the hope that the inhabitants will vote results that will be favourable to their cause.

This unsuccessful attempt by the Germans to put a good face on the military takeover of Luxemburg is a dismal failure for the Nazis.

Ninety-seven percent of those who vote in the plebiscite are opposed to the German presence.

* * * * *

- October Eleventh, Nineteen-Forty –

- Finland –

In an attempt to placate the sabre rattling Soviets, the Fins agree to de-militarise the strategic Aland Islands.

* * * * *

- France –

'Chef de lEtat Francais' (Chief of State of Vichy France), and Nazi puppet, Philippe Petain, makes a radio broadcast to the French people, telling them they must discard their traditional beliefs as to who are their allies and who are their enemies.

* * * * *

- October Twelfth, Nineteen-Forty –

- Operation Sea Lion –

Recognizing that the Luftwaffe has as yet been unable to take command of the English Channel and the coast of Great Britain, Hitler indefinitely postpones Operation Sea Lion, the planned German military invasion of the British Iles.

* * * * *

- October Fifteenth, Nineteen-Forty –

- Italy –

Despite Hitler's strong suggestion to Mussolini at their last meeting that Italy refrain from taking on any new military conquests, the Italians have decided to invade Greece.

They anticipate that the battle will last for only a couple of weeks and in view of Hitler's earlier comments purposely choose not to advise Germany of their intentions.

They schedule the invasion of Greece for the end of October.

* * * * *

- Germany –

Goring, having lost face with Hitler over his Luftwaffe's inability to take control of the English Channel, tucks his tail between his legs and slips off to restructure the priorities of the German air force.

The outcome of this re-evaluation defines new targets. These are aimed at bringing the English to their knees and seeking a peace agreement with the Nazis.

New priority targets are to be London, aircraft factories and industry, followed by British airfields.

* * * * *

- October Sixteenth, Nineteen-Forty –

- Japan –

Discussions take place between the Japanese and officials in the Dutch East Indies.

The Japanese are seeking a secure oil supply.

They demand the guarantee of forty percent of the East Indies' output over the next six months.

The British pull out all the diplomatic stops to prevent this from happening but realistically speaking, they recognize that those in the Dutch East Indies see little choice by to accede to the demands of the Empire of the Rising Sun.

On October the nineteenth the Japanese get their oil guarantee to cover the next six months.

* * * * *

The 4th Reich

- October Eighteenth, Nineteen-Forty –

- Vichy France –

The Petain led puppet government for the territories of unoccupied France institute anti-Semitic laws.

Jews will now be excluded from holding positions of authority in industry and the media and totally excluded from working at any level in the public service.

* * * * *

- Berchtesgaden –

Now secure within the confines of the compound surrounding his home in Berchtesgaden, Hitler takes time out to evaluate and assess his aims in regard to future diplomatic ventures.

He entertains little and spends most of his time alone pacing the rooms or out walking with his dog on the slopes of the Obersalzberg.

While holed up in Berchtesgaden the Fuhrer chairs regular military discussions and meetings to keep him abreast of the world and home front situations.

In addition, he uses the members of his inner circle as sounding boards during the vaunted dinners and entertainment that end each day.

After giving matters considerable thought he decides that he will make a brief stop in France while on route to his meeting with the Spanish dictator.

He is scheduled to meet with General Franco of Spain with the intention of achieving the pact with the Spaniard that he feels is necessary to further his plan to bring the British to the negotiating table and prevent the risk of facing a two-front war.

On October twenty-second nineteen-forty Hitler re-boards his personal train and departs for Montoire in west-central France.

That evening he is met by Pierre Laval, a staunch Nazi collaborator and deputy leader of Vichy France.

CHAPTER TWENTY-SIX

- Family –

- Eric –

Eric is living his dream.

He spends his weekdays aboard his new command, training the handpicked crew and working the huge U-boat through her sea-trials.

With only a few exceptions, which are quickly and easily rectified by dockyard workers travelling with the crew, she performs beautifully.

Eric's evenings during the workweek are primarily spent enjoying the company of at least one, and more often than not, both of the delicious blond twins.

The weekends leave him free to share, with the free-spirited blonds, the entertainment Kiel has on offer and he gives his household staff of two, Saturdays and Sundays off in order to freely avail himself of all the benefits that the large house he's been given provides.

Each weekend he and the girls settle comfortably into the large house for their own private party with him, assured that their blissful fun and games can proceed without outside interruption.

Eric finds that he no longer needs to exercise to keep fit.

Besides he has better things to do.

The blonds are constantly providing him with a daily physical workout that has toned him to perfection, to say nothing of dramatically improving his mental state.

* * * * *

- Gabriella –

Gabriella opened her eyes and waited for them to focus well enough to read the ornate carriage clock centered on the mantle of her bedroom fireplace.

Ten-thirty, how things had changed in just a few short weeks.

It was Sunday morning and her mother would have never allowed her to miss breakfast on a Sunday morning before Konrad had appeared on the scene.

She stretched luxuriously, enjoying the physical feel of her muscles working and then snuggled down beneath her down filled quilt and let her thoughts drift back to that first dinner on the night she and Konrad had met.

She'd been anticipating the worst of course...her family autocratically choosing a man for her.

Looking back on that night now she realized just how much she had changed since that dinner. She had a new whole new perspective on life today than she'd had then.

On first seeing Konrad that evening she'd initially assessed him in a physical sense only.

At the time, it had seemed quite normal to do so. It was how she evaluated any new man she met. Was it someone she could enjoy in bed or not?

Things had been simple then.

Evaluated in purely physical terms he'd impressed her immensely; my god what a hunk of man! From that simple point of view Konrad was definitely not what she had been expecting. She'd felt a flush of desire surge through her the instant she'd run her eyes over him.

She smiled to herself as she recalled her judgement.

Oh yes, this was most assuredly a man she would like to share a bed with.

What was even more surprising was that as the night wore on she did not sense the draining of that initial surge of desire as she conversed and gently flirted with him.

On the contrary, she found herself enthralled with him and there had been no reduction in her desire to possess him sexually.

He was bright, well versed in an array of topics, not overbearing, definitely gentlemanly and well-mannered, although

---

far from subservient or introverted.

A soft spoken man of few but well chosen words; supremely confident and sure-footed in whatever topic arose.

They shared an interest in medicine of course, she a nurse, well almost a nurse, and he a doctor, but she was amazed at how many other interests they seemed to share, everything from skiing to their taste in music.

It was almost uncanny and she had enjoyed his company throughout the evening.

She had not realized it at the time, but they had been lost in each other and had grudgingly spent only what time was required for politeness, to included the others at the table in their conversation.

She'd NEVER before experienced a man as captivating as this handsome SS-doctor.

Looking back on it now she could recognize that that evening had been the turning point and first step toward her making that major change in her outlook on life.

He had effectively swept her off her feet on that first night; she had changed enough after these few weeks that she was able to concede that to herself now, even if she had been incapable of recognizing it at the time.

She smiled contentedly and threw off her covers, stretched happily again and then vaulted out of bed and headed for her in-suite bathroom to run her tub, her thoughts of that first meeting still wafting gently through her mind.

Thank God for Ursula.

She found herself grinning as she adjusted the taps and then crossed to the sink and prepared to brush her teeth.

While brushing she let her mind drift back to that sisterly talk.

Ursula...the big sister who had always looked out for her and despite her behaviour, had supported her and helped her over all those early years, usually for a reward consisting of unguarded disdain.

But it had been Ursula who she'd sought out that night, Ursula who had stayed up until four in the morning with her, listening and carefully suggesting a course of action.

She wanted this man, not to sleep with, well that of course, but not only that.

She wanted to spend time with him and learn about him, she didn't know exactly what she wanted but she was afraid that she would not get the chance to find out.

What if he became aware of her activities over the past few years? How could he not become aware? How should she behave toward him, was he really interested in her, as interested as he'd seemed or was he simply a good dinner guest...

Ursula had let her babble on for what seemed like ages and then she'd smiled and sat back against the headboard of Gabriella's bed.

"Gabriella, I am so happy for you.

You've found a man who you actually think you want to have a long term relationship with and unless I'm blind he likely feels the same about you. You have nothing to worry about, well not nothing but you can certainly mitigate the damage."

Gabriella, her face reflecting the strain she was under, thrust her hands, palms out, in front of her.

"Well tell me then for heaven's sake. What do I have to do? I'll do whatever it takes."

Usual had laughed then; a full throaty chortle.

"You know, it surprises me to hear myself saying this, but I actually believe you might.

You will have to change, you realize, become a different women. For example, you won't be able to drag him into bed tonight.

You're going to have to show him that you are the kind of girl he thinks you are and while that won't be all that hard because he's already infatuated with you, it will have to be made apparent over a reasonable period of time.

The impression you leave him with once that time has passed must be one that he will not allow to be questioned by anybody else for the simple reason that he's convinced that he
knows you better than anyone else could possible know you.

That means that you don't sleep with him until his tongue is hanging out, he has given you a ring and I tell you that you can."

Gabriella's grin broadened to a beaming smile as she recalled her response to that statement and Ursula's instant reply.

"But how will I know how he is...you know, what he's like in bed? That may not be very important to you Ursula, but it certainly is to me and I don't want to find out about it when it's too late."

Ursula had arched her eyebrows and sucked in a deep breath.

"Gabriella it may surprise you to learn that I too appreciate a man who is good sexually now and then.

Unlike you, I just happen to keep that kind of thing private and that is exactly what you are going to do if you are really interested in a long term relationship with this man.

You will sleep with him before you marry him, but if you want my help in this, you will only sleep with him after you are properly engaged to him."

* * * * *

- Wilhelm –

The general parameters of Wilhelm's assigned duties had now settled into place.

After his transfer to Himmler's personal staff he had spent a few weeks receiving various orientation-type assignments, in the main an introduction into the various areas for which the SS held responsibility within the Nazi structure.

As initially indicated by the *'Reichsfuhrer of the Schutzstaffel',* now that he had completed this early orientation, his main duties revolved around two main areas, that of an administrative officer involved with Himmler's pet Lebensborn project and secondly of keeping the Reichsfuhrer apprised and updated on a regular basis as to new developments and advances taking place under his father's auspices.

Unlike others on Himmler's staff, he was not expected to account for his time to anyone other than the Reichsfuhrer himself; as long as the Reichsfuhrer was satisfied with his performance in the two areas he had been assigned, no further demands were made of him.

His immediate superiors in the Lebensborn project considered him to have been appointed personally by the Reichsfuhrer to act as his eyes and ears for the day to day operation of the program and as such he had been given a fairly free hand.

He had been instructed to make inspections of, and prepare statistical reports on, the expanding facilities. He was to evaluate efficiencies, offer suggestions for improvement of the systems being used and first-hand problem solve as he carried out his inspections.

The assignment was interesting and in consideration of what the project was intended to accomplish…the production of true Aryan German babies, it came with obvious fringe benefits.

He had posed for propaganda posters at Himmler's bequest with the result that his likeness had now been plastered all over the Reich.

Whenever he did his inspections he was inevitably recognized by the young women who were in attendance at the facilities with the intention of taking part in the Lebensborn program, and consequently found himself in high demand as an active participant in the process.

During every inspection he literally had his pick of the crop of a wide range of beautiful and willing young women who actively vied for his attention and like any other young, red blooded Aryan SS-officer; he did his duty by doing his level best to fulfill his responsibly in the service of the state.

It was a tough job, but someone had to do it.

When he was not directly involved with his responsibilities toward the project he spent his time with his father, publicly fulfilling his task of keeping Himmler updated on projects and privately keeping abreast of the expanding activities of ' *Operation Fatherland*'.

* * * * *

- Ursula –

Ursula had been sitting alone in her small office at BDM's Berlin head office staring vacantly at her phone for almost forty-five minutes as she struggled with her thoughts.

What the hell was she going to do!

She had agreed to take up her father's offer of the position of conservator for the seized artwork from the occupied territories at the family castle.

It was a job she very much wanted and she knew that, in accepting it, she would not only please her father but be happily immersed in work that would not only give her a real sense of accomplishment but also allow her to be of value to her country in a time of war.

At the time she'd met with her father there had been no complications around accepting the assignment.

But over the past few weeks a problem had arisen.

Well it wasn't really a problem as such, kind of a wonderful development to be honest.

She was now finding herself torn.

Who would have guessed that straitlaced independent little Ursula would suddenly find herself head over heels in love. It had all happened so fast.

Her mind drifted back to the start of it all, to that weekend long ago at the Castle von Stauffer when the guests had stayed over.

It had begun at the pool and continued on during dinner, the fireworks and as he saw her to her apartment door at the end of the night.

She found herself humming softly as she remembered.

It had all been so innocently romantic.

She hadn't even known his name. Well they'd exchanged first names of course, his was Friedrich, but with the informality of the setting around the pool, it hadn't really seemed necessary for full names.

He had obviously known who she was, but he'd never offered a surname during that visit and under the circumstances, she'd not felt it necessary to ask.

The pool had given her a clear opportunity to appreciate his physical attributes.

He'd been impressively built, a very handsome young fellow, tall athletic, blond, close cropped hair and deep blue eyes.

He had filled out his bathing suit very well as she recalled.

The remainder of the evening had given her ample opportunity to gauge his character.

She had enjoyed the attention he'd paid her at the pool and later, after the fireworks, when he had escorted her back to her rooms and behaved as a perfect gentleman, lightly kissing her hand and wishing her a pleasant good night.

She recollected that she had used her contact with him as an excuse to shift her mother's attention away from Ursula's activities during that day by way of expressing her interest in him, bringing him up and asking her mother to garner more information about him.

At the time her mother had been quite surprised at her request, obviously hoping, as Ursula had intended, that there was more to the question than met the eye.

As a result her mother had informed her over breakfast the next day that the young Luftwaffe pilot's name was Friedrich von Krueger, that he was of a titled and old family with money, and that he had a reputation with the ladies, but nothing that was not acceptable for a fighter pilot under the current wartime conditions.

Ursula would have probably simply considered the time shared between them on that weekend as an enjoyable social contact with a handsome man, and not pursued the matter further, if she had not received flowers on her next day at the office.

The card had provided no text, but had simply been signed Friedrich.

Even then she was inclined to dismiss the gesture as simply a polite response to a social weekend.

Then flowers had arrived for her the next day and had been arriving every day since then, either at her home on the weekends or at the office during the week.

Always, the same card...the only message, a simple 'Friedrich'.

Then one day there was a note over the name of the card.

'I have two tickets to the concert on Saturday evening...would you be free to join me for the performance and dinner beforehand?'

She had considered for two days and then sent him a note agreeing and providing him with her home telephone number.

All of that was history of course...they were now a regular couple on the Berlin social scene.

She had yet to sleep with him but she had reached the point where she definitely wanted to and knew it would happen soon.

They had already discussed a future together in vague terms, his concerns at making a commitment being the inherent risks of his profession and his likelihood to sustain injury or death and the unfairness of asking her to commit under those circumstances.

Despite how well they got on together, she remained a little uncertain of his ability to sincerely offer commitment in view of his earlier reputation with regard to women.

Since they had begun seeing each other she had noted absolutely no sign of his dalliance with other females and had been relatively amazed at his stated intent to respect her right to limit the depth of their physical involvement until they were both able to commit to a long term relationship.

As far as she could judge, they were open and completely honest with each other.

He was obviously sexually frustrated by their current situation, and he'd made it abundantly clear that he wanted to bed her, but he'd told her that he was prepared to wait until she was completely comfortable with that eventuality and he never pushed his obvious need too far.

On the past weekend he'd taken the entire equation to a whole new level by offering her a ring and she had accepted.

Her parents didn't know about it yet.

Emotions aside, by this point in time she was very much in love with this man,

Hence the current studious attention she was paying to the phone on her desk.

She needed to speak with her father.

Although plans had already been made and steps taken toward her new job, it was obvious to her now that she would have to back out of the agreement she'd earlier reached with him.

* * * * *

- Karl –

Count Karl von Stauffer was not surprised to receive the call from his daughter Ursula.

Whenever she was working in Berlin office she would routinely call to let him know that she would be dropping by his office to take advantage of a chance to ride home with him.

Subsequently when the call came he took it as routine.

It wasn't until he'd hung up that he took the time to reflect on the fact that Ursula had been uncharacteristically vague and evasive during the brief telephone exchange.

He briefly wondered what that had been all about before turning his attention back to the papers laid before him on his desk.

* * * * *

- Countess Erika –

Erika was tickled pink.

All her prayers had now been answered.

Ursula hadn't seen fit to let them know yet, but the Countess was on very good terms with Friedrich's mother and she had been fully apprised on the night of the occurrence by the wonderful news of Ursula's engagement.

Add that to the situation with Gabriella and there was little more a mother could ask for.

She had also found the answers to her two questions about Friedrich.

'Did she see him only as yet another prospective bed partner?'

No, that had become obvious fairly quickly.

'Why on earth was he still single?'

It turned out that it was because he had been engaged for several years and had just recently been jilted.

Then there was Gabriella.

She was certain that Doctor Kauffmann was going to offer a ring to Gabriella soon, as he had to take up his new position shortly and was certain to want her to accompany him. That would mean another engagement was in the offing.

Both her daughters were to be finally wed and each to an excellent match, what wonderful news.

God only knows she had waited long enough and had worked hard enough to achieve it.

Now her next endeavour would be to break the details of all this to Karl.

* * * * *

- Marshal of France –

Henri Philippe Benoni Omer Joseph Petain known affectionately to the French people as Philippe Petain, the *'Lion of Verdun'* or the *'Marshal'* was born in Cauchy-a-la-Tour in the North of France on April twenty-fourth, eighteen fifty-six.

A well-established French hero of the Great War due to his outstanding military leadership, Petain, had been promoted to the rank of *'Marshal of France'* on December eighth nineteen eighteen.

After the Great War Petain remained in the military and went on to hold various important Commands. One of his Protégés during this period of his career was one Captain Charles de Gaulle.

On February eighth, nineteen thirty-four Petain was invited to join the new French Cabinet as Minister of War. He held the position for a short time and then retired.

Despite his retirement he retained a post on the French *'High Military Committee'*.

The French General Election of nineteen thirty-six produced results of five and a half million votes for the *'Left'* and four and one half million for the *'Right'*.

A short time later in an interview, Petain, staunchly anti-Bolshevik and a political *'right winger'*, attacked both those who allowed Communists, intellectual responsibility in France and the Franco-Soviet Pact; this at a time when France had the largest Communist Party in Western Europe.

He claimed that France had lost faith in her destiny.

At the time of this interview *the 'Marshal'* was in his eightieth year.

In late May of nineteen forty the Germans were pounding the French and at that time French General, Maxime Weygand expressed his disappointment in the performance of their British allies.

The promised British air support had not materialized and the British Expeditionary Forces were retreating pell-mell. Both he and Petain recognized the military situation as untenable.

Paul Reynaud, the French Premier at the time, agreed with their assessment and felt they must seek an armistice.

Weygand indicated that he was in favour of saving the French army and *'wished to avoid internal trouble and above all anarchy'*.

On the thirty-first of May, Churchill's representative in France met with Petain and threatened France with a blockade and bombardment of the French ports it France agreed to an armistice with the Germans.

After this meeting Petain remarked to Reynaud; *'Your ally now threatens us'*.

After the fall of Dunkirk on June fifth, nineteen-forty Reynaud brought Petain, Weygand and the newly promoted, Brigadier-General Charles de Gaulle into his War Cabinet, hoping for renewed sprit in the resistance against the Germans.

By the eighth of June the Germans were at the gates of Paris and the government was preparing to flee the city.

Petain opposed such a move and during the cabinet meeting of that day Reynaud argued for an armistice.

On June tenth the government left Paris for the safety of Tours.

Their Commander in Chief, Weygand voiced the opinion that *'the fighting had become meaningless'*.

He was supported in this position by several other government members who were firmly set on a course toward seeking an armistice with the Germans.

On June eleventh Churchill flew to a meeting with the French leaders at the Chateau du Muguet near Orleans. Churchill was interested in having the French fight on but Weygand stood firm, bluntly stating that such a suggestion at this point in time was pure 'fantasy'.

A frustrated Winston then indicated that the French must then consider *'guerrilla warfare'* against the Germans until such time as the Americans entered the war.

The response to this thought was spontaneous and issued forth from several of the French in attendance.

'When might that be?'

Churchill had no answer and made none.

After a pregnant pause Petain spoke up stating that such activity would mean the destruction of the country.

Winston, ever the man for oratory, quoted Clemenceaus's famous words, delivered when he was Prime Minister of France during the Great War with Germany: *'I will fight in front of Paris, in Paris, and behind Paris'*.

With quiet elegance Petain replied that in those days the French had a strategic reserve of sixty divisions; now there are none. Making Paris into a ruin would not affect the final event.

The next day when the French Cabinet met, Weygand again called for an armistice to avoid what he foresaw as the danger of both military and civil disorder and the strong possibility of a Communist led upraising occurring in Paris.

Petain then read out a draft proposal wherein he pronounced *'the need to stay in France, to prepare a national revival, and to share the suffering of our people. It is impossible for the Government to abandon French soil without emigrating, without deserting. The duty of the Government is, come what may, to remain in the country, or it could no longer be regarded as the government'*.

Some ministers still opposed the seeking of an alliance.

An angry Weygand berated them for even leaving Paris and like Petain stated he would never leave France.

The government moved next to Bordeaux, repeating the action taken by the leaders of France during the German invasions of eighteen-seventy and nineteen-fourteen.

Here they grappled with the debate to seek an armistice.

A response to French President Lebrun's request to the United States for assistance arrived the next day.

It offered little hope of any such a possibility.

Two telegrams from the English arrived.

The first stated that the British would only agree to the French pursuing an armistice with the Germans if the French fleet was immediately sent to British ports.

The second offered joint nationality for Frenchmen and Englishmen in a Franco/British union.

Reynaud and five of his ministers thought these proposals acceptable.

The remainder of the cabinet did not, instead seeing the offers as insulting and a device to make France subservient to Great Britain, forming it into a type of extra Dominion.

At that point an exasperated and exhausted Reynaud asked President Lebrun to accept his resignation as Prime Minister of France and nominated Petain to take his place.

On June fifteenth a new Cabinet under Petain was formed.

By this point in time the German blitzkrieg was swiftly obliterating all attempts at the defence of France and rolling steadfastly toward Paris.

The Spanish Ambassador was promptly asked to submit to Germany a request to cease hostilities at once and to make known its peace terms.

CHAPER TWENTY-SEVEN

- A Plan Awry? –

After getting Ursula's agreement to assume the position of curator for the proposed storage of valuables and artwork at the family castle, the Count had finalized arrangements with Luftwaffe Major General, Gunter von Schmidt and the first shipment slated for the Castle von Stauffer was already being loaded onto railcars in Paris.

Karl von Stauffer smiled as his daughter was ushered into his office.

Registering the look on her face as she crossed to his desk and flopped uncharacteristically into an armchair across from him he recalled that she had behaved strangely when he'd spoken to her earlier in the day.

She wasn't her usual confident self. Something was wrong and it was serious enough that she wasn't trying to hide it from him.

He waited until his secretary had shut the door between their offices and then returned his attention to Ursula who had given forth with a large sigh as she adjusted herself in the chair.

"What is it…what's wrong?"

Ursula lifted her head and let her eyes meet her father's and filled her lungs before she responded.

"I know it's all been arranged and that I will be letting you down but I'm going to have to back out of the position with the art, Father. I won't be able to do it."

The Count was astounded.

He had already arranged her transfer from the BDM to General von Schmidt's personal staff and the first shipment was scheduled to be sent from Paris within a few days.

Ursula was supposed to be leaving in the morning for Lake Constance to take up her new position at the castle and oversee the construction that was to take place prior to the arrival of the first consignment.

"Why? What on earth is wrong?"

Ursula felt her eyes welling up.

My God! What is wrong with me? I haven't cried for years, and I'm bloody well not going to now!

She straightened in her chair and looked away from her father while she struggled to turn back the threatening tears.

It took her a few moments to pull herself together and the Count could plainly see that she was emotional and struggling to recover.

He averted his eyes as he busied himself reaching for the silver cigarette box on the right side of his desk.

He selected one and lit up in a leisurely manner to give her a few moments to recover.

This kind of reaction he would have expected from his youngest daughter, he would have taken it in stride as expected, but to see Ursula in this state was definitely unsettling.

He exhaled before he looked back up at her.

"Must be pretty serious, you'd better tell me."

Ursula let it out in a flood.

The Count said nothing as she spoke.

He already had some idea of most of the history she was laying out but some of what she was saying was new to him.

He'd had a vague idea that she was seeing the young flyer that she'd met earlier at the meeting at the Castle that he'd arranged as a first step in organizing 'Operation Fatherland'.

His wife Erika had been surmising that something permanent might come of the liaison, but he'd learned long past not to put a great deal of stock in his wife's ongoing evaluations of his daughters' various relationships.

He did however recall Erika mentioning that the fellow was a fighter pilot.

He tuned back to face Ursula who was finally getting to the point.

"...and well, last weekend he asked me to marry him and I said yes Papa. I love him. How can I go to Lake Constance now?

If I do I'll never get to see him. It's difficult enough now for us to get together as it is. Don't you see, if I go to the castle I'll rarely, if ever, get to see him?"

Ursula had run out of steam and she slumped in her chair and filled her lungs for the first time since she begun her obviously rehearsed speech.

The Count ground out his cigarette and sighed.

He was uncomfortable and didn't quite know what to say to her.

Ursula had raised her eyes to meet his and was clearly waiting for him to respond.

"Well, this is all new to me. Just give me a second to think it through. There must be some way we can work this out."

He reached again for the silver cigarette box and pushed it and the matching lighter toward his daughter.

Ursula smoked rarely, mostly only in a social context. He hadn't expected her to accept the offer, but she did.

She selected a cigarette from the box and lit it, giving him a chance to think.

He waited until she had exhaled a cloud of smoke and then, his features composed, he spoke.

"I believe he is a pilot. A Luftwaffe officer then, is he?"

Ursula nodded.

"Yes, he's a Captain."

Her father continued.

"I would assume that if he's proposed marriage the young fellow is as infatuated with you as you are with him. Would that be a fair statement?"

Ursula frowned across at him.

"I would say that our feelings have passed the point of mere infatuation, Father. We love each other, and in answer to your question, yes I believe he loves me as much as I love him; perhaps more."

The Count pursed his lips.

"My experience with these fighter pilots is that they live for their job. Would you say that this fellow…what is his name by the way? If he is about to become my son-in-law I should at least know the fellow's name."

Ursula laughed and under the circumstances, he was pleased to see that she was able to do so.

"Yes Father, you should definitely know his name and that way you can stop referring to him as the *'young fellow'*. His name is Friedrich, Captain Friedrich von Krueger. "

The Count smiled and nodded.

He features hardened and he let his eyes lock with hers.

"And what would be your honest evaluation of Friedrich's preference be if he was forced to decide between his love of flying and his love for you?"

Ursula frowned deeply.

"I don't understand the question, what are you implying father?"

Karl von Stauffer shrugged and held her gaze.

"I'm asking you to tell me what he would do if he had to choose between you and flying. Would he choose to be with you or to fly?"

Ursula was nobody's fool. She smiled for the first time since she had entered his office.

"If he had to pick one or the other he would pick me.

We have already discussed that point. Yes he loves to fly but he has been doing it for some time and has quite honestly expressed the realization that he has reached the point of exhaustion.

He has confided in me that he would like to move onto a new challenge, something different, and of course, when we marry, we would naturally want to spend our time together."

Her father raised his hands, placed the palms together and began to rub them.

"That being the case, I think I might be able to work this out.

You leave it with me and go ahead and catch your train in the morning.

* * * * *

- A Stop in France –

Hitler spent very little time with Laval once his train arrived at Montoire in Vichy France.

The Fuhrer treated the obligatory welcome from the Deputy Leader as his due and then they met briefly to complete the arrangements for Hitler's planned upcoming meeting with his German controlled puppet, the French Great War hero, Marshal Petain.

Hitler also used this short conference with Laval to advance the German intention to reduce France to a state of complete servitude to the Nazi Reich.

Hitler and Goring had determined that all Nazi occupied countries absorbed into the New Reich were to be promptly stripped of their wealth, valuables and raw materials and required to supply Germany with a steady supply of slave labour.

Vichy France, although not occupied, was to be no exception.

Hitler was fully prepared to use the force of full troop occupation to subjugate the Vichy French if that becomes necessary to reach his pre-set goals as to the rape of all subjugated territories.

During the brief meeting he found Laval subservient to a degree that left him confident that the plan for the Nazi pillage of Vichy could be readily fulfilled without his having to resort to a full occupation of the French territory, so called 'unoccupied' by German troops.

Hitler was more than satisfied with the exchange with Laval and as his train pulled out of the Montoire station that evening, all was right in the world and he was in a relaxed and confident frame of mind.

The Fuhrer's private train heads out into the French countryside for the overnight trip to the French border town of Hendaye which is located in south-western France near Biarritz.

This is where he will meet with Spain's new fascist leader, General Franco.

Hitler intends to deal with Franco personally in order to rectify what the Fuhrer considers as the previously unsatisfactory exchanges that have been conducted between the diplomats representing Spain and Nazi Germany.

He needs Franco to cease vacillating and quickly fall into line
to join the Axis powers and to play his part in the taking of
Gibraltar to assist the Axis powers in eradicating the British
presence in the Mediterranean.

The small border town of Hendaye is an unlikely choice for a
meeting of this importance but has been selected due to practical
necessity, for this is the point where the narrow-gauge French rail
tracks give way to the wide-gauge style of track used in Spain.

The meeting between the two leaders is scheduled for two in
the afternoon and typical of German rail punctuality, the Fuhrer's
train arrives slightly ahead of schedule.

There is no sign of Franco's train on the other platform.

Due to his mood and the clear afternoon sky Hitler, who
normally demands punctuality from others, is not affronted by this
failure of the Spanish train to make it to the station at the agreed
time.

A smiling Hitler accepts the situation as yet another example
of Spanish inefficiency and suggests to his staff that it should have
been expected.

The German Foreign Minister's personal train pulled in
behind Hitler' train and he and Ribbentrop strolled about the
platform discussing the impending conference.

Hitler made it clear that he would do the talking and Joachim
was to remain in the background, available to answer any questions
and provide any information the Fuhrer may require.

Hitler is planning on offering the Spanish dictator eventual
territorial gains as a part of the incentive to come on side with the
Axis.

These would be coming from what were currently Vichy
French holdings. The Germans had not discussed such future
intended land transfers with the *'Vichy French'* yet, as he was
eager to keep them onside in the short term until the British had
been marginalised in the Mediterranean.

He made it clear to Joachim that nothing was to be put into
writing about these intended territorial transfers as the Vichy
French would certainly be shocked and upset at such a suggestion

and if the territories in question heard about it they would in all probability transfer their alliance from Vichy to De Gaulle.

He wanted Vichy kept in the dark until Gibraltar had been taken and the Mediterranean had been locked down.

Hitler was scheduled to meet Petain on the return trip to Germany and at that time intended to induce the Marshal to instruct the Vichy French holdings in the Mediterranean to commence overt hostilities against the British forces billeted in the area.

Things were going very well for Nazi Germany, and Hitler was in extremely good spirits as he awaited the arrival of the Spanish train.

* * * * *

- Franco Arrives –

The armoured Spanish train carrying Franco rolled onto the International Bridge crossing the Bidassoa River at just after three in the afternoon.

The delay in the arrival had been intentional.

Franco knew exactly what Hitler wanted from him. He had known the details for some time.

Franco had come from simple roots and with the assistance of a lot of luck and often being in the right place at the right time he had managed to become dictator of Spain.

He was at his pinnacle, and he wanted to stay there.

He had no intention of setting his sights so high that he stood any chance of being kicked back down the ladder.

General Franco was a small, rotund, insignificant man whose tough opportunism had recently achieved greatness beyond his wildest dreams.

Franco strongly leaned toward aligning himself with the Axis; he was after all, a Fascist Dictator. However, he had joined the Spanish *'Falangists'* because he saw that party as the winning side in Spain's civil war, not from a strong belief in the principles of the movement.

Under the current world situation he considered it very likely that a direct Spanish alliance with Hitler's Axis could well be the straw that broke the camel's back for Spain and for him personally, it could well end of up as being a bridge too far.

Franco does not have a political death wish.

Since the day he'd taken control of his country he had been carefully dancing with Germany's Nazi leader, keeping to the *'Fascist'* tune but always taking care to keep out of a direct embrace.

He has every intention of continuing to talk the talk but he has absolutely no intention of walking the walk.

He isn't prepared to jeopardize either Spain or his own position by committing to one side, in what he believes will soon become a world war.

He and Spain will do whatever it takes to remain neutral until the outcome of that war can be guaranteed.

By arriving late he hoped to put Hitler off his game.

It is the first step in this new dance with the Nazi leader.

Franco is setting the stage for what he has determined will turn out to be a friendly conference, but one that will produce no change whatsoever in the current relationship between Spain and Germany.

Franco has no support among his own people for his decision to remain neutral in the war.

The members of his political party support the premise that Spain should join the Axis powers.

His own son-in-law, Serrano Suner, whom he has made Spain's Foreign Minister is staunchly pro-German and is convinced that the Nazi military is unbeatable.

He argues that point and pushes for an immediate alliance with Germany.

This, despite the ill-treatment he'd recently received in Berlin at the hands of von Ribbentrop.

The majority of Franco's generals agree with that theme but Franco remains sceptical.

On this trip to meet the Fuhrer he tells them that Hitler has failed to invade the United Kingdom and that anything short of an overwhelming invasion will mean that the British will not back down from the Nazis.

He is convinced that if necessary, the English will move the Royal Family and government to the safety of Canada, but that they will not give up the fight.

Additionally, he believes that the British will eventually draw the United States in on her side of the conflict and when that takes place the war will become one of attrition and therein not one Germany is likely to win.

Franco wanted to be on the winning side but he was looking over the long term, and his gut told him he had to remain neutral and on the sidelines until there was no doubt whatsoever which side was going to come out on top.

At the same time, he did not want to see Spain face the same fate as other countries who had failed to buckle under to the Nazis. By this time there was quite a list of those countries that had disappointed Hitler and had subsequently been crushed under the German military boot.

Therefore he had no intention of openly refusing Hitler outright and risking a German invasion of his civil-war-weakened state.

Instead he had to convince Hitler that he was completely onside with the Nazis and although, through no fault of his own but because of his country's crippling civil war, he could not commit immediately and that it was simply a matter of time before he would be in a position to join the Axis in their just struggle for a new and better world.

As his train pulled into the little station next to Hitler's the stage was set and to all intents and proposes General Franco was about to give what he prayed would be the performance of his life.

* * * * *

- Spanish/German Negotiations –

Pomp and Ceremony, the show was on, accompanied by a rousing military band as Franco stepped down from the train and crossed toward Hitler.

The Spanish leader immediately took the imitative, beginning with a long speech, richly spiced with good wishes and heartfelt assertions and declarations of Spain's historic affinity with and undying support of German people.

Spain was, without question, in full support of the aims of the Axis in the current situation and would unquestionably be honoured to fight at Germany's side.

Before inviting Hitler aboard his train for fulsome discussions, Franco laid it on so thick it was dripping.

The two sides sat down together - leaders, Foreign Ministers and interpreters - and Franco again opened the conversation, continuing on from his earlier speech.

'Yes, Spain would gladly fight at Germany's side'; however there were difficulties in doing so and these difficulties were already known to the Fuhrer.

Spain was suffering food shortages due to the stiff anti-Axis sentiment from America and Europe.

'Therefore, Spain must mark time and often look kindly toward things of which she thoroughly disapproves'.

This, he reminded Hitler was not unlike the position that the Italians had faced earlier in the autumn; when *'Il Duce'* had been forced hold back from joining the Axis, despite what had certainly been Mussolini's inherent wish to immediately join Germany in declaring war.

This was of course not unlike Franco's own current wish, but he, as had been Mussolini, was forced by unfortunate circumstances and conditions, to remain neutral in the short term.

It was not by choice that Franco was unable to instantly join with the Axis, but because of and for many of the same reasons, as had the Italians earlier.

Unhappily Franco was being forced by circumstances over which he had no control to adopt *'the same attitude toward the war as had Italy in the past autumn'*.

Hitler was obviously thrown off by this comparison to Italy's delay in overtly supporting the Nazis when he'd specifically asked Mussolini to do so.

He spoke up to change the topic, telling Franco that in exchange for Spanish collaboration in the war Germany intended to give Gibraltar to Spain once it had been taken, in addition to various coastal territories in Africa.

Franco did not immediately respond to this stimulus.

He sat quietly, his face a blank page for several seconds, then in a carefully calculated form, he returned to his pre-set discourse.

Poor Spain would receive the brunt of the effects of the British Forces allied in the Mediterranean should they enter the war at this point. How in God's name could they be expected to fend off the British in view of their current state of ill-preparedness?

The civil war had devastated his small country.

He had to have thousands of tons of wheat immediately just to fend off starvation for his people.

Would Germany be able to provide that wheat before Spain committed to face the British?

Spain had no large guns on her coasts to fend off the British navy, and would also need anti-aircraft guns to deal with the Royal air force.

Could he expect to receive these from Germany in the quantities needed in the near future?

Franco watched Hitler carefully and each time it seemed like the Fuhrer was prepared to speak the Spanish Dictator's discourse would change tack, bouncing from topic to topic.

How would Spain be compensated for the loss of the Canary Islands? Surely the Germans could see that this horrific loss would be inevitable.

He was of a mind with the Fuhrer.

Of course it was only fair that Spain should occupy Gibraltar, but it was clearly unacceptable for Gibraltar to be given to Spain by a foreign occupier.

No, it would have to be taken by Spain herself, and that would not be militarily possible without German assistance, planning and the provision of military training and equipment.

As to the African territories, he certainly agreed with the Fuhrer that these should by right fall under Spanish control after a successful campaign.

However, while he believed that the British could be driven out of parts of Africa, perhaps even out to the desert regions, his own personal experience told him that it was highly unlikely they could be driven off the continent.

He then expressed doubts that bombing alone would bring the British to their knees.

He suggested it might perhaps cause the British government to retire to Canada but that would simply put them nearer to the United States and therein further their endeavours to bring that nation into the war on the side of the allies.

He inquires as to how the Fuhrer's plans for the invasion of England were coming along?

Hitler couldn't believe his ears.

Frustrated beyond belief the Fuhrer leapt to his feet and exclaimed that there was obviously no point in continuing the discussions.

Franco was obviously unaffected by the uncontrolled outburst, which only served to increase Hitler's frustration level.

There was a pregnant pause in deathly silence while Hitler regained control and then sat back down, took a deep breath and calmly began to press his agenda for a treaty between the two countries.

Franco's response was immediate.

'Certainly, just as soon as Germany supplied the wheat, once the necessary armaments had been provided by the Germans and as long as Spain was extended the same courtesy as the Italians had been over the making of the final decision as to when it should enter the war on the side of the Axis; with those points met, of course they would then eagerly sign such an agreement'.

They were back at square one - just where Franco wanted them to be.

The meeting was promptly adjourned and an inwardly raging Hitler returned in disgust to his private car on his own train.

CHAPTER TWENTY-EIGHT

- Expanding Family –

Erika had ordered special preparations for dinner for the immediate family for that evening.

There was to be one absentee and two additions to the normal sitting.

Eric was in Kiel and physically unable to attend.

Ursula had agreed with her mother that her Luftwaffe Captain, who was in Berlin on a short leave until the next day, would be invited with the agreement between mother and daughter that the couple would officially announce their engagement to the family that night and Gabriella had specifically asked her to widen the circle to include Doctor Konrad Kauffmann, which Erika had of course immediately agreed to do.

When Ursula and the Count arrived at the house, Karl von staffer escorted his daughter into the formal drawing room where he found his wife sharing cocktails with Gabriella and Konrad Kauffmann.

He exchanged greetings and then left an uncharacteristically morose Ursula to join them as he excused himself to make a brief phone call from the privacy of the library.

His paused long enough to pour himself a stiff scotch from the side table to which he added a short pour of water and then left the room to go down the hall and make his telephone call.

Seated comfortably at his large desk, which was tucked into one corner of the library, he did justice to a good portion of his drink and then looked up the number for and dialled the home number of his good friend, Luftwaffe Major General, Gunter von Schmidt.

About fifteen minutes later he re-entered the drawing room and asked to have a private word with Ursula.

This request did not surprise the others in the room as Karl and his eldest daughter had been spending a good amount of time together of late over the planning for her new position.

Ursula carried her drink with her as she and her father went out and walked briskly down the hallway toward the library.

Once they had moved out of hearing range the Count turned to her and smiled broadly before speaking in soft voice.

"Problem solved, it will take a little time, probably about a month, but Captain Friedrich von Krueger will be receiving new orders tomorrow.

He is to be promoted Major and his new posting will be that of Commandant of the top-secret Luftwaffe security detachment that has been assigned to the duty of providing safekeeping for the state property during the period it is being stored at Castle von Stauffer."

A look of absolute surprise filled Ursula's face and was almost immediacy replaced by one of relief followed by tears of joy.

She threw her arms around her father and hugged him tightly, something she had not done in more than ten years.

When they parted moments later he handed her a clean handkerchief.

"Perhaps you should go tidy up a little before you go back in. Gabriella and Konrad will be joining us shortly."

Ursula dabbed her tears away and a brilliant smile broke out on her face.

"Can I tell him tonight…I will be leaving in the morning and I won't see him for awhile?"

The Count smiled and nodded,

"I don't see why not, but be sure to explain to him that he should keep the news to himself until he receives his promotion and should be appropriately surprised and pleased when he makes Major and gets his new orders tomorrow.

Away you go; they could arrive any time now."

* * * * *

- Foreign Ministers –

After Hitler left the meeting, the two Foreign Ministers, Joachim von Ribbentrop of Germany and Serrano Suner of Spain, walked together along the platform toward the Fuhrer's train.

They were discussing the meeting and the fruitless outcome and von Ribbentrop was trying to make some headway.

He complained to the Spaniard that Hitler was justly disappointed in what had transpired; explaining that the purpose of the trip had been to determine if Spanish needs and the Vichy French position could be balanced to meet the desires of both parties.

He indicated that The Fuhrer had Spain's interests at heart and was simply trying to act as an arbitrator with his two like-minded friends and that surely the Spanish Foreign Minister and his master, General Franco, could see that.

What difficulty could there be to a mutual agreement to sign a secret protocol to which Il Duce could later append his signature. This was a win-win situation for everyone involved, surely.

I have at hand the answer to all our desires.

Joachim then produced a copy of the proposal in question which had been translated into Spanish.

You will see here how the Fuhrer has planned carefully so all involved can benefit.

The protocol determined that Spain was to receive French colonial territories *'to the extent that France can be indemnified from British colonial possessions'*.

A look of surprise flooded Suner's face and he beamed, expressing pleasure at the fact the Germany's posture toward France had obviously changed.

Then he frowned and pointed out to von Ribbentrop that the document was not clear as to exactly what specific territories Spain would receive by entering the war.

He then expressed the opinion that under the circumstances the document was an affront to the Spanish people and Franco would demand these specifics included before any such protocol could be signed.

The leader of Spain would therefore need to study the

document in depth and provide a much more exacting determination of what Spain was to receive before agreeing to sign the document and it would only be reasonable, prior to doing so, to make the required changes in the document to reflect these specifics.

Before Joachim could respond, the Spanish Foreign Minister excused himself and darted off with the document, heading at a good pace back toward the Spanish train.

Von Ribbentrop, who was flabbergasted at such a response, was left speechless with his mouth hanging open.

* * * * *

- State Dinner –

The determined Germans invited the Spanish delegation to a state dinner that evening.

The meal was to be held in the Fuhrer's personal dining car.

The Spanish accepted the invitation with grace and expressed delight.

During the meal both Franco and his Foreign Minister behaved as privileged and genteel guests, conversing warmly and acting in an ingratiating fashion.

It was as if the earlier meeting had never taken place and by the time the meal was reaching its end Hitler felt there had been a change in the Spanish position and that they were finally coming to their senses.

By the time they rose from the table, Hitler was again in a good mood.

He cornered Franco and invited him to have a private discussion and a gregarious Franco eagerly agreed.

The two leaders talked privately at one end of the car for nearly two hours, during which time Franco pleasantly frustrated Hitler's every attempt to urge the signing of the protocol.

Franco simply would not agree with the German leader's reading of any given situation.

He talked Hitler in circles time and time again.

For example, Hitler's first target was to be Gibraltar.

Franco thought it should be the Suez Canal.

Hitler's renewed good mood faded rapidly and he eventually lost his temper.

Franco remained emotionless throughout, simply smiling and nodding genially as Hitler ranted.

Hitler left the dining car in a huff, and the Spaniards said their goodbyes and returned to their own train.

The Fuhrer stormed after the guests had left, shouting at everyone around him, issuing a flood of disparaging comments about the little Spanish dictator and threatening to break off all negotiations with the Spaniards.

He left Joachim in charge and ordered his train to prepare to leave the station and head back for his meeting with Marshal Petain.

After this row was over von Ribbentrop cornered Suner and his aids aboard the German Foreign Minister's own train and again tried to force the protocol upon them.

He got nowhere fast and quickly lost his patience and at that point he promptly dismissed them out of hand with the instruction that they were to sign the document forthwith and have it returned to the Germans no later than eight the next morning.

In the morning Suner decided not to meet at the appointed time with von Ribbentrop.

Instead he sent an aid with the updated document.

Joachim was so angry over this snub that his hands trembled while he read the adjusted document which now reflected that Spain was to be given the French territory of Morocco, among other changes in the original protocol.

When he saw that section he went ballistic, throwing the Spanish aide off the train with the instructions to resubmit a new draft of the agreement along the lines of the original.

Incensed, he then left the train and took a staff car to the nearest airport to catch a plane that would hopefully enable him to reach the scheduled meeting with Hitler and Petain on time.

CHAPTER TWENTY-NINE

– Bended Knee –

As soon at the family was seated and before the first course was served, Ursula announced her engagement to Friedrich.

Congratulations spilled out and wine glasses were exchanged champagne flutes which were then liberally filled and raised in toast.

When the last course had been served and the servants had left the room, Dr. Konrad Kauffmann, who was seated on Gabriella's left between her and her mother, got up and lifted his chair back out of the way before turning toward Gabriella as he dropped to one knee.

He then pulled the ring box from his pocket, flipped the top open and held it out to her.

The large diamond sparkled brilliantly as it picked up and reflected the soft light from the massive chandelier centered over the table.

"It would appear that I could have planned this for a better time. I had no intention of stealing anyone else's thunder tonight, but I'm afraid with this war on, we really don't have a lot of that particular commodity available to us.

Gabriella, will you do me the honour of becoming my wife?"

* * * * *

– Congratulations –

The men were in the library enjoying brandy and cigars over yet another round of congratulatory handshakes and backslapping.

The ladies were in the lounge indulging in a second bottle of champagne and Erika had taken centre stage as wedding plans were being sketched out.

Konrad was soon to leave for Norway on his new assignment and Friedrich's leave was over the next day and he would be returning to his squadron, if only to receive his new assignment at the Castle von Stauffer.

As matriarch, Erika was in her element and despite the challenge she was determined, before the evening was through, to have everyone's input as to a date and location for the now accepted notion of a joint marriage of her daughters.

* * * * *

- Petain –

On June twenty-second the French signed an armistice with Germany giving the Nazis control over the north and west of the country including Paris and the entire Atlantic coastline. It left the remaining approximately two-fifths of the French territory unoccupied.

On July tenth the French Chamber of Deputies and the Senate met together as a *'Congres'* to ratify the armistice.

At this meeting the Presidents of both chambers expressed the opinion that constitutional reform was necessary. The *'Congres'* voted on the suggestion and overwhelmingly agreed to grant the Cabinet the authority to draw up a new constitution, therein voting the *'French Third Republic'* out of existence.

The next day Petain assumed unquestionable powers as *'Head of State'*.

At that time, in an attempt to soften the change, Petain stated that: *'this is not ancient Rome and I have no wish to be Caesar'*.

Petain immediately took centre stage in the French political leadership.

Due to his background, temperament and education, Petain held robust, intransigent views. In addition, he now had absolute power.

The Cabinet had given him a platform and he didn't hesitate to use it.

His opening salvo was aimed at blaming the French Third

Republic and what he referred to as its *'endemic corruption'*, for the defeat of France.

He set up a regime that was clearly authoritarian and shot through with Fascist qualities. The previous republican motto of *'Liberte, egalite, fraternite'* (Liberty, equality, fraternity) was promptly changed to *'Travail, famille, patrie'* (Work, family, fatherland).

Fascist leaning and far right wing conservative factions now among those in government began an ambitious program which became known as the *'National Revolution'*.

This concept strongly rejected the former government's secular and liberal traditions in favour of a strongly authoritarian, paternalistic, Catholic society.

Petain held himself well clear of endorsing the term *'revolution'* to signify what was to him, simply a strictly conservative movement but his hesitation to use the word did not stop him from not only supporting, but often initiating the right wing addenda.

What had been a Republic had quickly become a State.

He told the French that the New France would be *'a social hierarchy'*, rejecting the *'false idea of the natural equality of men'*.

Petain's government used its new powers to bring in harsh measures.

They dismissed all republican civil servants, installed exceptional jurisdictions and proclaimed anti-Semitic laws while imprisoning opponents and foreign refugees.

Censorship was imposed. Freedom of expression and thought were effectively abolished with the reinstatement of the crime of *'felony of opinion'*.

This new French government was internationally recognized, the USA being one of the first countries to make such a determination.

* * * * *

- Montoire –

A still fuming Hitler arrived at Montoire in France for his meeting with Petain and was awaiting the Frenchman's arrival aboard his train.

The Marshal had recently changed his title from Premier to Head of State for Vichy in a step to visibly distance himself from the previous republican government.

Before Hitler's arrival at Montoire, Petain had received a call from Franco.

The Spanish leader's intention in making the call was to further muddy the waters and thwart Hitler's plans for Africa, in order to give him additional fuel to reasonably withhold taking the step of making an imminent commitment to bring Spain into the war on the side of the Axis powers.

Franco hinted at a Nazi intention to pressure the Marshal into playing into the German's hands with regard to French territory in Africa by involving himself in the ongoing peace talks with the occupied French territory and the Germans.

The Spanish dictator had advised Petain to avoid damaging his sterling reputation as a hero of the Great War, suggesting that he have no part in the signing of the final peace agreement with the Germans.

'You are the hero of Verdun. Don't let your name be mingled with the others who have been defeated.'

Franco pleaded with Petain to hold himself entirely separate from these negotiations, urging him to *'make your age your excuse'* and *'let those who lost the war sign the peace'*.

Pertain had responded with the simple facts as he saw them.

'I know General but my country calls me and I am hers. It may be the last service that I can do for her.'

* * * * *

- Command Performance –

An impeccably uniformed Marshal Petain, accompanied by Laval, arrived at the railway station for the scheduled meeting with Hitler.

As Petain entered the station, he was greeted by Germany's top military man, *'Generalfeldmarschall'* (Field Marshal) Wilhelm Bodewin Johann Gustav Keitel, head of the *'Oberkommando der Wehrmacht'* (Supreme Command of the German Armed Forces) OKW, the de Facto War Minister under Hitler.

Keitel was accompanied by Joachim von Ribbentrop who had been successful in arranging for a flight that could get him to the meeting on time.

Keitel and the Marshal exchanged salutes.

Keitel then led Petain past the German honour guard and von Ribbentrop and Laval dropped in behind.

Stiff-backed, silent and with his eyes locked directly ahead of him, Petain moved rapidly past the guard and through the station.

As he emerged from the other side and onto the platform fronting Hitler's train, The Fuhrer appeared and walked toward him with an outstretched hand.

The two men shook hands, Hitler looking slightly downward at the shorter Frenchman.

Their expressions were formal and in no way welcoming, after which Hitler led Petain to his private coach and the two men sat down facing each other with the German interpreter between them and their entourages seated nearby.

Hitler was the victor and he led the exchange between the two men, opening with the statement that he was aware that Petain had not been among the French leaders who had declared war on Germany and concluded by saying that *'if this were not the case, this talk could not have taken place.'*

Hitler then moved on to enumerate the French misdeeds which had been committed by those who had made the determination to declare war against Germany before repeating to Petain what he'd recently said to Franco.

We have already won the war; England is beaten and will eventually have to admit it.

He then alluded to the fact that someone was going to have to pay for the resulting war and that responsibility would have to fall on the shoulders of one of the two initiators of the conflict, those being France or England.

If it was to be England who faced this horrific burden then France would find itself in the position of taking her place in the world that was her due and not only be allowed to maintain her colonial empire but retake her territory in the central African colonies that had foolishly chosen to follow De Gaulle.

Petain sat straight-backed and silent to this point, at no time agreeing to or supporting these comments

In an attempt to draw him out, Hitler asked Petain how he felt about the English attacks on the French fleet.

Petain, without emotion, replied that the attacks affronted most Frenchmen but that his country was in no position to wage another war and promptly changed the subject by making a request that Germany reach agreement for a final peace treaty *'so that France may be clear about her fate and the two million French prisoners of war may return to their families as soon as possible.'*

Hitler made no direct response to this request, instead indicating that France should give serious consideration to the entering of the war on the side of the Axis.

Petain again made no direct reply to that veiled suggestion, instead professing to a personal admiration for the Fuhrer, expressing the wish for collaboration with the Germans on numerous levels and leaving the impression that he agreed with many of Hitler's opinions.

* * * * *

- Return to Germany –

When Hitler was unhappy, those around him were nervous and despondent.

A cloud of dejection hung heavily over the Fuhrer's train as it headed back toward the German border.

Hitler had made the trip to Hendaye to bring the Spanish dictator onside with a commitment to join the Axis in the war.

He had made the trip to Montoire to bring the Vichy French into the war firmly on the side of Germany.

Franco had danced around him and made no real

commitment.

Petain had espoused pleasantries and been complimentary to Hitler personally but still intended to remain neutral.

To add insult to injury, The Fuhrer had received a letter from Mussolini as his train crossed out of France and entered Germany. The letter was dated a little less than a week before.

It contained an intense tirade against the French of such magnitude that Hitler became concerned that if such words of condemnation ever managed to reach the ears of the French he would never be able to achieve a future agreement with Petain to join the Axis powers in the fight against the Allies.

Hitler immediately ordered von Ribbentrop to move up his scheduled meeting with Mussolini in Florence, to October twenty-eighth.

Joachim's telephone call to Rome moments later threw the Italians into alarm.

What had happened during the conference with Petain that would necessitate Hitler rushing to see Mussolini? What kind of agreement had the Nazis made with the French that might thwart Italy's claims against France?

The new date was subsequently agreed upon and Hitler ordered his train to change direction and head for Munich instead of Berlin to offer him a chance to rest and prepare for the updated trip to meet Mussolini.

* * * * *

- Duplicity –

On the afternoon of October twenty-second as Hitler was preparing to leave for Italy he received word from the German Military attaché in Rome that the Italians were intending to attack Greece the next morning.

Hitler was at his wits end.

On his last meeting with Il Duce he had made it very clear that he did not want Italy to take on any additional military campaigns in the near future.

As they ate dinner that evening von Ribbentrop, in support of his Fuhrer, voiced his displeasure at the news.

'The Italians will never get anywhere against the Greeks in the autumn rains and winter snows. Besides the consequences of war in the Balkans, are quite unpredictable. The Fuhrer intends at all costs to hold up this crazy scheme of Duce's, so we are to go to Italy at once, to talk to Mussolini personally.'

In line with this view Hitler's staff drew up a crisp message of condemnation for the invasion of Greece with the intention that it be immediately forwarded to Mussolini under The Fuhrer's signature.

Everyone in the inner circle was surprised when Hitler refused to sign the missive.

The Fuhrer had by this point been given time for sober second thought in respect to his initial reaction.

It wasn't that Hitler wasn't still angry that his advice had been dismissed as inconsequential. Quite the contrary. But Mussolini was his strongest ally and he was hesitant to risk jeopardizing that relationship by issuing a personal chastisement of a decision already taken by Il Duce.

As his personal train *'Fuhrersonderzug Amerika'* raced south he still had hope that he would somehow be able to reverse, even in these final stages, this foolish move on the part of Mussolini, before it became a reality.

That slim hope was shattered as *'Amerika'* traveled through Bologna. At ten o'clock, Hitler received a message to the effect that the Italians had just marched into Greece.

An exasperated Hitler, still hesitant to publicly condemn the Italian leader, lashed out at those around him, spewing profanities and heaping scorn on the German Diplomatic core and liaison staffs for failing him yet again.

He eventually worked himself up to such a state that he shifted his remarks and began berating the Italians.

He spoke in general terms however, never singling out Mussolini personally.

CHAPTER THIRTY

- Bordeaux –

Night was falling as Karl von Stauffer arrived in Bordeaux aboard his personal rail cars which were attached to a freight train returning empty to France from Germany before preparing to make the return trip to Germany with a refill of consigned plunder.

Although he was the only member of his family on board, he was using both cars in order to facilitate the safe transport out of Germany of a good number of German citizens who were interested in immigrating to South America.

The group aboard the Count's cars, primarily of Jewish extraction, consisted of the last assemblage of a considerable number of men who would be making up the cargo that would shortly be boarding a neutral, Brazilian freighter for a trip back across the Atlantic.

Like those that had gone before it, this freighter was nothing to look at, having just delivered a Brazilian cargo consisting of copper, nickel and iron destined for rail shipment to factories in Germany, however it suited the purposes of *'Operation Fatherland'* perfectly.

When the Nazis came to power, they had quickly worked towards removing all Jews within the New Reich from positions of importance and over time, with a few exceptions, all Jews period.

A good number of these people were at the top of their fields, many were the world's best minds in their areas of expertise.

While the Nazis did not value these people, the members of 'Operation Fatherland' did.

Karl had considered their removal from leadership within the various fields of endeavour by the Nazis, simply because of their race, nothing more than a politically dogmatic and stupid exercise in fulfilling Nazi Party policy.

He and others within the organization had been quietly and

prudently offering these men, and a few women, a chance to start a new life, in a new country, where they could safely continue their research in their chosen fields.

Acceptance of this offer by these various individuals had obviously been a leap of faith.

For them it meant going to a new location and trusting that the advanced facilities and materials required for further research and development in their disciplines would be in place to allow them to continue to work for the betterment of themselves and the fatherland. Never mind that this was a country whose new Nazi masters had recently named them human garbage and *'persona non gratis'*.

Under the current circumstances available to them in Nazi Germany, it seemed, if not an easy choice, really the only choice for them to make. This was not the first of what was anticipated to be several groups of their kind, about to board ship here in Bordeaux to begin the long voyage to Brazil.

Publicly, von Stauffer was seen to be aiding in the plan to help the new German government to move Jews out of Germany.

Privately, Karl had arrived in Bordeaux to see them off and wish them well, for he recognized them not as the pariahs the Nazis did, but instead as the long-term key to Germany's future in a rapidly changing world.

A distant cousin of Karl's would be meeting the ship in Brazil

* * * * *

- Florence –

The sky was heavily overcast and rain, at times heavy, was falling as Hitler's train slowed and began to roll along the line into the swastika festooned station in Florence at eleven in the morning on October twenty-eighth, nineteen-forty.

The mood of Hitler and those aboard the train tended to match the weather, dark and gloomy.

The Fuhrer had moved to stand by a window and was looking

out as the first of the well-wishers standing at the edge of the tracks raised their hands to give the Fascist salute and wave at his slowly moving train.

The crowd of waving arms began to grow in size as the train edged closer into the station and the sight of hundreds of Italian citizens enthusiastically braving the dreary downfall, many huddled under their umbrellas, quickly brought about a change in Hitler's demeanour.

The Fuhrer had the window unlocked and lowered as a smile formed on his face and he raised his hand and began to acknowledge the fervent waves of welcome.

Moments later the train slowed yet again as the platform came into view and the crowd swelled yet again, becoming a sea of arms and hands, raised in the Nazi salute.

Many of the women in the mass of humanity before the German leader could be seen wiping tears of joy from their eyes and as the train came to a stop the civilian throng was replaced by a glut of uniforms, arms raised in salute which gave way to a red carpet backed by floral arrangements upon which Mussolini stood waiting.

He was backed by his son-in-law, the foreign Minister.

Hitler moved to the door of his private car and dressed in uniform and wearing a leather greatcoat he dropped briskly down out of the coach and onto the red carpet.

Il Duce hurried forward to greet Hitler and the two men exchanged the fascist salute and then Hitler reached out with both hands to accept Mussolini's extended right hand, grasped it and shook it warmly.

As they were shaking Mussolini leaned forward slightly and eagerly blurted.

'Fuhrer, we are on the march!'

Other members of the German entourage had by this time stepped down from the train and an array of necessary exchange of salutes took place, giving a clearly displeased Hitler an opportunity to bite his tongue.

The Fuhrer made no response, instead he moved away from Il Duce to exchange salutes with the others in Mussolini's welcoming delegation.

This done he turned and moved back to stand by Mussolini.

Without speaking the two leaders began to lead their delegations along the platform, past the Italian honour guard which Hitler acknowledged, reviewing and saluting as he strode by.

The two men exited the station and entered an open car which was sitting at the front of an awaiting motorcade.

The line of vehicles quickly filled and drove off toward the Palazzo Pitti where the meeting was to take place, slowly passing through the enthusiastic crowds lining the streets, standing in the rain, shouting their adulation: '

'Fuhrer, Heil Fuhrer... Duce, Duce!'

Once the cars had delivered their charges to the Palazzo and the meeting began, a buoyant Mussolini made no further mention of Greece.

Il Duce considered his failure to advise Hitler about his intended move on Greece as a *'tit-for-tat'* with Hitler in view of the Fuhrer's dispatch of German troops into Romanian just days after their meeting in the Brenner Pass, where the German leader had agreed to take a hands off approach to the Balkans.

At the time of the Nazi move into Romania a surprised and angry Mussolini had commented to his son-in-law, Ciano that *'Hitler always faces me with a fait acc*ompli'.

Later referring to the Italian invasion of Greece he remarked to Ciano *'This time I am going to pay him back in his own coin. He will find out from the papers that I have occupied Greece. In this way the equilibrium will be re-established.'*

For his part, Hitler did not raise the matter of Greece.

Instead the German leader spent the time giving Il Duce his take on his recent meetings with Franco, Laval and Petain,

Of Franco he described their meeting as a nightmare of astounding dimensions and remarked that rather than repeat it he would: *'prefer to have three or four teeth out'*.

He advised Mussolini that the Spanish leader had been *'very vague'* about his intentions to join the Axis and had left Hitler wondering how on earth the man had ever managed to become Spain's leader.

He shared his impression of Petain, who he considered to be an honourable and dignified soldier and that of Laval who Hitler felt demonstrated a layer of false servility that suggested future unreliability.

The meeting, filled with smiles and warmth on both sides, went on for some time and the cries for viewings from the massive crowd waiting outside under the rain in the large plaza in front of the palazzo meant that the two leaders repeatedly acquiesced to the pleas and appeared together on the balcony overhead to receive the adulation each considered his due and thereby appease the sodden mass of enthusiastic admirers.

The conference finished with Hitler fortifying his earlier promises made at Brenner Pass wherein he had assured Mussolini that he would: *'on no account conclude peace with France if the claims of Italy were not completely satisfied'* and Il Duce reiterating his long held belief that their countries were and would always be in full harmony.

Back aboard his private train and headed for Germany Hitler, ensconced within the safety of his own circle, gave vent to an honest expression of his displeasure over the Italian decision to invade Greece.

'Why on earth didn't Mussolini attack Malta or Crete? That would make some sense in the context of their war with England in the Mediterranean, particularly with the Italian troops in such straits in North Africa that they had just requested a German armoured division'.

Radiating out from Hitler, a dark cloud of melancholy quickly returned to encompass those riding within the *'Fuhrersonderzug', 'Amerika',* as it made its way back to Germany through the snow-capped Alps.

The Fuhrer's eager expectations for his diplomatic forays over the past few days had come to very little.

On his own over the past few months, he had become the historic master of national expansion by way of military force. He'd surpassed the iconic leadership of both Napoleon and Alexander, and he had done it alone.

Now, in order to complete his creation of a new world order

he wished support, not major support, and not support that should have been predictably or reasonably withheld.

By traveling to Hendaye, Montoire and Florence he had come to three supposed like-minded national leaders to seek from them agreement with what seemed to him as both sensible and obviously self-serving co-operation with his immediate plans, and what had he received by way of support?

The ineffective little man that he had personally helped to win the Spanish civil war and therein the leadership of that country had failed to join the Axis powers as he had previously promised.

The new leader of a conquered France, a man who currently enjoyed his position only because Hitler had found it acceptable, had decided that his country was in no position to join the fight against England.

His, so far steadfast, Ally had seen fit to disregard his sound advice and attack Greece and in so doing was foolishly jeopardizing Hitler's plans to destroy the British strength in the Mediterranean theatre.

Additionally, Goring's ongoing Luftwaffe attack against England was showing little sign of forcing the British to the peace table as had been promised but was slowly but surely decimating German airpower which he was counting on for air cover in his upcoming move east to gain necessary German 'Lebensraum'.

A dismayed Hitler was seemingly inconsolable as he complained vehemently about the obvious stupidity of those with whom he was forced to deal.

In the end, it was Franco, unappreciative of Germany's aid and despite the need by the Axis for his full support in the Mediterranean in order to take Gibraltar - a man who had now decided on neutrality, who was to receive the bitterest tirade. .

Mussolini, who for his personal glory, was playing at conqueror of useless territory took second place, and Petain, who Hitler knew he could crush on whim, brought up the rear.

Hitler's attempt at personal diplomacy had fizzled badly and the trip back to Germany seemed to take forever for those surrounding the Fuhrer.

CHAPTER THIRTY-ONE

- Porto Alegre, Brazil –

The city of *'Porto Alegre'* (Merry Harbour) is situated on the eastern bank of the *'Rio Guaiba'* (Guaiba Lake), where five rivers converge to form the *'Lagoa dos Patos'* (Lagoon of the Ducks).

The large freshwater lagoon it deep and is easily navigable by large ships.

Porto Alegre began as a large farm which was surrounded by several different tribes of Indigenous Indians.

A small village was formed there in seventeen fifty-two by settlers who arrived mainly from the Azores, Portugal.

Porto Alegre had grown to become a city of twelve thousand inhabitants by eighteen eighty-two, the year Brazil gained its independence.

The main port facilities for the town were constructed between eighteen, forty-five and eighteen-sixty.

In the late nineteenth century immigrants from other parts of the world, principally from Germany, Italy and Poland flooded into the area and by nineteen-forty, the vast majority of the population was of European decent.

By the end of the nineteenth century the population of Porto Alegre had reached seventy-three thousand people.

The first immigrants from Germany, primarily those involved in agriculture, arrived at the port itself but were sent on to what is now the city of *'Sao Leopold'*, which was approximately seventeen miles away.

Between eighteen twenty-four and nineteen-fourteen, fifty thousand Germans arrived in *'Rio Grande do Sul'* where they spread out to form rural communities in the countryside.

In the early twentieth century there was a large rural exodus in Brazil and this brought many German-descendents to Porto Alegre.

By nineteen-forty these German expatriates composed a
large percentage of the city's population and had become involved
in many commercial enterprises.

A branch of the von Stauffer family had formed part of the
earliest emigration from Germany to Brazil when the youngest son
of a member of the family had brought his bride and young family
to seek his fortune and they had settled to farm near Rio Grande do
Sul.

Since that time the Brazilian von Staffer's, who had been
fortified over time by additional family emigrants, determinedly
held strongly to their Catholic faith, had proven to be accomplished
procreators.

The family, like the German communities it inhabited, were
close-knit and supportive of each other and each new crop of von
Stauffer children had been guided and assisted by an earlier
instituted family trust which saw them individually and
collectively grow successful in their various career endeavours -
the girls to good marriages, benefiting the family and the boys each
set up in their chosen field.

Initially their ties to the land had set the standard for success,
more land being purchased and put into production until the family
was the largest landowner in the area by far, but as is always the
case, some members of the extensive progeny had turned their eyes
to pursuits of other than agricultural endeavours and by nineteen-
forty the name *von Stauffer* had become prominent in a vast
number of commercial enterprises, many of them having nothing
to do with the subject of agriculture.

It was to these distant relations that Karl had turned when
he'd first envisioned the course of *'Operation Fatherland'* and had
come to the realization that for the future of the German nation
those looking ahead would be better to leave the instability of
Europe and seek a safe harbour elsewhere in the world.
Somewhere they could work productively and without unwanted
interference until Europe regained stability, of whatever nature that
might be.

Over the past two years he had taken pains to reopen regular
contact with the Brazilian side of the family and had recently

strengthened his ties with them by way of mutual investments in several promising commercial enterprises, including shares in the new mining operation, which, it was thought, would not only be successful within its own right, but also act as camouflage for its true purpose.

* * * * *

- November First, Nineteen-Forty –

- Greece –

The British send Greece air support, moving approximately half of their Egyptian based air fleets to assist the country in its defence against the Italian invasion campaign.

The English can ill afford to strip the aircraft from Egypt at this point but feel compelled to honour their previous guarantees to the Greeks with a view to strengthening neutral opinion in the area, especially that of Turkey and the Balkans.

* * * * *

- November Third, Nineteen-Forty –

- Battle of Britain –

For the first time since the first week of September of this year, the German's do not bomb London.

The respite brings a sense of hope to Londoners', but it is short-lived as the city is hit on the next night and the attacks continue nightly for the next ten days.

* * * * *

- Battle of the Atlantic –

On November third, U-99, Captained by Otto Kretschmer,

sinks two Auxiliary Merchant Cruisers (Armed Merchant Ships), the *Laurentic* and the *Patroclus.*

Despite the fact that twenty-six Italian submarines have joined their German counterparts in the U-boat attempt to sever the shipping lines from the new world to the British Isles, the earlier levels of successes in this endeavour are not repeated.

* * * * *

- November Fourth, Nineteen-Forty –

- Greece –

The Italian invasion has begun to flounder as the Greeks begin to counter attack in the northern sector of the front, this despite their overwhelming strength in Italian numbers.

* * * * *

- November Fifth, Nineteen-Forty –

- Atlantic –

The fifteen thousand ton German pocket battleship, *Admiral Scheer*, which had left port on a war patrol on October twenty-third, spots the British convoy, code named HX-84, which consisted of thirty-eight ships, at fifty degrees North and thirty degrees West.

The German pocket battleships have been specifically designed for the task of seeking out and destroying convoys in a time of war.

HX-84 had sailed from Halifax Nova Scotia in Canada on the twenty-eighth of October under escort by two Canadian destroyers, the *HMCS Columbia* and the *HMCS St. Francis.*

Once the convoy was safely clear of the coast of North America, *HMS Jervis Bay* relieved the Canadian escorts of their charges, taking over the unenviable task of singlehandedly escorting the convoy the rest of the way across the Atlantic to Britain.

The *Jervis Bay* was a converted liner which had been built in nineteen twenty-two and had been re-commissioned by the British government for use as an armed merchant cruiser.

She had been fitted out with eight, ancient, six-inch guns before being assigned to Atlantic convoy duty.

It was late afternoon when the *Admiral Scheer* came upon the convoy and her Captain chose to make an immediate attack in order to provide himself with what remained of daylight before the fall of darkness could offer his quarry protection.

Upon sighting *Scheer*, Captain Fegen aboard the *Jervis Bay* didn't hesitate to move to defend his flock of merchantmen.

He immediately ordered the convoy to disperse and steamed his ship at full speed toward the approaching heavily armoured and gunned German pocket battleship in hopes of bringing the big ship into the range of his guns, all the while frantically dropping smoke floats in an attempt to cover the fleeing convoy behind him, as he closed.

It was a David versus Goliath stratagem in every sense.

Within fifteen minuets of the *Scheer* opening up with her guns the *Jervis Bay* was dead in the water and sinking.

The heroic intervention of the *Jervis Bay* coupled with the onslaught of darkness minimized the destruction brought about upon the convoy by the German battleship, but by the time the smoke had cleared six ships had been sunk and one had been badly damaged.

When the *Admiral Scheer* returned to base in April of nineteen, forty-one she had sunk a total of ninety-nine thousand tons of Allied shipping.

Early British fears of the devastating effectiveness of these swift, well armed predators when applied to the purpose for which they had been built, - convoy hunting and destruction - had come home to roost.

* * * * *

- November Seventh, Nineteen-Forty –

- West Africa –

Under the command of General Leclerc, a contingent of Free French troops land at Libreville and against only sporadic opposition over the next week, successfully bring French Equatorial Africa over to the Allied cause.

* * * * *

- November Eighth, Nineteen-Forty –

- Greece –

Greek counterattacks against the Italians encircle the *3rd Alpini division* near Pindus and the Greeks soundly thrash the invaders, in the process taking in excess of five thousand prisoners of war.

* * * * *

November Eleventh, Nineteen-Forty –

- Mediterranean –

On this date the British Mediterranean fleet takes the offensive, using the aircraft from the carrier *HMS Illustrious* to launch a torpedo attack on the warships at anchor in the Italian port of Taranto.

The recently completed Italian battleship, the *Littorio* receives three torpedo hits inflicting serous damage and putting her out of service for five months.

Four other ships in the harbour are also struck and damaged by torpedoes.

Navies throughout the world are surprised by the effectiveness of such an attack against capital ships, carried out by the dropping of torpedoes from aircraft, against a moored fleet.

They are also impressed by the slight losses on the part of the British during the engagement, that of only two planes.

The Japanese Navy took very special note of the method of attack and its results, studying and adapting it in great detail, a fact that was soon to become apparent in a new Pacific Theatre of War in the not too distant future.

* * * * *

- November Twelfth, Nineteen-Forty –

- Berlin –

Despite the fact that the Soviet Foreign Minister is in Berlin for talks with Germany on the possibility of their joining the signatories of the Tripartite Pact, Hitler issues Directive Eighteen, which includes the initiation of the planning for an invasion of the Soviet Union.

* * * * *

Agreements between the Japanese government and the major oil companies in the Dutch East Indies are signed.

These guarantee that Japan will now receive one million, eight hundred thousand tons of oil annually.

* * * * *

- November Fourteenth, Nineteen-Forty –

- The Blitz –

Approximately five hundred German bombers from *'Luftflotte 3'* led by pathfinders from *'Kampfgruppe 100'* attack Coventry on the night of the fourteenth.

The British had broken the German enigma code by this point

in the war and as a result did have some notice of the Nazi intention to bomb Coventry that night. However there was only a short timeframe between the decoding of the intent and the attack itself and subsequently little could be done by the British to prepare for the raid.

The intended targets for the raid were the factories and industrial infrastructure, although it was recognized by the Germans that the collateral damage to the city would in all likelihood be extensive.

The first wave of craft to close on the city was made up of thirteen specially modified *Heinkel He 111* aircraft equipped with *X-Gerat* navigational devices.

This type of equipment was the latest model of the radio navigational devices that were being continually developed and upgraded by the Germans for the express purpose of aiding in night bombing missions.

There was, at the time, an ongoing scientific battle raging between the two countries as the British worked feverishly to develop distortion and jamming devices that would interfere with the effectiveness of the Nazi's application of these new radio directional beams.

The Germans would come up with a better, more sophisticated apparatus and the British would shortly respond with a device that would render the latest German creation ineffective.

Unfortunately for Coventry, the British had as yet to come up with the technology that would effectively interfere with the *X-Great*, by November the fourteenth of nineteen-forty.

Consequently the *Heinkels* assigned to path finding duty that night had no difficulty in completing their task efficiently and the target was subsequently well marked for the bombers who followed.

The initial wave of follow-up bombers dropped high explosives with the intent of knocking out utilities and cratering the roads to prevent the capability of an effective fire fighting response, as well as collapse roofs to open buildings to the next air fleet.

This wave was followed by aircraft loaded with a

combination of high explosive and incendiary bombs, some containing magnesium and others petroleum.

Coventry's air defences consisted of twenty four 3.7 inch AA guns and twelve 40 mm Bofors. Over the course of the raid in excess of sixty-seven hundred rounds were fired.

Only a single German bomber was shot out of the sky.

More than two hundred fires were ignited across the city; the main concentration was in the city centre.

There was a resulting firestorm, and with communications, water mains and roads damaged or destroyed, firefighters were very quickly overwhelmed.

In that one night, more than four thousand three hundred homes were destroyed and a full two-thirds of the city's buildings were damaged.

One third of the factories were destroyed or suffered severe damage and another third were badly damaged.

Almost six hundred people were killed and over one thousand were injured.

Although both the size and payloads of aircraft was to expand as the war went on, the methods used in this raid were to set the standard for future strategic bomber raids conducted by both the Axis and Allied forces.

* * * * *

- Greece –

By November fourteenth the entire Greek military is in full attack against the Italians and some British troops and airfield staff are in Greece.

The Italians have been stopped in their tracks and are beginning to fall back in disarray to lick their wounds.

* * * * *

- November Eighteenth, Nineteen-Forty –

- Directive 18 –

Hitler releases Directive 18 on the twelfth of November.

Part of that missive is a plan to deal with England without the necessity of having to directly invade across the channel.

The Fuhrer intends to unleash a series of strikes that he expects to destroy the British ability to make war in the Mediterranean and force them to retire from the area.

If he can accomplish this while his Luftwaffe bombs the British Iles and his U-boats and heavily armoured surface vessels destroy the Atlantic convoys he believes he will leave the English with little choice but to seek an immediate peace with Germany.

It will mean sending German forces to Egypt and Greece to accomplish what the Italians had started but were proving to be unable to finish and then to seize Gibraltar, the Canaries, Azores, Madeira and parts of Morocco.

Once this has been accomplished England will be stripped of a good portion of her empire and this will bring her to her knees.

For this plan to work he has to take control of the Axis powers in the Mediterranean in order to reverse the Italian's dismal performance and additionally bring both Petain and Franco to heel.

His first move is to hold yet another meeting with the Spanish Foreign Minister, Serrano Suner, which is scheduled for November eighteenth.

Hitler opens the meeting with a statement.

'I have decided to attack Gibraltar. All that is required is the signal to begin, and a beginning must be made.'

What he received in response from Suner was yet another dance.

Spain would of course join the Axis powers as soon as possible, but must for now remain neutral in order to import much needed wheat from the west to feed her people, etc, etc.

The meeting quickly drew to a close as Hitler's frustration level rose.

The conference had again accomplished nothing but Hitler was still convinced he could eventually bring Franco into the Axis.

The 4th Reich

* * * * *

- November Twentieth, Nineteen-Forty –

- Hungary –

In Vienna, Hungarian Prime Minister Count Teleki and Foreign Minister Csaky agree to sign on to the provisions of the Tripartite Pact.

* * * * *

- November Twenty-First, Nineteen-Forty –

- Greece –

Greek forces enter *Koritza*, capturing two thousand Italian prisoners and some heavy equipment.

They have now driven pretty well all of the invading Italian forces back into Albania.

* * * * *

-November Twenty-Third, Nineteen Forty

- Rumania –

In Berlin on this date, Ion Victor Antonescu, Prime Minister and *'Conducator'* of Romania, agrees to join the Tripartite Pact.

Talks also take place with regard to the intention of the Nazis to take part in the invasion of Greece, using German forces already based in Rumania.

Further demands are made by Germany for sufficient supplies of food and oil to meet the needs of this invasion.

This agreement has been brought about by the Nazis pressing the Balkans to come on side with the Axis

Bulgaria and Yugoslavia have not as yet succumbed to the

pressure but progress it also being made in those talks.

* * * * *

- November Twenty-Forth, Nineteen-Forty –

- Balkans –

After meetings in Berlin, the Prime Minister of Slovakia signs up for inclusion in the Tripartite Pact.

* * * * *

- November Twenty-Sixth, Nineteen-Forty –

- Poland –

Described as a *'Health Measure'* by the occupying forces, the Nazis begin work on the creation of a Jewish ghetto in Warsaw.

In fact, this is the first concrete step being taken to deal with the *'Serious Jewish Problem'* that the Germans inherited when they invaded Poland.

The party's clear goal is the removal of Jews from German territory and a good portion of Poland is now part of the Reich.

All Polish Jews are now to be herded into a central location in preparation for an, as yet undetermined method, of finally dealing with them.

CHAPTER THIRTY-TWO

– Wedding Bells –

On Sunday December first, nineteen-forty Ursula and Gabriella von Stauffer are married in a joint Roman Catholic service.

Their husbands are in uniform for the ceremony and as they leave the cathedral the two couples pass under the raised swords of dual honour guards composed of both Luftwaffe and SS officers.

Due to the social stature of the von Stauffer family and Karl von Stauffers elevated position within the Reich; the service is attended by a large congregation which is comprised mainly of the social, military and political elite of the day.

After the reception, Gabriella and Konrad immediately leave for the train station as SS-Hauptsturmfuhrer; Dr Kauffmann has to take up his new assignment in Norway the next week.

Ursula and Friedrich travel with them to the station and see them off before boarding the family's private railcars which will take them to Frankfurt where they will stay with Friedrich's family for a week before travelling onward to castle von Stauffer to take up their separate duties relating to the care and storage of treasure being transported in for storage from recently occupied territories.

The Count and his two sons attend at the station to join in on the send-off of the two von Stauffer girls and their new husbands, while Countess Erika remains to oversee the winding down of the aftermath of the wedding and reception.

Erika will be leaving from the same station in a few days to travel to the castle with a view to opening it fully and making it ready for her daughter and new son-in-law's arrival.

She will then remain in residence there for an indeterminate period of time at the request of the Count, this in view of the recent bombings of the German capital by the British and his desire that she keep herself safe from harm.

After the two newly wedded couples leave the station Eric, Wilhelm and the Count leave the Berlin Bahnhof for a small restaurant nearby where they are able to find a private table tucked away in a corner.

While they are awaiting the passing of the hour and a half before Eric's train is scheduled to depart for his return trip to Kiel, they snack on a tray of sausage and cheese and enjoy some favoured local beer.

An animated Eric spends some time telling them about his new assignment and the wonder of the new U-boat he now commands. In response to his brother's enquiry about how he spends his free time, he flushes slightly in consideration of his father's presence at the table and then without delving into any great detail, makes mention of the blonde twins he has befriended.

From that point the conversation moves on to the current activities of *'Operation Fatherland'* as Eric is brought up to speed on that front.

A good deal of the time left to them before Eric's train leaves is spent in discussing the plans for both the mine and the family's purchase of land with a view to building in Brazil.

The Count refreshes his sons on the extent of their distant relative's holdings in the area and gives them a general overview of the number and status of the members of that branch of the family.

Wilhelm and Eric already had a general understanding that they had relations in Brazil and other countries, but both expressed surprise when informed of the size and accomplishments of that particular offshoot of the family.

* * * * *

- December Fourth, Nineteen-Forty –

- Albania –

The Greek forces continue their successful counterattack against the Italian invasion.

Having, by this point, pushed the Italians well back into Albania, they advance toward and take *Premeti.*

* * * * *

- December Fifth, Nineteen-Forty –

- Berlin –

Hitler's request of the High Command for an outline of their proposed attack on the Soviet Union is presented to him.

As was the case in an earlier version this new one envisions providing for a three-pronged attack with the stronger, centre force aimed directly toward Moscow.

Hitler gives tentative agreement, although he suggests some modifications.

Hitler is wary of making the main drive at Moscow. He has no desire to repeat Napoleon's mistakes. He comments.

'Seizure of the capital is not so very important.'

Field Marshal Brauchitsch responds to Hitler's statement, protesting that Moscow was of supreme importance not only as the focal point of the Soviet communications network but as an armament centre.

Hitler snaps back at him.

'Only completely ossified brains, absorbed in the ideas of past centuries could see any worth-while objective in taking the capital.'

There was a brief heated exchange between the two men but as Hitler grew angrier he simply out-shouted the Field Marshal and began to lecture him as to the difference between purely military objectives versus politically astute points of view.

A properly chastised Brauchitsch arched his eyebrows and shut his mouth.

At this meeting Hitler orders that the planning for a German offensive in Greece be continued at an accelerated rate.

* * * * *

- December Sixth, Nineteen-Forty -
- Rome –

A clearly displeased Mussolini orders changes in the Italian military command structure; among others, the Commander in Chief is replaced.

* * * * *

- Albania –

The Greeks continue to force the Italians back deeper into Albania.
Sarande is taken and held.

* * * * *

- December Eighth, Nineteen-Forty –

- Albania –

The defending Greeks capture both *Argyrocastro* and *Delvino*.

* * * * *

- December Ninth, Nineteen-Forty –

- North Africa –

Despite lacking the necessary numbers to take on a major target, the British, armed with new Matilda tanks, go on the offensive in the western desert of North Africa.

The Italians have done very little to fortify their positions on the front and have their troops in a series of camps which are not set out in a manner that will allow them to support each other in the event of a targeted attack upon a single settlement.

The British launch their limited force in the shape of a left hook behind and around the Italian coastal positions.

They unleash the lumbering Matildas to successfully break through the defensive lines of the first camp at *Nibeiwa* and take it before repeating the procedure on the *Tummar West* camp, with the same positive result.

* * * * *

- Albania –

The Greeks continue their advance into Albania, as they take the city of *Pogradec* which sits on the shores of Lake Ohrid.

* * * * *

- December Tenth, Nineteen-Forty –

- USA –

With hopes of slowing the continued Japanese military expansion, President Roosevelt extends the coverage of the export-licence system, binging on board all manufacturers of iron ore and pig iron.

* * * * *

- Berlin –

For several days, German Field Marshal Milch has been in Rome taking part in discussions to diplomatically access the Italian campaign and discuss providing assistance for the Italian navy.

On this date the OKW, *'Oberkommando der Wehrmacht'* (Supreme Command of the Armed Forces) orders the transfer of *X Fliegerkorps* (German Tenth Air Corps) to south Italy and Sicily.

* * * * *

Dr. Goebbels, the German Propaganda Minister, keeps himself aware of the pulse of the German people.

In the early stages of the war, Hitler's diplomatic triumphs coupled with the swift Nazi military victories had provided the propaganda machine with a continuing series of positive achievements that had assured an optimistic response toward the policies of the New Reich and its leader.

However over the past few months these had slowed considerably and Goebbels, realizes that Germany was probably facing a longer than anticipated and more difficult battle ahead.

He senses a need to shift his messages aimed at the German public and begin tailoring them toward the dissemination of a specific message, one of a need to prepare for hard times ahead.

Gathering his staff together he announces that the first step toward this end is to be a strong avocation for a reduction in the length of the upcoming German Christmas celebrations.

The previously enjoyed yuletide season of several weeks is to be shorted to a period of two days only.

Germany was at war and the attention and efforts of all good Germans was to be directed toward the winning of that war. Intense and long-lasting celebration should rightly result from the winning of the war and in the meantime, pleasure and gratification were not to be wasted on the frivolous festivity surrounding the Christmas Holiday.

He further ordered that morality within the Reich needed to be strengthened in preparation for, what could be a, long battle ahead.

A general cleansing of German moral character was needed in order to remove unclean thoughts and galvanize the single desire to one's duty for the fatherland.

Outside temptations like those of lust and self-satisfaction had to be removed from the public area so that the German soldier could concentrate on his duty to fight and protect the fatherland.

Public erotic exhibitions of entertainment for men were to be banned, theatrical comedic routines that relied on political satire and negativity or lewd material for purposes of sexually oriented titillation was to be demonized and banned.

* * * * *

-North Africa –

British forces in North Africa take the Egyptian city of *Sidi Barrani* which lies approximately sixty miles east of the Libyan border.

They have now taken twenty thousand Italians prisoner and have cut off the use of the International Coast Road to the Italians at *Bug Bug*.

* * * * *

- December Eleventh, Nineteen-Forty –

- North Africa –

The British roll up another fourteen thousand prisoners as they take on the Italian *Catanzaro Division* which they clean out of strategic positions in the area of *Bug Bug*.

* * * * *

- December Twelfth, Nineteen-Forty –

- North Africa –

General Archibald Wavell, commanding the British forces in North Africa, loses his 4th Indian Division which has been withdrawn from his command in order to fortify the Sudan.

As a result he is obligated to slow the progress of his attacks against the Italians.

* * * * *

- Belgrade –

Yugoslavia enters into a treaty of friendship with Hungary.
They take this step in an attempt to improve their relations with the Germans.

* * * * *

- December Thirteenth, Nineteen-Forty –

- Berlin –

On this date Hitler issues another directive.
Directive 20 orders the further preparation of the plan for the German invasion of Greece, now code named *'Operation Marita'*.
Accordingly, the OKW orders more German troops into Rumania.

* * * * *

- Libya –

The British send a limited force into Libya to cut off the road leading west from the large and strategic Italian contingent stationed at the Mediterranean seaport of *Bardia*.
They achieve their objective.
Over the next nine days the Italians use their navy to support their troops and in response the British navy comes into action against them.

* * * * *

-December Seventeenth, Nineteen-Forty –

- Berlin –

The OKW presents the revised plan of attack for Russia to Hitler for his approval.

After examining it Hitler changes it to retard the advancement of the center prong of the attack that is aimed at *Moscow* and to initially use that force to swing north to assist in the taking of the *Baltic States* until both they and *Leningrad* had been captured.

Only after this had been accomplished would *Moscow* be taken.

Satisfied after those adjustments Hitler removed the working title of the plan which had been *'Operation Otto'* and renamed it *'Operation Barbarossa'*

* * * * *

- USA –

Roosevelt introduces the concept of Lend-Lease to the Americana people.

Lend-Lease is the President's way of responding to the needs of Britain for military aid while being fully aware of the fact that they do not have the funds to pay for it.

In his usual folksy way, the President justifies the program to, the mainly-isolationist American public, with the simple argument that *'If your neighbour's house is on fire it is only sensible to lend him a hose to stop the fire spreading to your own house, and that it would be stupid to think of asking for payment in such circumstances.'*

He gets some negative feedback, but surprisingly, less than he had anticipated.

He'd sold the programme to his citizens well.

Helping a neighbour and protecting your own ass at the same time was not going to war after all, it was simply every day common sense.

* * * * *

- North Africa –

The Italians have removed their garrisons from *Fort Capuzzo*, *Sollum* and three lesser position on the Libyan/Egyptian border, sending them to the relative safety of the *Bardia* fortress.

The British quickly move in to occupy the positions.

* * * * *

- December Eighteenth, Nineteen-Forty –

- Berlin –

Hitler issues Directive 21 ordering that, regardless of the situation regarding the British at the time, the German Armed Forces must be prepared to in future overrun Soviet Russia in *'a rapid campai*gn' of occupation.

The final preparations for this attack against the Russians are to be in place no later than May fifteenth, nineteen, forty-one.

Few of Hitler's Generals support this new campaign, certainly not if it is to commence prior to the occupation of, or treaty with, England.

Privately and whenever possible, with Hitler, they council a different course, one of pausing to consolidate and enjoy the successes of what has already been achieved and that of rebuilding their forces before seeking further conquest.

However, Hitler has no patience with these military men who do not seem to recognize his extraordinary powers and genius for military planning and execution.

He is at the peak of his power and has proven his worth surely. How dare they question his planning?

Hitler does not hesitate to verbally attack any of them who suggest any other course and he does this openly in front of their peers if the occasion to do so arises.

It has become apparent that if any one of them disagrees with him too strongly they jeopardize their positions.

He will discard and replace any man who does not fall into

line with his own plans.

For the most part the Generals bite their tongues and do what they can to work behind the scenes.

* * * * *

- December Twentieth, Nineteen-Forty –

- Bulgaria –

Bulgaria steps into line with Nazi polices, proclaiming new laws aimed at destroying the *Free Masons* and other, what are referred to as, *'secret societies'*.

Anti-Semitic laws are tabled which are clearly solely aimed at the Jewish members of their population which numbers fifty thousand.

* * * * *

- December Twenty-Third, Nineteen-Forty –

- Albania –

The Greeks continue their successes in Albania, taking the old town of *Himarra*.

Other Books by Patrick Laughy

Paperbacks

The Little Black Book

Alumni

The 4th Reich Book 1

E-books

The Little Black Book

Alumni

Atlantis-Ship of the Gods-a fantasy series

The 4th Reich Book 1 Part 1

The 4th Reich Book 1 Part 2

The 4th Reich Book 2 Part 1

The 4th Reich Book 2 Part 2

Made in the USA
Charleston, SC
16 May 2013